THE LAST ADAM

J. W. Price

27 APRIL 1966
(BATH)

James Gould Cozzens was born in Chicago in 1903. His first published work, an essay, appeared in *The Atlantic Monthly* when he was a sixteen-year-old schoolboy at the Kent School, in Connecticut. He attended Harvard University and during his sophomore year published his first novel, *Confusion* (1924). A year later he left Harvard to go to Cuba, where he wrote *Michael Scarlett,* a novel about Elizabethan England. Since that time he has published ten other novels, including: *S.S. San Pedro* (1931), *The Last Adam* (1933), *Men and Brethren* (1936), *Ask Me Tomorrow* (1940), and *The Just and the Unjust* (1942). *Guard of Honor* received the Pulitzer Prize for Fiction in 1949. His most recent book is *By Love Possessed* (1957).

JAMES GOULD COZZENS

The Last Adam

A HARVEST BOOK

HARCOURT, BRACE & WORLD, INC.   NEW YORK

With affectionate esteem
to Willard F. Read, M.D.

The snow storm, which began at dawn on Tuesday, February 17th, and did not stop when darkness came, extended over all New England. It covered the state of Connecticut with more than a foot of snow. As early as noon, Tuesday, United States Highway No. 6W, passing through New Winton, had become practically impassable. Wednesday morning the snowplows were out. Thursday was warmer. The thin coat of snow left by the big scrapers melted off. Thursday night the wind went around west while the surface dried. Friday, under clear, intensely cold skies, US6W's three-lane concrete was clean again from Long Island Sound to the Massachusetts line.

With the storm had come a necessary halt in motor traffic. Both Wednesday and Thursday it was scanty and uncertain. Friday, fine and sunny, all the main roads were crowded by the delayed appearance of heavy vehicles; 150 h.p. tank trucks distributing gasoline crawled out from their depots; the five-ton truck-and-trailer combinations supplying chain grocery stores took the road. Although the day was one of the coldest of the winter, a remarkable number of private cars came out, too.

Through the wide bay window to her right, May Tupping could find a moment from time to time to watch, across the corner of the New Winton green, this never quite ceasing procession. She could amuse herself by noticing the number plates. Bound north went plate after yellow New York plate. Bound south passed the frequent green plates of Massachusetts, the dingy ultramarine of Vermont. From both directions appeared a scattering of white number plates; presumably from New Hampshire when they came down, and from Rhode Island when they came up. She saw one which she knew was Maine's black and white; and one which was probably New Jersey, but the colors happened that year to be practically the same as Connecticut's own.

Two of the gasoline trucks paused at Weems's garage, thrust their hoses into the buried storage tanks for a few minutes before moving on, but most of the traffic had no business in New Winton. Cars going through as fast as they could flickered behind the bare elms on the west side of the green all afternoon. At the south corner the rigid batteries of pointed arrows turned a few west to cross the river; but, as a rule, May could make a safe bet with herself. She knew what each southbound driver was going to do before he did. Abreast of the white board, suspended from a neat signpost arm and carrying the black inscription: *New Winton, 1701,* a discovery would be made. At that point, driving, one saw both that the bridge road was deserted, and that US6W, leaving New Winton, dipped gently, stretched a level, exhilaratingly straight two miles to the river bend. Each car suddenly went much faster. Given the book on her lap, the various colors of the number plates, and this little ingenuous trick practiced so faithfully by driver after driver, May Tupping managed to pass the time.

"I'm sorry, Mrs. Talbot," May Tupping said, "Doctor Bull does not answer."

Her right hand twitched the plug from 11. On the other line there was a halt, a sort of silent whine, while Mrs. Talbot's harassed mind wrestled the vain little it could with her worry. "Well," she said in necessary surrender, "well, all right, May—"

May released the key, dropped the plug back. Looking away from the electric glow shining off the complex surface of the switchboard, she saw three New York plates succeed each other, but abstractedly, concerned about Mamie Talbot. She wished that she could be surer that these calls of Mrs. Talbot's were just Mrs. Talbot's nervousness. Whether by nature, or because of the amazingly bad luck she had, Mrs. Talbot was always upset, apprehensive, hysterically expecting the worst. You couldn't tell what she really meant by Mamie having a bad turn. In Mrs. Talbot's words, Mamie didn't rouse. A person with pneumonia was naturally pretty sick, might not feel like rousing every time Mrs. Talbot had a mind to rouse her.

Still, with nothing else to do, May presently plugged in 11 again. Doctor Bull's house was at the other end of the green, and if she were looking she could see his car arrive. But she might not be looking; he could have come while she had her eyes on the number plates. Then, too, car or no car, Mrs. Cole might have got back from wherever she was. Or she might even have been in the house all the time. Mrs. Cole was very absent-minded, and if she happened to have a door closed, she might not realize that the telephone bell meant anything. It was even possible, May thought privately, that Mrs. Cole would simply decide to be deaf. Though she seemed quite able to keep house for the doctor, who was her nephew, and to go unescorted to the motion pictures in Sansbury, people said that she was ninety years old. Perhaps at that incredible age you ceased to see the use of answering telephones if you had anything better to do.

Whether the old lady was at Sansbury in a motion picture theater, or merely letting the phone ring while she philosophically puttered about the kitchen, made very little difference. Soon, tired of the throb of the futile ringing, May disconnected, sat passive again, regarding the book in her lap. It was the sixteenth volume of a set of books in the library. The set was said to contain everything ever written with which an educated person should be familiar and volume by volume May was getting through it. She let her eyes focus, reading again, for she was not yet tired of it: "—*My marks and scars I carry with me to be a witness for me, that I have fought his battles who now will be my rewarder.*

[4]

When the day that he must go hence was come, many accompanied him to the river side, into which as he went he said, Death, where is thy sting? And as he went down deeper, he said, Grave, where is thy victory? So he passed over, and all the trumpets sounded for him on the other side."

How Mrs. Talbot got on at all, May didn't know. Mrs. Talbot took in a certain amount of laundry work, but most of what money they had Mamie made laboriously in the Bannings' kitchen, washing dishes and doing things that the cook and the maid did not care to do. May doubted if she were paid very much, especially when Mamie got her keep and clothes which Virginia Banning no longer wanted. Of course, it let Mamie get away from her mother, but May was astonished that Mamie could stand it, even so. Mrs. Banning made her go to the Episcopal church. Mrs. Banning also told her that she would lose her job if she went out evenings with a man.

The man, May learned from Doris Clark, who had Morning on the switchboard, had been Donald Maxwell. Donald worked for Miss Cardmaker on the hill. Very coarse in moments of intimacy, Doris said that she would eat her hat if Mamie (the phrase was Doris's) hadn't been laid. "Listen, I *know* Donald," she explained.

May didn't doubt that anything Mamie might have been, Doris had been first. Both the Clarks and the Maxwells lived in the handful of houses a mile or so west of the river known as Truro. It wasn't that Doris resented it; she seemed to take a personal pride in Donald's achievements. Like her sister, Clara, who had 2nd Night on the switchboard, Doris showed a quality which May Tupping could only describe as horrid. A good sample of it was the brazen use both of them made of a building company's calendar on the far wall, and minute pencil checks for a calculation which May felt violated decent reticences.

Disquieted, not liking her thoughts, either of the Clark girls, or of Mamie's illness, or Mrs. Talbot's misery, May looked down now, read once more: "—*though with great difficulty I am got hither, yet now I do not repent me of all the trouble I have been at to arrive where I am*—" A kind of courage and sober cheerfulness seemed to come to her out of the fine plain words in simple succession. Looking through the window, she could see over the veranda rail, down the short slope of lawn under snow; then, the packed soiled snow of the uncleared side road; the snow, clean again, deep and undisturbed, blanketing the elongated trapezoid of the green. At the far corner, diagonally across from the carefully kept high hedges of the Bannings' place, was the old Congregational church, standing on the green itself. It was all white, with six tall multiple-paned windows on this side; four plain white columns on the front; and a steeple rising beautifully from two polygon lanterns. Down at this end was only a pedestal, lonely; and more lonely still, on top of it stood the stiff, a little less than life-size figure of a Civil War soldier.

While May looked now, into sight at the corner came a low gray car, traveling north very fast. Its top was down. It was occupied by a single fur-coated driver. Guy Banning, she recognized, up from college for the Washington's Birthday week end. He must have been going some, for two hours ago he was still in New Haven, telephoning his mother that he was coming. May watched the gray car pass all the way up the green, turn into the Bannings' hidden drive. Though Guy would probably have to think a minute to be sure of her name, it pleased May to consider how much she knew about him. She even knew all about the gray car. Although it had been built in Europe and had cost ten thousand dollars, Guy had managed to buy it from another Yale boy for only a few hundred. Getting gas at the garage, he told Harry Weems about it, and Harry told Joe, and Joe told her. Harry had gone over the engine and was ready to admit that it was a fine car; he'd never seen one to touch it. It was five or six years old, but it was so well made that it was just as good as new.

Her reflection was interrupted. Turning off US6W to pass right in front of her came a big scarlet truck. The closed doors of its cab bore the gold words *Interstate Light & Power Company*. May reached and plugged in 145. "Mr. Snyder," she said, over the bend of the Cobble to the power line construction camp, "that truck of yours is just going by now . . . you're welcome."

She had hardly finished speaking when, distinct even indoors here, she heard the long arrogant whistle of a locomotive, warning motors which might be approaching the bad crossing US6W made a half-mile north. That must be a freight train; and she concluded, glad to have something more to think about, that they would better side-track it. The evening train, upbound, ought to be already at Sansbury. She waited a minute, still looking out, and presently she saw the locomotive's voluminous plumes of steam jetting above the bare tree tops, an intenser white on the sharp snowy slope of the Cobble behind. The train itself she could not see because of the houses, the hedges and trees on the rise of ground to the east of the green. Very dimly, peals from a swinging bell reached her. Yes, she decided, relieved; they were going to side-track it. The puffing crash of steam expelled in new, laborious movement sounded. The round white plumes went back past the station roof.

Presently it would be dusk. At some point the western hill shadow, coming silently up the fields from the river, had reached the green. The slanting flood of sun diminished, finally was gone. It was perfectly light still, a sunless lucid light with no direct source. The sky was a hard northern blue; sun itself shone a bright sad orange on the crest of the Cobble. Increasing cold could be guessed from an elusive, fragile clarity of air in the valley shadows. By contrast, the heat about her permeated May; it seemed to sink to her bones, pleasurably, the way cold painfully does. She hoped it would stay there, that she could absorb it and carry it home and keep it in the cold of the kitchen. The kitchen floor was practically on the ground, and the inside of the walls had never been finished so you couldn't expect an oil cooking stove to help much. All the while she worked, May's hands were either aching with cold or seared with heat. She only hoped it would be warm in the living room where Joe had his bed.

On the switchboard the first position pilot light awoke. She cut off the buzzing, noted that it was 44. "Oh," said a surprised voice, "that you, May? Well, May, would you ring Doc Bull? Pa"—it was Sal Peters, down the river, and she seemed exasperated—"ain't a bit well—"

The plug went into 11, and, ringing, May listened, suddenly hopeful, meaning to mention Mrs. Talbot too, if he answered; or if Mrs. Cole had come back and knew where the doctor was. She rang it for a full minute. "I'm sorry, Mrs. Peters," she said. "Doctor Bull isn't there."

Now it was really dusk. New Winton's street lights would any minute now wink on. May could imagine a man in the power plant, miles and miles away down the next valley, looking out a window and saying: "It must be getting pretty dark in New Winton." He would throw a switch. At once, all around the green here, lights jumped up. In New Winton itself you couldn't do anything about it. Forty miles away they decided whether you needed light or not. Or perhaps a machine took care of it all, turning itself on by a clock with nobody paying any attention. May wasn't, actually, much interested in that event. Purely mechanical things didn't interest her. At least, not in the real sense of interest, as when she said that she was interested in books. Once or twice she had tried to understand the telephone system more completely. Joe had described it to her several times; but either he didn't describe very well, or she just couldn't keep her mind on it. Joe knew. He had been Assistant Mechanic on the Emergency Repair Squad.

She would never have met Joe if he hadn't been; and surely it would have been just as well if she never had met him. That was, Joe would never have come to live in New Winton. If he had never come to live in New Winton, he never would have met Harry Weems. That certainly would have been better as far as Joe was concerned. For herself, May never expected things to be very good. As long as she lived, she more or less expected to realize that whatever was, was a pity; and how much better it would have been if—

Facts were facts, and May didn't mean to do anything but face them and make the best of whatever misfortunes they implied. Still, she couldn't help seeing—the same turn of mind which made her patient in reading so many books made her patient in reflection—that there had been a point in every course of events (and usually countless points) at which the littlest, most incidental change in any one of a hundred interlocking details of time, place, or human whim, would have turned the whole present into something entirely different. For instance, Joe almost didn't go with Harry Weems that day. The members of the Emergency Squad were scattered up and down the valley; here, a lineman; there, a mechanic; the superintendent at one point; the truck, its driver, and a line engineer at another. The sensible plan was that everywhere would be some one close at hand. Most often, he could handle minor difficulties alone. If he couldn't, the truck would gather up the full crew. That morning, a man somewhere thought he was going to need help. Joe was just waiting for the truck to pick him up. At the last minute, the man who was going to need help decided that he didn't need it. Much pleased, Joe went squirrel hunting with Harry Weems.

The perfect pattern of things as they were still had half a day and a thousand chances to break up, change to something else. Through this tangle of alternatives, choices—now a delay, now an acceleration—events made up their mosaic of cause and effect with superlative delicacy and skill. At four o'clock Harry Weems returned. Although he was older than Joe—say, twenty-eight—and gave you a great impression of cheerful sophistication and calm assurance, he was all to pieces. He didn't know how the gun went off. He was walking behind Joe, and they had just seen another squirrel. Joe said: "You get him." Harry Weems was a good shot. He raised his gun to knock the squirrel off the oak limb, and the next thing he knew—indeed, before he knew anything—he had put a .22 bullet in Joe's back.

Doctor Bull said at first that Joe would be all right in a week. He removed the bullet. He pointed out how lucky it was that they had been hunting with .22 rifles instead of shotguns. Fired so close, a shotgun would have blown Joe's back out. It was also lucky that the light single bullet had hit one of Joe's ribs, close to the spine, doing no more than cracking it a little. Though Joe's back hurt him a good deal, they all agreed that it was lucky. Joe didn't complain, except to mention once or twice, after Doctor Bull had dressed the wound a second time, that his wrists seemed to feel queer. Four days later he woke up in the morning unable to move his arms at all. He could move his legs all right; but for some reason he couldn't stand erect. Not yet, that was. Doctor Bull said that it would pass off, but May could see that he had been very much surprised. He got Joe over to Torrington and had an X-ray taken but in the picture nobody could find anything wrong. That was why Doctor Bull told her not to worry.

As November changed to December, and December to January, presumably there was still nothing wrong. Joe was perfectly well except for his useless arms and not being able to stand up. Inside May something took the conviction out of the phrase, not yet. A sick person had either to get worse or get better; but there wasn't any need for Joe to get anything. He could just go on. *You don't mean not yet*, the inner voice advised her, *you mean not ever. . . .*

Buzzing broke about May's ears. To her right, one of the seven toll line lamps was glowing. Twitching back the key, she bent her head to the curve of the mouthpiece horning up off her breast. "New Winton operator."

"Sorry, New Winton!" cried a snappish voice. "Boston, Massachusetts, calling New Milford. My error."

There was an empty humming of the lines. May was conscious of the light, firm pressure of the metal headband; she seemed to feel it on the bone of her head through her never very thick

[12]

blond hair. Half-past five, she saw. Everywhere shifts were waiting to change, and the relief of impending escape worked with the intolerable slowness of that last thirty minutes to make them a little inaccurate. "Only," thought May, "I wish I could stay here; I wish it were only four o'clock." Four o'clock would mean two whole hours in which to sit and be warm; to muse on what caught her eye or came to her ear; to read her book.

Now the buzzing broke out, and, not so tranquil, she noted the light. She took 11 in her left hand and shot it in. "Yes, Mrs. Talbot," she said quickly. "I'm ringing him."

After a while, she said: "I'm sorry, Mrs. Talbot. Doctor Bull can't be back yet. I think probably Mrs. Cole went to the movies in Sansbury, so she ought to be up on the evening train any moment. She may know where the doctor is. I'll try to get her as soon as the train's in."

Mrs. Talbot said nothing at all. There was simply a silence; then the click of her hanging up. Immediately came another sharp signal, a new light glowing. Mrs. Banning's precise voice gave May the number of the house behind the Cobble where Mr. Hoyt, the artist, lived. "Thank you," May said carefully, for Mrs. Banning was supposed to be the one who had complained to the district superintendent about what was called "indifference and slovenly service." Although May guessed what the purpose of the call was, and although the company had been known to discharge people for this seriously regarded offense, May remained quietly, the key caught toward her, listening in.

[13]

The voice which answered was Mr. Hoyt's daughter; a soft, flat yet fresh voice, distinctively Southern, skipping the hard consonants with an air of trustful sweetness. "Oh, Valeria," Mrs. Banning said, sweet too, but severe under it, "has Virginia left yet? I want to speak to her."

"She's right here, Mrs. Banning. She's just this minute going."

Plainly Valeria had now put, ignorant of the result, the mouthpiece against her breast. Slightly hollow, but clear to May and of course to Mrs. Banning, she could be heard saying: "Ginny! it's your mother. She sounds kind of mad, honey."

The faint jar of some one taking the telephone came through, and Virginia Banning's voice, vehement, said: "Yes, Mother. I'm coming!"

Mrs. Banning said: "Virginia, I think this is very inconsiderate of you. You know perfectly well that Larry wants the Ford to go to Sansbury."

"Lord!" said Virginia Banning. "It's hardly half-past five! Even if he were going to New York, he wouldn't have to hurry—"

"Now, Virginia, I am not going to argue with you. Larry has his evening arranged, and he's all ready—"

"All right! I told you I was coming, didn't I? I can't come while I'm on the telephone, can I?" She was inspired suddenly and said, violently ironic, "Why don't you make Guy let Larry have his car? Nobody's going to use that tonight—"

"Virginia, if you are not home in fifteen minutes—"

May could hear the crack of the replaced receiver. Mrs. Banning hung up then, but not before her voice, faint as it turned, probably toward Mr. Banning, observed something about such a problem.

May guessed that it was a problem. Four months ago, Virginia had been sent home from a girls' school she went to. Doris Clark had listened in on enough of the telephoning which attended this to be able to report that Virginia had so far forgotten the lady-like requirements of her sixteen years as to slap what Doris called the Principal's face. "She was so mad, she was crying," Doris added. "She said the Principal was a God damned old fool, right to Mrs. Banning; if you can imagine—"

May could imagine. She saw Virginia Banning from a distance, but with a special sympathy. May, who hardly ever got anything she wanted herself, could feel for some one in practically the same situation. The fact that Virginia had, or could have, almost every single thing May would like but didn't get wasn't the point. Whether you ought to want what you wanted wasn't the point, either. She felt quite sorry, sitting there facing the switchboard. She even wished that she were intimate enough with Virginia to be able to tell her the importance of one great truth that merely being six years older than Virginia had taught May. There was a mercy in the world which you might not at first recognize. If you just kept on not getting what you wanted, you would stop wanting it in any painful way. It would be all right. You would learn to like what you had.

May looked out the window and saw that while

she had been absorbed the lights had come on up and down between the thick lower trunks of the elms. She arose, her wires following her, and pressed the switches, lighting first the porcelain-faced sign with the deep blue silhouette of the bell on the lawn, and then the bulb over the door on the porch. The room lights she didn't want; there was great comfort in this warm dusk.

As though it had chosen to take advantage of her momentary moving away she saw the pilot light glow. Construction camp, she noted. "Number, please," she said, not taking time to seat herself.

"Listen," said an annoyed voice, "get me New York—quick, will you? The office will be shutting up."

"I will connect you with long distance at Torrington," May said. "One moment, please, Mr. Snyder." She drew out a toll line plug.

There was a click, followed by the words: "Torrington operator."

May said: "New Winton calling, New York, New York, please." The line hummed higher and a snappish voice, strangely familiar when you remembered that she had no idea what the girl who spoke with it looked like, chanted, "My Danbury lines are engaged, New Winton. I will connect you via New Haven." Out of the murk of sound a voice like one from Heaven observed, "Hello—hello—hello—:" The ring and click augmented with a noise like the rush of winds on the miles of dark wires.

"New Haven operator," remarked a new voice, remote, intensely articulate.

"Would you kindly ring New York for me?"

That was Torrington, May knew; and at once it turned back on her. "New Winton! Have you a number?"

When she had obtained it from Mr. Snyder, she twitched the key for Torrington's attention. "This is the New Haven operator," protested the far-away voice. "I am holding this line for Torrington. Please get off."

"My call, New Haven," May said. "New Winton calling New York."

"Thank *you*—" the far-away voice sharpened officiously. "Kindly route through Danbury, New Winton. We aren't supposed to take calls—"

"New York City," said a disinterested, new voice. "Number, please?"

"I will give you Torrington, New York—"

"Hello!" objected May. "Here's your call, New York. New Winton, Connecticut, calling Ashland-four. . . ."

May could hear the final throb of the ringing. The ease of these long leaps from city to city more distant absorbed her. She felt translated, gone from here; just as it gave her a small, ever-new pleasure to know that the ringing she heard so clearly was heard, too, through the mutter of New York. The voice that sounded next would be from an office somewhere in the jumble of great towers, looking out on the long angling shadows and glowing murky gorges between enormous buildings, thick pinnacles lighted for the end of the afternoon.

"Interstate Light and Power."

"New Winton, Connecticut, calling," answered May.

[17]

She held the key a moment, refreshed by distance, reluctant to return. Mr. Snyder was saying: "Interstate? Transmission Line Construction. Division three. Snyder speaking. Hughes there? Yes—" he broke out, "Yes! Well, stop him, sister, stop him! This is important."

After a moment, he cleared his throat, adding: "Oh, hello. Hughes? Snyder. New Winton. Sure, the truck came. Is anything wrong? Say, what the hell was the idea of sending those insulators? Haven't they got any specifications? What? They're five-unit strings. Well, all they need is some common sense! How are you going to hang two-twenty kilovolt conductors on them? Yeah, I know. He ought to be back selling coffee percolators. Sure, my fourteens probably went down to the Delaware job. Well, listen, Hughes; straighten it up, will you? This damn storm has held everything up. We're scheduled to be through next week—"

Regretful, May let it go, making a mental note to ask Joe right away what five-unit strings were. It cheered him, she found, if, as soon as she got in, she could tell him something which he would then have to explain to her in great detail. She was still standing, and now she heard Helen Webster's overshoe muffled feet on the porch. It was two minutes to six.

"Hello, darling," said Helen. "Say, this is like an oven!" She parted her coat. "And how about some light?" She turned it on.

After that she shrugged her coat off, jerked the hat from her head. Holding both in one hand,

[18]

she stooped unsteadily, loosened the fastenings of the overshoes, kicked them off against the wall. Then she hung up the hat and coat, patted her hair, and came down and hopped on the stool.

Blinking in the hard blaze of light, May slipped off the ear phone, unhooked the noose of the mouthpiece. She said to Helen Webster: "You have the camp there, talking to New York, via Torrington, New Haven."

The buzzing broke out, the pilot light glowed. "That's Mrs. Talbot again," May said, glancing at the panel. "She's been trying to get Doctor Bull all afternoon."

Helen shoved the ear piece down her disordered black hair. "Number, please?" Her hand with the plug out ready to ring 11 faltered. She slid her other hand over the mouthpiece, turned her dark eyes back on May.

"Oh, my God!" she said. "Listen, May. That poor kid is dead!"

2

In bad weather, or in winter, few cars attempted the climb to Cold Hill. It would be absolutely impossible for the school buses, so Cold Hill continued to have its small, shabby, one-room school for the children of the families living in the dozen poor farms which succeeded each other along the cleared strip of barren upland. No one of any means or influence lived on these drearily windswept acres, fifteen hundred feet, every foot difficult, above New Winton in the valley, so there was no reason for New Winton to add the

[19]

great expense of making the road passable to its already sufficient troubles with roads.

In the case of the Cold Hill road, there was a further paralyzing point. At the end of the seventeenth century the first white men to see and covet the valley had stood at this edge of the eastern hills. They descended—or if they did not, their wagons and ox-teams must have for it was the one possible place—just where the Cold Hill road still came down. For at least three-quarters of a century this road, not then so much worse than other roads, was the way to New Winton. They called it the Hartford Post Road. Now described for the purpose as the Historic Hartford Post Road, its plight was pressed regularly by New Winton's representative in the legislature, to the attention of the Committee on Roads, Bridges, and Rivers. As New Winton was, if possible, less important to Hartford than Cold Hill was to New Winton, for thirty years it had been just as regularly disregarded. The State Highway Department had never been instructed to acknowledge responsibility. Perhaps it never would be; but as long as New Winton hoped the state might sometime take it over, there was little likelihood of the town doing anything.

*

Though this was Friday morning, Joel Parry hadn't seen any one try the Cold Hill road since the storm Tuesday. At nine o'clock, standing aimless in his barnyard, not sure yet how best to waste the day, he was interested to notice a motor car. It was rounding the dammed-up, frozen pond which, fenced about and posted with No Trespassing signs, was the reservoir of New Winton's water supply system.

Joel's eyes were not good. Blinking against so clear a morning and so much painful snow filling this high hollow behind the Cobble, he couldn't tell who it was. It might be some one coming to see him; or some one going on around the Cobble to the Lincolns'. People going to the Hoyts' usually came the other way, but most cars were bound for one or the other. He took several steps down toward the roadside to ask the driver, because he could tell him that the Lincolns weren't there. Like Mr. Hoyt, Mr. Lincoln was a painter—an artist, that was—and had a good deal of what Joel understood was temperament. It had made him gather up his wife, infant son, and servant, close his house, and depart Monday with fantastic violence for New York. He had stopped to make an arrangement with Joel about keeping an eye on the place.

At the roadside, huddled in his mackinaw and ready to triumph over the driver with his information, Joel saw first, in the corner of the windshield, a white oblong card with black letters. Not yet able to read it, Joel did not need to. He knew at once that it said: *Board of Health.*

He turned squarely around, retiring with surly preoccupation, as though on some important errand to the barn. He heard the car come abreast and pass him. His curiosity made him look to see which way it would go at the fork beyond. To his astonishment, it went right, and he could not stop himself from shouting out, sour;

in a sense, jeering: "You never make Cold Hill!"

Not heeding him, the car jolted into the lower woods. The angle of the barn hid it from sight.

*

Doctor Bull heard Joel. Joel was one of his inveterate enemies. Joel had been, without the least relenting, ever since the summer afternoon eight years ago when his boy, Joel, died. Nothing like the course of events to establish a diagnosis; and young Joel's complaint had been appendicitis after all. They got him to the Torrington hospital twenty minutes before his advanced peritonitis finished him. An interne there, not aware that any physician had been consulted in the case, chided Joel. The patient should have been brought in two days ago. Joel, interpreting the information in his own way, said widely that Doctor Bull had killed his son. When you got right down to it, George Bull guessed he had, for he had administered a dose of castor oil and told them not to worry. On the other hand, if he were to send everybody he had found in forty years' practice with symptoms of a moderate belly ache over to a hospital miles away for observation—

Now, actually seeing the Cold Hill road begin its climb, George Bull saw too that Joel was probably right; it looked impossible. More pleased than not, he roared out loud, exhilarated by the freezing blue sky, the bold rise of the snowy woods, and something to get to grips with. He opened his engine wide and rushed to the attempt.

There was a quick loss of headway; a slowing,

vain jangle of his chains searching for a hold. Snow fanned up furiously, spurting under his hind wheels. Since he was presently making no progress, his engine stalled. He eased the car down to the bottom, turned it around, started up hill again, uproarious, backing this time.

To his slight surprise, he was successful. The snow, mauled to the underlying dirt by his first attempt, gave him some traction to start, and so, just enough momentum to continue. Grunting, his face scarlet with cold and exertion, he peered over his shoulder, out and up, his hands busy with the wheel, twisting to take every advantage the surface gave him. In this way, uncertainly but steadily, he covered slightly more than half the ascent. He saw then that the bad curve ahead was going to be too much. He swept his eyes about, jerked powerfully to the right, and backing straight through an unbarred gate in the rail fence found himself in an open field. Wheeling on this wind-thinned, never trodden snow, he was able to go into second. Picking a low place, he rode down the overgrowth of small bushes separating this field from the next, drove on up the slope between the spaced corn shocks, elated by the excellence of his inspiration. With surprisingly little difficulty he reached at last the fence behind the Crowes' barn.

Out, he put his bag on the running board, stamped in the snow, shaking his shabby raccoon coat into place. The red fleshy mass of his cheeks, the great bulging sides of his nostrils, red, too; the red, strong solid lips and blue eyes, wrinkled by the years at the corners but very bright and shining, gave him the air of a robust, benevolent

Santa Claus. He beat his gloved hands together, hard, making a sound like Olympian applause while he looked down on the whole white valley.

New Winton lay there, but George Bull could not see it. The crest of the Cobble, now far below, concealed the village. He could see fields just west of it; the red brick, extensive slate roofs and cupola with golden top of the new village school; and part of the Episcopal cemetery. Beyond that, the fringe of bare trees marked the edge of the frozen river. He could even make out a small truck moving down the road to the heavy-beamed steel arc of the bridge.

Looking down more directly, between the slope of the hill he stood on and the low bump of the Cobble on which a thin screen or scruff of trees had been left, there was the round spot of the reservoir, adequately isolated. Two brooks, which joined with a now sunken spring to feed it, could be traced by their rocky courses some distance up and back through the irregular hillside. North, were the roofs of Joel Parry's house and barns. Seen from here, it looked very much as though Joel's barnyard would drain into the reservoir. George Bull wished that such a thing could be suspected. Then, as Health Officer, he could have Joel's whole place condemned and make him a lot of trouble. As a matter of fact, Joel's land was on a lower level, sloping into the gentle depression widening on, north, between Cold Hill and the northern point of the Cobble. Following this funnel-shaped falling away, one could see, well north, clear through the naked trees, the French provincial outlines of the house Norman Hoyt's cover-designing for a popular weekly had financed. It looked very pleasant this snowy morning. Thin blue smoke mounted, it seemed as much as fifty yards, straight up from the chimney at the end.

Out the small gap where the bridge road went west through the hills to Truro came the newest feature of the valley. George Bull hadn't seen the Interstate Light & Power Company's high tension transmission line with all the steel up before. It was said to be the most considerable yet erected in the East and George Bull could believe it. Even at this height the towers marched in tremendous parade. Gray skeleton galvanized steel, they crossed the narrow river, the flat fields, and, high above a special wire guard, US6W. They were hard to overlook; they were to carry 220,000 volts and it was deemed expedient to lift up such a thunderbolt on towers ninety-seven feet tall where there was any chance of people moving around and under them. Once across the valley, they shortened to get over the wooded rise which turned the railroad and US6W into two separate southbound channels. The line took, in effect, four relatively squat steps up hill and across the summit. Now the great towers were resumed again, three of them standing at thousand-foot intervals between the south slope of the Cobble and the north end of a marshy sheet of water close to the railraod track, called Bull's Pond.

Through a denuded swath in the succeeding second-growth woods, the line stepped up the eastern valley wall. It straddled the roofs of the

[25]

construction camp, lying southeast, behind and above the round spot of the reservoir. By turning, staring that way through the haze and shine of sun on snow and the blur of white bottomed woods, George Bull could see the tower tops in unbroken sequence, departing majestically to the hazed horizon. It couldn't be said to add much to the rural beauty, but it was something to see. George Bull laughed, for Mrs. Banning had made an awful fuss about it—as it happened, belatedly, when the right of way had been quietly secured and the concrete footings for the towers were being put in.

He supposed it was quite an outrage to Mrs. Banning's proprietary feeling about New Winton. Looking back to the extreme high end of the Cobble, he could see a part of the aged, almost orange brick of the Cardmaker house set in its great trees, and he laughed again, for Mrs. Banning had had trouble there too. Four or five years ago Janet Cardmaker and her house had thrown New Winton into a turmoil of the sort which George Bull most enjoyed.

The Cardmaker house was the fourth of four houses actually dating from the eighteenth century. Of course, it was a close thing; it had been built in 1790. Levi Cardmaker, who happened to have lost his ears in England, was doing better in America. About the middle of the century he had shrewdly possessed himself of what was then regarded as an iron mine, a few miles west of Truro. By the river he had built and owned New Winton Furnace. In 1777 New Winton Furnace cast fifty cannon for the Continental Army, and they were paid for, gold in advance; a fortunate turn for Mr. Cardmaker, for the Continental Army never got them. When, in April, the patriots ran from the Ridgefield barricade, allowing the British to escape from burned Danbury, these cannon, unmounted and cradled for shipment, made the choicest item of the spoils. Mr. Cardmaker had better luck in keeping his gold. The house he built when he judged (even in his timorous old age) it was safe to build houses was much the finest and most elaborate in that whole corner of the state.

At any rate, New Winton had been taking this fine house calmly enough for rather more than a hundred years. Since it was not down on the green, it was as good as forgotten when a Mr. Rosenthal happened on it. Mr. Rosenthal was excited. Janet herself said that she thought he was going to have a stroke when she told him anything he wanted was for sale.

Recovering, Mr. Rosenthal had wanted a good part of the furniture in the front rooms. Plainly he would have liked the whole house, but since that was impractical, he took mantelpieces and paneling. Carefully and expertly, men he brought up for the purpose removed the long curved stair rail in the hall. They took the semicircular porch with four thin white columns; door, lintel, fanlight, and the beautiful scrolled iron work done by a blind German at the long-gone New Winton Furnace forge. Mr. Rosenthal gladly had his carpenters build Janet a new door at no expense to her. The truth was, he paid very well for what he took.

Now, led of course by Mrs. Banning, came the uproar. No possibility of doing it remained, but warm talk turned on the advisability of buying so fine and historic a mansion. A queer creature like Miss Cardmaker actually had no right to it; it belonged to posterity. Most of the uproar necessarily subsided when Mr. Rosenthal, personally supervising every operation, departed for New York, shepherding a truckful of spoils. The victory was his, if one excepted the spectacular triumph of Henry Harris, then a Justice of the Peace.

No one in the village was too humble, or too indifferent to resent (once told of what it consisted) this brigandage; but only Mr. Harris could find effective expression for the feeling. After consulting the town records he was able to announce that if Mr. Rosenthal was so keen on antiques, here was another for him. It was an ordinance passed in 1803. It provided a fine of twenty-five dollars for trespassing on the village green by a non-resident without written permission from a selectman. Once it had served to keep itinerant peddlers from camping there. Henry Harris guessed that it would apply just as much to Mr. Rosenthal, seen to be impudently walking around the old Congregational church which stood on this public land. Mr. Harris sent for Lester Dunn, one of the constables, and Lester went and arrested Mr. Rosenthal, who was examining the edifice with painstaking appreciation. Mr. Harris read him the regulation. If Mr. Rosenthal didn't think it applied to him, he'd better send for his lawyers and let them show Mr. Harris why not. Mr. Rosenthal paid. There were, he remarked, somewhat redder in the face but quiet and patient, many quaint and interesting things to be found in the old records.

Mrs. Banning, Doctor Bull guessed, was having quite a time, since in natural operation the course of events went against her. She got there late in the process. In 1774, nine hundred more people lived in New Winton than lived there now. They must have lived in houses; but only three of the houses they could have lived in were left—what they would have called the new Cardmaker house was almost twenty years in the future as they saw it. Changes and accidents which had reduced the count of eighteenth-century houses to four, would naturally proceed until there were none. The Bannings had two of them —that was, their own large house had been developed out of one and then restored back as far as practicable, and they owned the little Allen house, which figured in all books on the subject, across the way. George Bull knew that they coveted the Bull house; but their hostility to him personally kept them from making an offer. If Mrs. Cole—Aunt Myra—died, he wouldn't mind selling it—he supposed it would have to be to the Bannings; but, he reflected, grinning, not before he'd made an effort to find a wealthy Jew who might like to buy it—to live in, that was, not to take away. Mrs. Banning, bristling with upper middle-class New England abhorrence of New York Jews, would do some squirming then. That would really get her. He could imagine her saying: "Some dreadful people named Oppenheimer

have that fine old house. They're the most odious
and pushing sort of Jews. But what can you do?
They simply force their way in everywhere. . . ."

George Bull's laugh boomed out unabashed by
solitude. Suddenly remembering what he had
come for; that he had at least a dozen of those
damn brats to vaccinate, he took his bag. Walking around the bleak, unpainted corner of the
barn, he swung open a gate and so approached
the back door of the Crowe house.

It was after three o'clock when George Bull,
down from Cold Hill, drove into Janet Cardmaker's road. He had just gone through the shadows
lying along behind the Cobble, past the white, restored Colonial of the Lincoln place, past the
Hoyts'. He was later than he had meant to be.
The Crowes had given him dinner after he finished with the children—great quantities of
tasteless scalding food and tumblers full of hard
cider. He felt very cheerful. When, just past
the Hoyts', he encountered Virginia Banning,
driving a new Ford coupé, he roared, "All right.
Wait a minute." With some difficulty he backed
a hundred feet to a point where she could pass.
She said, curt, unsmiling: "Thank you."

George Bull didn't resent the attitude, copied
from her mother, for he guessed that Virginia was
a longer thorn than he was when it came to prick-
ing Mrs. Banning. "Got a bit of old Paul in her,"
he decided, remembering Mr. Banning's father.
He liked her frail, still adolescent face; the cheeks
a little hollowed; her sulky small mouth. Virginia

Banning's blue eyes had a defiant gleam, as though she would like to tell every one to go to hell. There was, too, a wiry rebelliousness about her narrow, fleshless buttocks—he could picture her best walking down to the post office, the wind tightening her skirt around a frank, limber stride; a short, fur-collared leather jacket buttoned across her practically breastless chest. Only one of the lot with any guts, he always thought; and that amused him, for he guessed if she had been born fifteen years later, a hell-bent for science fellow like Doctor Verney at Sansbury would have changed her altogether. Irradiated ergosterol might have done the trick. Verney would tell you all about it—a trifling deficiency of the antirachitic vitamin D, with a consequent shortage of actually assimilated lime and phosphorus. That accounted for the constriction of the jawbones, giving her face that fragile, determined shape; a flattening of the chest cavity; a narrow, somewhat rachitic pelvis. Normal parturition would probably kill her; but fellows like Verney considered the course of nature undignified and poorly planned anyway. All that waiting around and mess, when a nice little Caesarian section—

He laughed, thinking: "I guess I needn't figure how to get it out until she finds somebody to put it in"; and then he laughed again, with relish, for he could imagine Mrs. Banning probably having a stroke at the impropriety of such gross speculations. He blinked into the golden sun and brought his car to a halt. Stepping out on the snow, beaten hard, stained with horse dung, polished in spots by the runners of a big sled, he went and banged on the kitchen door.

There was no answer. Turning, he saw yellow electric light in the small square windows piercing the concrete foundations of the big barn. Janet might be down there.

As he pressed his bulk through it, the narrow opening left in the wagon doors was forced wider. His boots resounded on the planking while he walked familiarly to the stairs in the corner. Down their dark turnings the cobwebs came off on his swinging fur. He shoved the door at the bottom open with his foot and stepped out.

"Hello, George," Janet nodded. "I could tell you a mile off. Harold thought it was an elephant upstairs."

Harold Rogers, her farmer, sallow, unshaven, in overalls and a black leather coat, grinned. " 'Lo, Doc," he said. "One of those little Devons is kind of sick. Don't know what's wrong with her."

Janet Cardmaker wore a garment which she had made herself—eight or ten red fox skins sewed over an old cloth coat. Though the cows filled the long cement stable with a humid, ammoniacal warmth, she hadn't bothered to unbutton this. A round cap, also of fox skin, was crammed casually down on her head. The big bones of her face made her look gaunt, but she was, in fact, very solid; stronger than most men; almost as tall as George Bull, and fully a head taller than Harold Rogers. From under the circular rim of the cap's yellow fox fur some of her dark hair escaped, disordered. Her black eyes

[32]

rested contemptuously a moment on Harold. She said: "Look at her, will you, George? She's an awful sick cow."

Harold said: "Might be a kind of milk fever, Doc. I—"

"Let's see," answered George Bull. "Oh. Down there."

He walked along the row of placid rumps; the cows, their necks in hangers, patient, incurious. On the cement, the last of the line had collapsed. Released from the hanger, she lay on her side, her lean, bony head against the feeding trough. In her terrible prostration, her ribs rose like a hill. Her great eyes were fixed in a stupor, hopeless and helpless; her legs inertly pointing.

George Bull stooped, put out a gloved finger and poked her udder.

"Milk fever, hell!" he said. "And listen to her breathe!"

Stepping over the stiff out-thrust of the hind legs, he pulled off his glove. Stooping again, he felt along the stretched neck until his big fingers discovered the artery in the lower throat. Compressing it, he looked at his watch. After a moment he announced, "That's better than one hundred." Unbuttoning his coat, he pulled a clinical thermometer case from his pocket, extracted the thermometer. "Good as any other," he said. He shook it, pushed it between the folds of skin where the hind leg lay half over the udder. "Bet you it's a hundred and five," he said. He looked at Harold. "Kind of milk fever, huh? Don't you even know what pneumonia looks like?"

He recovered the thermometer. "Hundred and

[33]

four and a half," he observed. "Probably really more. Do you want to try to save her? Devons aren't much use to you anyway."

"They cost money," answered Janet. "It's not your cow."

"All right, get together about an acre of mustard plaster. Harold can beat it down to Anderson's pharmacy—" he fumbled until he found a notebook. Tearing out a sheet and taking a pencil, he began to write, reading aloud: "Twenty drops of aconite and one ounce of acetate of ammonia in—oh, say, a half-pint of water. Every two hours or so. Get a blanket and cover her up. In the morning, she ought to be dead, so you needn't bother to telephone Torrington for a vet. Harold can fix it."

"Fix it, Harold," Janet agreed. "Come on up to the house, George."

The front rooms of the Cardmaker house were as Mr. Rosenthal had left them, stripped of furniture, the stairs with no rail. The new front door was never used. Janet lived in the kitchen wing, principally in the enormous kitchen, sleeping in a small bedroom up the back stairs. A Mrs. Foster came every day in summer, but in winter, when walking was harder, only twice a week, to do what washing and cleaning was done. Janet, when alone, fed herself. Harold Rogers lived with his wife in a cottage on the slope beyond the barn. This Belle Rogers was one of a locally recurring pale, wan, blond type, descended probably from a single, pale, wan, but prolific individual five or six generations back. Janet ignored Belle's existence and George Bull didn't doubt that Belle tried to pay Janet back by spreading the continually resowed crop of scandalous rumors about his own intimacy with Janet. It was the sort of pale, wan, reprisal you'd expect from Belle; such rumors were an old story and Belle could hardly animate them into interest. George Bull didn't care in the least, remarking to Janet: "Somebody's started them chewing on the same old stuff. By God, I'm sixty-seven years old! They ought to get up a delegation to congratulate me."

Janet made no comment beyond shrugging her shoulders. Her indifference to talk in the village was so complete that George Bull doubted if she ever felt any of the pleasure he had in disregarding what was said. At moments like that he could understand Janet best. In her despoiled house, her grotesque clothes, her solitary existence, she was entirely free from the ceaseless obligations of maintaining whatever appearance you pretended to. Many people soothed themselves by saying that Miss Cardmaker was crazy; but George Bull guessed, when you thought it over, that they were the crazy ones. Other people—it would be the Bannings—thought that it was terrible. They meant that James Cardmaker's daughter had no business to live in a kitchen, eat her own cooking, care for her own cows. Her father, they said, would turn in his grave if he—

George Bull could remember Mr. James Cardmaker perfectly. Janet was about eighteen when her father finally died. She had been away for a year or so at some women's college, and it was Mr. Cardmaker's grave illness that brought her home. George Bull used to come up once or twice a week. The complaint had been, or had appeared to be, a multiple neuritis. Though Mr. Cardmaker was no drinker, his affliction showed many of the symptoms of an alcoholically induced one. George Bull couldn't help him; all he could do was charge for his visits.

Janet was around, of course; receiving his orders and instructions, of which Doctor Bull gave a good many, making up—he'd been younger then himself—learnedly for his actual helplessness in the case. Janet he'd known—in the sense that it is possible to know a child—for years. Meanwhile she had grown into a big, plain, dark girl. His head was as active as most men's on the subject, but George Bull was sure that the idea of seducing Janet had never entered it. Being Janet Cardmaker, she could be expected to order her life on the accepted lines of a dreary, drily educated, consciously high-thinking, virtue. Everything agreed with it—her plainness; her father's intellectual and moral tastes; her going away to college. George Bull certainly hadn't been prepared, that afternoon—well, he guessed it was twenty-eight years ago.

About this time of year, too; for he could remember Janet—the indelibly fixed details of great surprise assured that—standing by the window at the end of the upper hall, looking out at snow on the ground and the bare limbs of the maples. He had just left Mr. Cardmaker. Hearing him, she turned, coming down toward him, and he paused halfway, meeting her, ready to give her some needless directions. She said: "This is my room. Come in a minute."

"What do you want?"

It wasn't, even in this, her so startlingly arranged initial experience, at all an emotional matter with her. George Bull was free to enjoy, at least, the great relief of not having to pretend that it was with him. Janet simply said: "Go on. Go ahead." Even her own ignorant awkwardness did not disconcert her. She frankly expected him to instruct her. It was his problem, not hers; and to the solutions he found, she assented with a violent inexpert willingness.

The old man procrastinated. He considered himself a genealogical authority, because the Boston *Transcript* had frequently published letters of his about Connecticut families on its Saturday page. The hobby gave him something to do, or try to do, through the miserable tedium of dying. He took notes which he did not appear to recognize as the almost letterless scrawls his drooping hands made them. At least once Doctor Bull found him puzzling, in a bewilderment more grim, or even ghastly, than comic, over pages of books held upside down. Like his pendent wrists, his skin-covered face without flesh, his shoulders humped to his little round head, this confusion of aimless, vaguely human activity suggested one thing only. When you saw him shaking and shifting the book held upside down, you saw, too, what James Cardmaker—his notes in the *Transcript*, his historic house and name, his college-educated daughter, aside—really was. Not merely evolved from, or like an ape, Mr. Cardmaker was an ape. The only important dissimilarities would be his relative hairlessness and inefficient teeth.

George Bull came twice a week to look at this phenomenon. Janet, adroitly arranging occupations for the servants, would follow him upstairs and go into her room to wait until he had seen as much as the collection of his fee required of Mr. Cardmaker's inane persistence in living.

This was all right, so long as the old man did manage to live. In the village everybody knew how sick Mr. Cardmaker was. Doctor Bull's willingness to go up so often was, if anything, a credit to him. Going up after Mr. Cardmaker was dead would be different. George Bull planned, as a matter of fact, to end the affair with Janet altogether. He expected to be tired of her; not realizing that mere beauty was what custom staled. Until a man withered into impotence he would not tire of Janet's vital, almost electric sensuality.

It was the summer of 1903 that Mr. Cardmaker died. George Bull could remember the very warm, very clear and beautiful day of his funeral. The doors of St. Matthias's Church were standing open on the sunlit green and the hot wind in the trees. Afterwards, they went out to the cemetery behind and stood in the sun. Several women put up parasols. He could remember the strong south wind shuffling the pages of Doctor Hall's prayer book. The cast-up earth of the hole was dried to a crumbling yellow.

There, then, around that grave, George Bull had been able to see New Winton—every person who could be said to matter, with many who did not. They stood sweltering together, formally seeing the last of James Cardmaker. Here were the ones he had to think of; old Paul and Mathilda Banning; Joseph Allen and his two elderly sisters; Samuel, his wife Sarah, and his brother, Daniel, Coulthard; the Herrings from Banning's Bridge; Micah Little from Truro—not one of those was left alive now. Perhaps thirty other adults, important only in so far as their talk might bring a matter to the superior handful's attention, and a scattering of restless, unwilling children raised the total attendance to sixty or seventy. Because of these people, he could not, plainly, continue to visit Janet Cardmaker.

In the early nineteen hundreds it hadn't occurred to George Bull that he could go anywhere, with or without proper reason, as often as he pleased; and if New Winton—that was, the Bannings, Allens, Coulthards, Herrings, Littles— noticed the improper conduct of two, by birth of their own small number; why, let them notice! Let them notice until they burst! George Bull thought that he would need to be above suspicion if he wanted New Winton as a place to live and practice in. He dared say that he had been right, then. Times had changed as much as he had, since; like himself, the age seemed to grow in experience. The naive sharp edge of shock and social outrage was gone from all the simpler improprieties.

Even in 1903 he had soon modified his view. What he needed to be was no more than careful. That meant some weeks when he could contrive neither to visit nor to meet Janet at all. Many of the meetings were marked by inconvenience of time or place which he had to laugh to remember. "By God," he thought, "we were pretty keen about it in those days."

In the kitchen, his fur coat off, George Bull sat down at the table. He could see one of those electric clocks on the shelf, its third hand a slim gilt needle crawling the steady circle without relief or rhythm. From it you got a glimpse of time as it must be, not as man measured it. It was all one, no beginning, no middle part, no end. He remained absorbed in it a moment while Janet took off her things. She was wearing a flannel shirt, so deep blue as to look black, and corduroy breeches. Her shapeless waterproof boots were laced to her knees. Leaving him, she disappeared into the pantry. When she came out she carried a gallon glass jug three-quarters full of hard cider.

"Have a drink, George," she said. "It's all I've got."

Knowing that she did not like cider, he finally found the booklet of government prescription blanks, unscrewed a fountain pen. "There you are," he said, "and take it to Sansbury. Anderson has in some new whisky so bad a bootlegger wouldn't sell it." He balanced the jug lightly. "I don't mind this stuff," he said.

The cooking stove had been removed from the kitchen, and where it had been, out from the sealed chimney, stood a Franklin stove, taken from Mr. Cardmaker's one-time study. Janet did her cooking, or had it done when Mrs. Foster came, on a gleaming, extensive electric range set against the east wall, out of the way. Bent, busy at the basin in the other corner, soaping her hands, she said: "How's Mrs. Cole?"

"Oh, Aunt Myra's a little vague, now and then," George Bull answered. He filled his glass half full of cider and drank it off thoughtfully. "She's quite a girl, when you think that she was born in 1846. I overhauled her last week, just for fun. There really isn't anything wrong with her; I mean, nothing you could put your finger on. She's spry as you please; got all her teeth. I don't see anything to stop her. I wouldn't be surprised if she lived to be a lot over a hundred. Every now and then she takes to calling me Kenneth for a few days—that was her son. Died of typhoid at Tampa in the Spanish-American war. But she does practically all the housework—you can hear her dropping dishes in the kitchen and telling the little Andrews girl to let things be, she'll do them. She gets to Sansbury twice a week to the movies. Won't bother to go down to the station for the bus. She just goes out to the road and waves at the driver, so now he stops for her. The Bulls are pretty hard to kill."

"What's all this I hear about a row in town meeting last week?"

George Bull roared. "Row is right! I guess you could have heard me having moral indignation all the way up here."

"Well, go on."

"What do I have to go on about? I just told Banning the Board of Health was going to fine him fifty dollars for letting Larry use the river bank for a dump. I told him I'd make it my business to see that water the children of New Winton used to swim in wasn't polluted. What did he think of that?"

"I heard Mrs. Banning wrote some letters to the County Health Officer."

"School Board stuff. I hadn't had a chance to vaccinate the brats at Cold Hill until today. She'll have to do better than that. Lefferts sent me the letter. He just took a pencil and wrote on the

[41]

corner: 'Dear Bull: Here's your prize belly-acher again.' "

"What did you do?"

"I just told you. I got Lester Dunn to scout around until he found where Larry had dumped a lot of junk up the river. Then I fined Banning fifty dollars."

"Quite a coincidence."

"Banning didn't seem to see it; but I'll bet Mrs. B. guessed. It's just the sort of thing she'd do herself, the bitch. Well, one good turn deserves at least two others. I told Mrs. Talbot—and for all I know, it's true—that she ought to have more sense than to let Mamie live at the Bannings'. Mrs. Banning would feed her what the dogs didn't want and put her up in the back garret with no heat. Of course she gets pneumonia. I hear all over town now that Mrs. Banning practically fed her pneumonia with a spoon."

"George, you're a confirmed old devil, aren't you!"

Janet's amused voice was almost as deep as his. From talking mainly to men, her tones had taken on something male. Hearing that plain accent, that ruminative inflection given to words sober, positive, well-considered, you could see best not Janet, but out of a strangely vanished past, certain composed, farm-weathered faces; the men of an older Connecticut standing quiet, their grave eyes in direct regard, their opinions simply and unhesitatingly spoken—for they were as good as you were; a reticent, unpolished courtesy made them willing, for the moment, to assume that they were no better than you were.

Moved by these authentic, almost stilled tones,

George Bull, who belonged here by blood, found himself regretful. When, after his father's death and his Uncle Amos's, he came East there had seemed to him to be something here which he liked and wanted. Part of the feeling might have been mere relief, to have his father dead, Michigan so far away, the hard, cheerless business of his youth there definitely done. Perhaps all of it was that. It was on Memorial Day, 1889, that he first saw New Winton. He got off the morning train and heard a band playing—*land where my fathers died, land of the Pilgrim's pride*—blaring distantly down the green. They were, it happened, that day unveiling the little Civil War soldier to the somewhat belated memory of those brave men who fought for liberty and union. Half a company of the men in question could still assemble, wearing the dark blue of the Grand Army. Every one for miles around was listening to the remarks of one of Connecticut's own generals. Everything looked festive—bunting sagged from elm to elm at that end of the green. The people in their best clothes looked well-to-do; the town looked well-kept and prosperous—even, with this crowd, populous. Almost at once somebody had said to him: "You Eph Bull's boy, may I ask?" The speaker could, it developed, recall the Reverend Ephraim Bull when he was a child in New Winton, and had never thought either of the ministry or of Michigan.

Remembering that holiday morning, it was possible to deduce from it and mourn a lost comfort, a lost ease and peace in the intimacy of small valley, small farms, small towns with a couple of church steeples, small hills and ponds; rivers

[43]

passed by insecure covered bridges. George Bull wasn't sure that such a land had ever actually existed, except on some summer or early fall days for an hour, or an afternoon. In the same fanciful way, life here seemed to him kind and friendly; the men were simple, but honest and happy, to a point not known in Michigan. Of course, the truth was that men were always the same everywhere; Michigan had been full of his own terrors and chagrins. He hadn't, for instance, wanted to be a doctor particularly; but what he wanted was not important to his father. The Reverend Ephraim Bull thought in vague stern terms of humanity. Some form of the urge he had felt to preach to the Michigan backwoods, he expected to find in George. There were not enough doctors out there.

Made miserable by poverty and poor preparation, George Bull was certainly not promising. The exacting Doctor Vaughan soon advised him to leave Ann Arbor, where the new university medical school was beginning to get on its feet. Bull had mistaken his calling. George Bull couldn't leave; he had been afraid to go home. His father, getting older, got blinder, as though he had seen the glory of God to his permanent hurt. The old man went groping around, his hands out warily, and though George Bull could have broken him in half, the terrible voice, hoarsened and resonant, shouting as from a pulpit, paralyzed him; the blind, uncertain hands seemed sure to catch him. With desperation in his efforts, he did better; Doctor Vaughan, pleased, let him stay.

"That was pretty long ago," he said, and grinned, seeing Janet looking at him. "Thinking," he explained. "I'm getting a little vague, like Aunt Myra. Well, Banning paid his fifty dollars all right."

"I guess he can afford it."

George Bull laughed. "He can. But he's lost a lot of money. They figured it out in the post office that he got no less than seven notices of passed dividends last quarter—intelligent girl, that Helen Upjohn. What she doesn't know or can't find out from smelling the mail isn't worth knowing. Well, I'll have some more of this hog-wash, and then I ought to be going. I want to see Mamie Talbot."

"Is she very sick?"

"No. She'll get by. Not as bad as your cow. Sort of puny, like her mother, though. I ought to take an interest just for the looks of it. Mamie insisted on going home when she felt bad, so she kind of got out of the Bannings' hands. Mrs. Banning wanted Verney to come up—for a consultation. He wouldn't do it. Said it was my case. Damn delicate of him."

"How do you get on with him?"

"We're pretty polite. All he wants anyway is a little professional chit-chat about how slick he is. He sort of fancies himself as a surgeon. Sometime I'll beat him to it. I'll tell him about those orchidectomies I performed on your calves. 'What you say is very true, my dear Doctor, but, in my limited experience, I find that I get the most satisfactory results—this was the technique I found so effective when I was attending the King of Iceland; you may have heard—by grasping the balls firmly—' "

"Now, listen," said Janet, "if you think you're out behind the barn talking to—"

"Slip of the tongue," said George Bull, refilling his glass. "Good thing Verney didn't hear me. He'd have a piece in the State *Journal* about the dangerous abuse of the Basle Anatomical Nomenclature in rural counties—well, hallelujah, I think I'm tight! Let me try that again. Basle Anatomical Nomencla—"

"You must have had a drink or two up Cold Hill."

"I did, for a fact. You ought to see Crowe, that pot-bellied little rat, put it away."

"Well, don't fall in the fire. I've got to get over and help Harold. When he hasn't some one working for him, he never gets the stripping done."

"What happened to that Truro boy—Donald Maxwell? Didn't you have him?"

"Harold thought he was fooling around with Belle. Not that it was the first time. It was just the first time Harold thought of it."

"So what?"

"Harold came to me and said he wanted me to fire Donald."

"And you did?"

"Well, Donald's always been the village satyr, and so he probably wouldn't be able to stop. I was afraid Harold might mention the matter to him and get half killed. Donald said to me: 'Ain't I a good worker, Miss Cardmaker?' I told him he'd better ask Belle about that. He said: 'Miss Cardmaker, you don't mean to say you think there was anything wrong between me and Mrs. Rogers?' Since pretty nearly every morning, when Harold took the milk down, I'd see him walk up to the cottage and then somebody would pull down the shade in the bedroom, I thought he had plenty of brass. 'Listen, Donald,' I said, 'what do you want with that half-dead little slut? Why don't you go marry yourself a real woman and stop taking candy from kids like Harold?'"

"You must have scared him to death."

"I guess it gave him quite a shock. He said he would, he knew a girl in Torrington; only he hadn't any money. I took his note for five hundred dollars. Since it wasn't any good anyway, I told him I'd tear it up when his first son was born."

"Get it out and start tearing," said George Bull. "I helped a girl have his first son up to North Truro about five years ago."

"Yes, I know. But I told him no monkey business this time. Last Thursday he mailed me a clerk's copy of a marriage certificate from Torrington."

"Well, I'm damned," said George Bull. "You're quite a moral influence. But that doesn't help you milk the cows, does it?"

"Time was, " Janet said, "when I could milk every cow in the barn with my two hands. With a machine to do all the real work, Harold can't even strip them."

"Well, of course," George Bull said, "you only have about twenty more cows now. That might make a difference. Let me know how my patient is."

Left alone in the warm kitchen, George Bull went and turned on the radio in the corner beside Janet's desk. Almost immediately—this was a much better set than the one he had got for Aunt Myra at home—a voice said: "WTIC, the Travelers, Hartford, Connecticut." With the suddenness of a switch swung closed, dance music of great volume and elaboration burst out, filling the room.

George Bull stood quiet a moment. Outside it had somehow got dark and he looked at the clock with the relentlessly turning gilt needle. It was practically six, and he decided that he could see Mamie Talbot in the morning just as well. The blurred glow of alcohol filled his big frame. It gave the music in his ears an unearthly sweetness, rich, intricate, and gay. Presently his pleasure in it had reached such a point that he felt impelled to dance; and so he did, after a fashion; performing a careless and exuberant two-step around the room.

After a time, the door opened; but he saw that it was Janet and did not stop. She looked at him and laughed. "George," she promised, "you'll be on your ear in a minute."

"Go milk your cows," he roared. "I'm fine."

"Harold brought Pete Foster up with him."

"Fine. How's my patient?"

"She looks pretty near dead."

"Fine. Best thing could happen to her."

"Want some supper?"

"Hell, no!"

"Well, I'll go up and change my clothes."

"Fine. I'll help you."

"You'd better stay down here, George."

"Sure, I'd better."

"Listen, George, it's cold as a barn. I left all the windows open. Wait until—"

"Wouldn't be the first barn we'd been in."

[48]

"I guess it wouldn't, at that," she admitted. "Come on, then."

"First," said Mrs. Talbot, "it was Bill; and then it was little Bill. Now it's her. I knew it as soon as she was sick. You needn't think I didn't know—" Her voice mounted on each word, and now she screamed; broke off, wailing faintly as she got in breath to scream again. "I knew it all the time." She clung to that; as though her foreknowledge justified something, made a point in her favor.

This was the way Mrs. Talbot had been going on, by herself. May Tupping could identify the awful sound which had brought her out across the back, hatless, shivering in her thin coat. "You've got to stop that," May Tupping said. "Mrs. Talbot, you've just got to stop it! Where's your coat? You come over to our house—"

"Long about six o'clock," Mrs. Talbot said, "she starts making this noise. No one just sleeping ever made a noise like that. I—"

In the anguish of her desire to hear no more, May's eyes blurred with tears. It wasn't about Mamie. Death, she saw, in Mamie's case—and why shouldn't it be that way in every one's?— was a thing time passing took care of. Time arranged it and carried it safely through. The key to understanding, knowing how it was, came to her in a matter so simple as her trips to the dentist in Torrington. The dentist hurt her so much she would be worrying all week. When the day came and she started, she would say to herself that at five o'clock, just three hours from now, she would be getting into the bus to come home. It would be all over. Time would take care of it; it had to be five o'clock not long from now; and when it was, as soon as that, everything would be all right. Death too might be bad to go to—there was that apprehensiveness of the trip to Torrington; nothing helped her any; you could not look out the windows in peace or read a magazine with attention. Death, too, might be worse even than you thought, when you reached it—the dentist never hurt her less than she expected. Yet it would be past soon; a matter done with and no longer important. She stepped out into the end of the afternoon lying over Torrington. She walked slowly, liberated, to the place where the bus stopped. On a pillar before the bank, the great four-faced clock said five; and, as she had known it would be, all was well.

The peace of this idea wasn't shaken, even by Mrs. Talbot; but with nothing to make her cry about Mamie, May had nothing to justify herself. She thought: I feel as if I could hardly stand it. By it, she knew, she meant Mrs. Talbot. She was appalled to find herself taking this moment to be base enough to abhor Mrs. Talbot's dirty clothes and dirty house. She backed away at heart from Mrs. Talbot's loathsome weeping. Who could support the cumulative effect of such unhappiness, illness, dirt, poverty? Mrs. Talbot's hair— had she ever washed it?—lay in a scanty offensive snarl, matted to the back of her neck; and, looking down on it, May had to swallow twice before she could say: "You get your coat on. I'll be right back."

She closed the door, stepped down the two wooden steps and fled, her heels catching on the foot-marked path, yesterday's slush frozen hard as iron. She kept her mouth open, gulping in the clean air. Entering her own back door, she saw— it had been impossible for her to remember—that she had left nothing in danger on the stove. From this frigid shed of a kitchen, she passed into the warm room. "Joe," she said, "I've got to bring Mrs. Talbot over here. She's pretty near crazy—"

"Hello, May," Harry Weems said. He was sitting on the other side of the stove and she hadn't seen him at all. "What's the trouble?"

"Mamie Talbot died."

"Say, that's too bad!" Harry got to his feet, agitated. Joe had gone pale, his mouth tightening in a sort of sullenness. Joe wanted his supper, not Mrs. Talbot. Joe couldn't stand Mrs. Talbot anyway—who could?—and May didn't blame him. "I couldn't help it," she said. "She can't get herself anything to eat. Harry," she added in sudden appeal, "could we get a bottle of gin or something? We've got to give her something—"

"Sure thing," said Harry Weems. "Get you one right away."

"Wait. I'll pay you."

"Don't be dumb," he said. "Anything I have you can have. Gosh, May, what do you think I am?" He was a little redder; hurt; pulling his cap on as he went out.

"He'd never miss it," Joe said. Joe really tried, but he couldn't hide the bitter edge on his words.

Look at Harry and look at him. "He made a hundred and seventy-two dollars last week," Joe said. "He brought five cases over from New York state last night, and he says practically all of them are spoken for. Listen, for God's sake, what's the good of bringing Mrs. Talbot here?"

"Joe, I tell you she's pretty near crazy. I don't know what she'd do. One thing: she wanted to go up and tell Mrs. Banning she hoped she was satisfied, because she's killed Mamie, all right."

"Well, I hear it's the truth."

"No, it isn't! It's just craziness. I think in some ways Mrs. Banning was pretty mean to Mamie. But I happen to know this, because Mamie told me. All this fall, Mrs. Banning came out herself and saw that Mamie drank a glass of milk with every meal."

"Larry keeps three Jerseys for her. She has to get rid of the milk some way, I guess."

"Another thing Mamie told me was when it got so cold last September, that week, Mrs. Banning came up to their rooms at ten o'clock at night herself to see if they had enough blankets."

"Banana oil!"

"I can't help whether you believe it or not. Mamie told me."

"Well, what's so wonderful about it? You keep saying, 'Mrs. Banning herself,' like she was God or something."

"Well, lots of people wouldn't have bothered."

"Yeah, and she's one of them."

"Well, Joe, I'm sorry. I've simply got to bring Mrs. Talbot over for a little while."

"Go and get her and let's get it over with!" He shifted a little on his back. One arm slid inertly sideways; but before she could help him, he pulled up his shoulder, turned, making it fall back. "Go on," he said. "Get the hell after her!"

*

In that wing of Bates's store which was rented to the United States Government, the post office window was not yet open. Behind the high screen formed by the mail boxes, Helen Upjohn and Mr. Bates's daughter Geraldine could be glimpsed in hasty movement under the tin-shaded lights hung above them. There was a constant sound of paper striking glass softly as envelopes went into their proper boxes. Suddenly whole small oblongs would be blocked up with rolled afternoon papers from Danbury, Bridgeport, or New York. People who cared to pay for boxes from time to time stepped forward, twisted the small combination dials, drew out whatever there was and retired to lean against the varnished wainscoting, looking at it. A row of windows let those otherwise unoccupied gaze out.

All along the front, ample, mellow light flooded the section of cement sidewalk. Between this paving and the triple concrete lanes of US6W stood half a dozen motor cars, several of them with their headlights on, their front wheels against the sidewalk edge. Out of the dark, new figures kept appearing on this well-lighted little stage. Some went to the doors of the store and came over inside; some walked past outside and came in the post office door. This opened and closed constantly, admitting people who were brought to a halt by the press, distributing themselves as they could along the bits of unoccupied wall, against the board covered with notices about fourth-class mail, the Postmaster General's obsolete request to mail Christmas packages early, and the poster, in colors, of what was being shown at a Sansbury moving picture theater.

Above, under dusty glass, hung a framed picture displaying the leaves and flowers of the mountain laurel with an ornately lettered plea to spare it—*The Mountain Laurel, kalmia latifolia, is made, constituted, and declared to be the state flower of the State of Connecticut—Public Acts of 1907*. Up to it floated a general haze of tobacco smoke, a general murmur of voices and confusion of conversations.

Here, or stepped out a minute, or just coming in, were most of the men who had a stake in New Winton; power in its government, or position in the sense of running a business or owning a farm. Since every one knew every one else clothes had no symbolic value here. Their good suits were at home. They wore old overcoats, old boots and overshoes; hats and caps meant only to cover the head. Mr. Bates, moving behind the grocery counter, his threadbare jacket hanging open on a sweater of sagging gray, was First Selectman. In a very old black overcoat, Matthew Herring, the Treasurer, retained by his tall thin frame and composed face a distinct air of gentility. He came, of course, of superior people, living, well enough to-do, in a large house in the unfortunate taste of the '70s above Banning's Bridge. Charles Ordway was more citified. As Representative in the Legislature, he felt the need to be presentable in Hartford. He made up for bringing his

[54]

new clothes home by great affability; he and Henry Harris, on several occasions his defeated Democratic opponent for his position, stood together in the friendliest possible intimacy. The clock now said ten minutes past six and Lester Dunn called loudly: "Let's go, Helen! Read what he wrote afterwards!"

There was a glimpse, for those against the notice board, of Helen Upjohn's fleeting pale smile beyond the glass-fronted pigeon holes; a little laughter rewarded Lester Dunn. The door opened and George Weems came in from his adjoining garage. Several voices saluted him. Henry Harris lifted his brown, pointed face and said, "What do you know?"

"Not so much, Henry," George Weems nodded. "Hello, Charley." He paused a moment and added, "Harry just came by and tells me Mamie Talbot's dead."

Silence fell instantly. There was a following murmur; surprise; disinterested consternation; then, in a gradual, grave lament, separate voices: "That's too bad—"

"Why, that's a shame—"

"Why, yes, Mr. Weems says Mamie Talbot's dead—"

"Don't seem right. How old's she? Not more than seventeen, I should say—"

"I doubt she's more than sixteen—"

"I surely feel sorry for Mrs. Talbot. You'd think she'd had her share of—"

"You can't hardly believe it. She was just as lively and—"

Henry Harris looked around, and seeing no one except Matthew Herring who could be called

[55]

really intimate with the Bannings, allowed himself, for he had a long-standing political feud with Mr. Herring, to say: "I hear she took sick through overwork and underfeeding."

Matthew Herring, though he could not help hearing, paid no attention, so Henry Harris went on: "I noticed they didn't keep her. Sent her home when she felt too bad to earn her pay."

Matthew Herring removed the mail from his lock box, snapped it shut, and turned about; his high thin shoulders stooped a little; his long reserved face expressionless. "You oughtn't to say things like that, Henry," he observed. "We know what you say never means anything; but strangers might take you seriously." He nodded to Charles Ordway and went out the door.

There was a stir and snicker of applauding laughter. Through this relieved sound, a voice, harsh in an old bitterness re-aroused, came clear, heard by every one: "What you expect when you got a horse doctor treating her? Just give him time, I say, and old Doc Bull can kill us all."

*

"That's all right, Virginia," Larry Ward said. "It's only about six or a little after. I told Mrs. Banning not to hurry you; you'd be along soon enough."

In the light-flooded garage, Larry's face had a beautiful warm bronze color. The carefully shaved skin was firm and very fine textured. What should have been handsomeness was subtly spoiled by a too great regularity of feature. It gave him the blank, insensitive look of a wax model. Like a model, too, his eyes were astonishingly bright, China blue, shaded in his bronzed face by an expression of perpetual mild perplexity. Virginia Banning got out of the Ford. "You'd better not keep Charlotte waiting," she said sharply.

"We're going to the dance at the Odd Fellows Hall in Sansbury," Larry said. "I guess she'll wait, all right." Showing at once his idea of the splendor of the proposed entertainment, and his pleasure in Charlotte Slade's probable docility, he came innocently close to smirking.

"Well, you needn't be so damned conceited," Virginia told him. "If I were Charlotte, I'd drop you cold!"

Larry looked at her, stunned to the customary confusion which afflicted him in matters not connected with farm animals or gasoline motors. He laughed a little uncertainly, straightened the bright orange necktie which he had knotted into a starched linen collar, and got into the Ford. The engine was still running, so he backed out promptly, halted. "Go on," Virginia said. "I'll shut the doors."

"Thanks!" he shouted, waving his hand, backed about and started down the drive.

Virginia made a slight, contemptuous sound between her teeth. She pushed her gloved hands into the pockets of her leather jacket, moving speculatively to look at Guy's car.

Standing on the clean cement of the garage floor next to her father's dark, sedately shaped, carefully kept, sedan, this car of Guy's had a wonderfully violent air. Guy got something when he got that. She hoped, each time she saw it, that it would please her less, look more ordinary and less desirable; but it didn't. Its great power and tremendous potential speed could not have been more quietly, entrancingly evident. It had none of the shiny ostentation of lesser cars, turned out thousand after cheap thousand. Slate gray, its not too new enamel was flat and dull under a hardened film of dust and oil; its metal, of a luxurious tough thickness, showed the same lusterless practicality. A lean, three-pointed star was hung in a metal ring poised on the radiator cap; simple and severe badge of makers who didn't make cars for everybody, not a tricky little statue or ornament.

Virginia's gloved hand caressed one of the great headlights couched inside the long strong swoop of mudguards slightly dented here and there on the edges. Out the sides of the formidable hood came fat tubes, like ribbed worms of soiled metal. They passed diagonally astern, ducked out of sight again. Virginia was not sure what they did, but they seemed to imply a power too titanic for any ordinary hood to cover and hold. She moved along the side, glanced into the open driving compartment. The keys were there.

Carefully, unhurried and absorbed still, she passed on, examined the tires, glanced at the dial on the underslung gas tank behind. Very quietly returning, she opened the door, slid across the much-used leather of the open seat. There she sat a moment, buttoning her jacket, pushing the fur collar close under her chin, tucking her skirt tight under her narrow thighs. She laid a hand on the wheel, reached and turned on the ignition. The headlights snapped up to a mighty glare on the radiators affixed along the back wall.

The motor turned over vainly a moment. It caught then with a shocking thunder and she throttled it down, wincing; opened it up again, jerking the choke. With a wheel-spoke in one hand, the choke held out against possible stalling, she let the clutch engage gingerly, gazed over her shoulder, watching the long stern push out onto the drive. It bent majestically to the right until, looking front, she was pointed for the gate. Letting go the choke, she stamped on the clutch, snapped over the gear lever. Gathering momentum with a great roar, she swept down to pass the house.

Upstairs, a window slammed open, and though she did not bother to look, she heard the sound of Guy's outraged shouts. Glancing hastily right and left, she slid through the gate, turned south in a pool of radiance from a street light at the corner. Down the ghostly sweep of US6W her long-shafted lights poured ahead. She saw a movement among the cars before the post office and jabbed her thumb on the button, sending the shattering blare of her horn down to them. The red taillights of one or two, starting to back, stopped, frightened; a single dark figure scurried across the down-flung brilliance. She was into high; and, given the accelerator, the motor picked up marvelously. She was doing forty-five when she roared, horn rasping out, past the hesitant parked cars; the lighted windows of the store; the glowing glass globes on Weems's gasoline pumps. It was fifty-five when the half shadowed, half arc-lit shape of St. Matthias's Church at the corner hid the bridge road from her. She punched the horn button and took a chance. She was past it then; the star-scattered sky opened like an immense southern dome as she dipped down beneath the last street light and off on the fine straightaway to the river bend.

Lighted like the other dashboard dials from some secret inner source, the shaking band of the speedometer showed now, now hid, the numeral 6 of 65; and that was certainly fast enough. The air lashed stinging around the low windshield, so fiercely cold it scalded like fire blown along her face. She could scarcely breathe; the blast of it drove, chill, right through the leather of the buttoned jacket.

Seeing that sixty-five was fast enough; already a little afraid with only this unfamiliar wheel to direct the great machine moving her, Virginia found that she was going faster. A perverse desire, born half of the awful beauty of speed, half of her fear's delectable pain, tried its edge on her shaky stomach. Not really wishing to, not able not to, she saw a black 7 shaking into sight; a thin line; then, the companion 5. To her right, the gigantic frail gray shape of a tower in the new transmission line went up against snow, dark hill, and at the top, stars. It was gone, and she saw, instead, the long low mound of a tobacco barn. It appeared, telescoped magically, disappeared. Two big elms were levered past the side of her eye.

Now she saw the starlight distantly on the flat snow covering the river bend. With a pain of fear, an anguished faintness, fleetingly on the speedometer she beheld an 8 coming up. At once, its zero joined it. Her far-flung headlights had found the precise low line of the white fence, curving at the bend with the great arc of the curving road. She started to say: "Oh, Jesus . . ." but the solid wind crammed in her parting lips, choked her. With an insane and paralyzing fatality she knew that she was going to be killed. She could never get around there at such a speed. She would have to drive through the fence, over the bank, break out a great hole in the snow-covered ice; and everything would be quiet, freezing, star-lit on the empty road with no one stirring.

A fear so great as to be more an agony of rage at the folly of killing herself when she did not want to die, for no reason at all, convulsed her. She locked her left hand on a spoke of the wheel, put her right hand on that, ready to bear down. The foot, so senselessly on the accelerator, recoiled; she cried out in surprised minor anguish as the sharp heel of that shoe dug the instep of her other foot, bracing, both of them, on the foot brake. She didn't even think of the emergency brake; she closed her eyes, her lungs bloated in despair; her belly caved in.

Instantly a horrid jolt took out her breath; she drew on the wheel with all her might and her eyes, forced open, saw the white fence leaping toward the headlights. There was a rasp and slurring screech. Pain sank in her armpits as the steering gear attempted to escape her. The car wobbled right, then left; it hovered in a delicate indecision, poised to overturn. Two wheels fell jouncing back on the concrete; the engine stalled. Her headlights brought up across snow-covered field and boulders and small, rotting apple trees. She was three-quarters of the way around the bend, pointed diagonally across the road.

Virginia lay back in the seat, her hands limp in her lap. The bright stars seemed to quake toward the blackness of the sky as though they were going out. A taste like blood was in her mouth; the wind, gentle, overlaid her face with a killing pain of ice. Brushing her glove distracted against her cheek, the leather came down to the dashboard radiance stained dark with sweat. She had one thigh locked over the other, the toe twisted tight around her ankle. Wincing, she realized with a sharp horror of disgust that she had wet her drawers a little; and at once she began to cry, for, safe and alive or not, that was really too sickening to bear.

*

Mrs. Cole, boarding the train at Sansbury, had inadvertently picked the steps of the smoking car; but she was out of breath and sat down there anyway. "You be more comfortable in another car, Mrs. Cole?" the conductor asked.

"Oh, no," she said. "I don't object to smoking. My boy Kenneth smokes the whole time. Tell them not to stop on my account."

He went away then and she was able to settle herself and get her copy of that morning's New York *Mirror* open to the daily true story. She was wearing her old bifocals instead of her new reading glasses, so the small print occupied her for most of the twenty-five minutes taken by the train to get up to New Winton. Finished, she

[62]

turned to the serial then and, holding the sheet close, read the synopsis of preceding installments: *Coral Wright, beautiful and seventeen, is left alone in a little seaside hamlet upon the death of her mother. Hobart Nixon, an unscrupulous and distant relative, has long annoyed her. Roger Clark, young mining engineer and beau of Coral in her school days, is back to sell some property before going West again. He falls in love with Coral and says that someday, when he makes good, he will come back and marry her. Coral thinks it's just a line with him. Maurice Maxwell, millionaire playboy, has built a great summer estate in the village. He has met Coral and asked her to his opening house party and she has half promised to come. Nixon, whose wife is deaf, sneaks into Coral's room that night and begins to overpower her. Now Continue—*

At this point the conductor opened the door and came down the aisle. Ahead, the locomotive broke into a doleful wail for the crossing on the Cobble road just south of New Winton. The conductor held the top of the next seat and said: "This is your station, Mrs. Cole."

Mrs. Cole objected: "I gave you my ticket, young man."

"Yes, I got it. This is New Winton. This is where you want to get off."

"Is this Bridgeport?"

"No, ma'm. This is—"

"Well, I'm going to Bridgeport. Will you tell me when we're getting in?"

"This train don't go to Bridgeport, Mrs. Cole."

"Why didn't you say so when you took my ticket? Land sakes, where does it go to?"

"You don't live in Bridgeport any more, Mrs. Cole. This is New Winton."

"Well, have the train stop, please. That's where I want to get off." She arose, flurried, and the conductor bent down, recovering her packages. "Those are some little things I bought at the five and ten," she told him. "Thank you very much." She hooked her umbrella over her arm, clasped her handbag tight and poked the newspaper under one elbow. Three or four amazed faces watched her leave the smoking car.

"Will you be kind enough to assist me, young man?" she said to the conductor. "I have all these things."

"Don't you worry, Mrs. Cole. We'll get you off." He opened the door of the other car and shouted perfunctorily, "New Winton, New Winton. . . ."

When the train had moved on, and most of the cars and light trucks waiting for it had either got into motion or shown no immediate sign of doing so, Mrs. Cole judged it safe to cross from the gravel platform of the station to Fell's Meat Market. She looked sharply at the wide closed doors of the Station garage to be sure that no motor was going to sally out on her. Continuing she went briskly by Fell's lighted windows to the corner, where the short street led up to the green, between Upjohn Brothers' store and the bulky building known as Upjohn's Hall across the way. At this point she stopped, made a slight clicking sound with her tongue, turned about and went back to Fell's.

Warner Fell himself, in a dirty apron, was behind the hacked cutting block. "Good evening, Mrs. Cole," he said.

Mrs. Cole sniffed. "Something don't smell very fresh here," she remarked, generally.

"Why, Mrs. Cole, I'm sure everything—"

"Well, something isn't. How are your lamb chops?"

Warner Fell pushed up the latch of the big refrigerator doors, produced, dropping on the block, a chunk of bone-backed meat. Mrs. Cole bent down and sniffed it, looked a moment at the faint round government inspection stampings in purple ink. "Hm," she said, "it's a poor cut. Well, I'll take a dozen. Cut them thick."

Warner Fell drew out a long knife, sliced to the bone, chopped through with a cleaver. When he had done this four times, he said appraisingly, "Don't you guess four would be enough, Mrs. Cole? These are good thick ones."

"Yes. Four's right. That's two for the Doctor, and one for me, and one for Susie."

She added this to her other packages, went out and walked up to the green. Crossing the road, she passed the lighted windows of the library, looked carefully to be certain that the fire truck wasn't on the point of coming out the adjoining driveway. In front of Weems's house at the corner, she paused, glancing up and down the deserted road. Then she crossed over and passed along the upper end of the green. When she got beyond the Ordways' house she saw that there was no light at home; the Doctor couldn't have got in yet, and she remembered that she had let Susie go. The Doctor could eat the other chop, or it would do for Susie tomorrow.

Passing through the gap in the lilac hedge, she reached the door. Here on the steps, she had to set down most of her packages in order to find her key and use it. Once inside, she got a light on, went directly to the kitchen where she deposited all her things on the table.

This was hardly done when the telephone rang, for, up at the other end of the green, Helen Webster saw the light. Mrs. Cole came pattering back again and took off the receiver. "No," she said, "I don't know where he is. I just this minute got in. Oh! You say she died? Oh! Now, that's too bad. Please wait a minute until I get something to write with. I'll make a note for him—"

She laid the receiver down and went back to the kitchen, turning over her things on the table in search of a pad and pencil. Not finding them immediately, she paused, perplexed. Out of a page of photographs which her paper, thrown down, had exposed, the nostalgic word *Bridgeport* arrested her. It went on—*Beauty Victim of Maniac's Retribution?* The photograph of a dark, thick-featured girl regarded her. *Revenge hinted in murderous attack on pretty Nita Popolato. Story p. 2.* Mrs. Cole made a clicking sound with her tongue and turned to page two.

February 19th, Bridgeport, Conn. Near death in St. Vincent's Hospital, Nita Popolato, dark-eyed Bridgeport beauty of seventeen, gasped out a tale of primitive vengeance and passion which set police scouring the city for—

After a while Helen Webster shrugged. Having no facilities for a howler circuit, the most she could do was keep ringing the line. This effected a small, discontented clucking noise, audible a few yards around the unhooked receiver in the hall. Mrs. Cole, who had found her reading glasses and pulled a chair up to the light in the kitchen, was not disturbed by it.

*

"Guy, darling!" Mrs. Banning called, "Guy!"

She heard the violent opening of his door and his quick step in the upper hall. "Oh, never mind, dear," she said. "I just thought I heard your car. It was probably one on the road."

"You did hear it," said Guy. His voice was constricted with fury, and Mrs. Banning turned from her dressing table. "Come in, dear," she said. "Why, what is the trouble?"

Guy pushed the door open. A pattern of half-dry lather, left from his interrupted shaving, decorated his face. He knotted the cord of his dressing gown hard about him. "Why, Guy," repeated Mrs. Banning, "what on earth has happened?"

"What you heard," Guy said, "was Ginny taking my car out. And I won't have it. I've told her twenty times that it isn't safe for her to drive it. It's not a Ford. If she thinks I'm going to let her smash it up just for fun—the crazy little fool!"

"Oh," faltered Mrs. Banning, "how did she get it? Why, how dreadful! She couldn't hurt herself, could she?"

"I don't care what she does to herself; it's the car I'm worried about. She got it because I was fool enough to leave the keys in it. How did I know she was going to sneak around and take it when I wasn't looking? If you and Father can't make her stop, I can. I'll spank the pants off her—"

"Now, Guy!" interrupted Mrs. Banning. "That's enough! I want you to control your temper. I quite understand that you're upset; and there's no excuse for Virginia. Your father will deal with it—"

"He won't do anything to her; he never does—"

"Now, darling, we aren't going to spoil this week end with quarreling. Virginia is younger than you are. She doesn't always understand—"

"Understand?" he groaned. "What doesn't she understand? The English language? And, my God, she's practically seventeen. You talk as if she were about ten. That's the whole trouble, really. Everybody treats her like a baby. She ought to be at school. Except, I suppose, no decent school would take her, after she's been fired from everywhere on the map."

Mrs. Banning arose. "We won't talk about it when you're so excited, dear. You go and finish dressing. I'm not excusing Virginia; it was very wrong of her to take your car without your permission, and I know she won't do it again. And, Guy, try to be a little patient with her, won't you? She's not very strong, and she's not very happy. She really hasn't a friend her own age except Valeria Hoyt—"

"All right," he said, "all right! I suppose you would make her behave if you could; and if you don't, you just can't." He turned and went out.

His mother, following him, went to the stairs. The slight weight of her small, but carefully recorded and clearly seen concerns made her frown a little. She could, almost simultaneously, be anxious about Virginia; regret Guy's violence when annoyed; remember to speak to Mary about the mint sauce. From the afternoon's meeting of the School Committee, she kept her resolve to do something—perhaps appeal to Hartford—about Doctor Bull's utter neglect of his duties in regard to the compulsory vaccination of the school children at Cold Hill. Plainly the county authorities weren't going to do anything about it. Her own personal distaste for Doctor Bull, his boorishness, his coarse, roaring manner, his callous, undoubtedly ignorant neglect of his work and his patients, she tried to keep out of it; but really it was almost incredible that a family like the Bulls could have produced such a person!

From her encounter with Doctor Wyck, the Rector, she had the matters of seeing that flowers for the altar, in the proper, seasonally difficult red of an Apostle and Martyr, were on hand Tuesday. When Doctor Wyck spoke of Tuesday, she had, with the greatest presence of mind, been able to remember that it was St. Matthias's Day, and say so, before he made his own reference to the Feast of Our Patron. She was, after all, one of the few that Doctor Wyck relied on for a decorous High Church attitude, and she would have been much chagrined if she had let him down.

Then there was poor Mamie Talbot. She must really go over tomorrow and see for herself if anything could be done to make the child more comfortable. Mamie's illness brought back the never welcome thought of Doctor Bull; and she wondered if Doctor Verney couldn't be persuaded—Doctor Bull's gross negligence and incompetence made it really Doctor Verney's Christian duty—to come up and—

In the hall and along the stairs, the walls were papered in the modern copy of an old pattern. Vertically, horizontally, and obliquely, in exact alignment, three sage-green designs repeated themselves on the white ground. One was a stiff, heraldic eagle, his claws full of furled American flags; one was a laurel-wreathed bouquet of cannon, swords, muskets, and infantry drums. The third showed the gaunt face of President Jackson. Below his bust, the cleft streamer read: *Our Federal Union it must be preserved.* Mrs. Banning halted and studied it, startled, for she thought that she had seen a stain near the top at the end. Her mind jumped instantly to the chance of a tub overflowing in the bath between Guy's room and Virginia's. Relieved, she realized then that it was only a shadow, and went on.

Turning back through the hall, the half open door gave her a glimpse of the warm dusk in the library. A mixture of lamplight and failing firelight shone up the paneled, urn-topped doors of a secretary desk from her great-grandfather's New Haven house. Her husband sat before it, the pen in his hand moving steadily. Beyond his small neat shoulders and upright head, she could see the books climbing the wall in unbroken rows through the aureate twilight, gilt titles catching the glow. From this glimpse, as from the tranquil hall, and from the dining room (now that she went through it) with the fine sideboard, the laid oval table with candles unlighted, the four good Chippendale chairs—she wished that she had four more, instead of three more; but seven, when they were such exceptionally good and authentic ones, was a respectable number—Mrs. Banning could take the quiet, never-ending, often not even conscious, pleasure of a house by years of patient effort made exactly the way she wanted it, and functioning serenely under her attentive eye.

The pantry and kitchen were glowing, full of a savory warmth of good cooking, a cheery cleanliness and shining order in the porcelain and enamel, the glass and noncorrosive metals of modern equipment. Mary, seated by the prim burnt orange curtains, was reading the morning paper. Ethel was calmly busy over pots steaming on the long stove. Mary put down the paper and stood up. Ethel said: "Good evening, m'am."

"Oh, Ethel, that smells very nice," Mrs. Banning said, contented. "Mary, will you remember to use the little silver boat for the mint sauce, please? And will you bring me some ice and a shaker into the library in about five minutes? I think Mr. Banning and Guy would like a cocktail."

Laying down the tapering black shadows of screening cedars, gilding the enclosing fence of woven chestnut paling, Virginia watched her headlights sweep the garage and stable. Immediately mounted up the boom of deep throated barking. Virginia could see, now that she was past the fence, the twin dog houses near the door of Larry's living quarters. Out them were thrust the smooth piebald heads, large ears cocked bristling, belligerent, of the Great Danes. Observing that this car was going right into the garage, first Delilah, then, eagerly, Samson, planted massive thick-toed forepaws on the trampled snow. Their splotch-marked bodies emerged. First one, then the other, barked; monitory rather than excited. With diligent haste, majestic in their mere stature, they bounded together to investigate.

Virginia brought Guy's car to a halt beside her father's; switched off the ignition and then the lights. She could hear the pad of heavy feet on the cement. Samson's sharp ears and bold, big muzzle appeared, face to face with her, his paws supported on the doortop at her side. He made at once a gratified whining sound. Jostling him, up came Delilah, pawing Virginia's leather covered shoulder with her blunt claws. Virginia sat still a moment and Samson's wide wet tongue slapped vigorously down her cheek. Recoiling, she pushed his head away, opened the door, forcing them both down, and stepped out. Delilah made a half wheel, collapsed, displaying her long nipple marked breast and belly to be scratched. Virginia started to put out a foot, but her knees, she found, were not yet steady. Samson pushed his heavy head confidingly against her hip, crowding closer.

The kindness of this reception seemed enough to kill her. Virginia could feel a violent tingling in the bridge of her nose; tears swam warm into her eyes; a trembling came over her and her chest swelled to suffocation. She sniffed a little, and Delilah rolled back; disappointed, arose to her feet. Both of them tilted their heads up to regard her face, tongues hanging in mild wonder.

She managed to say, "Leave me alone, you damn fools!" for she knew that they were going to do that in a moment. Their instinctive, reasonless jubilation at sight of her would be innocently exhausted. The dog houses, slightly warmed by their big bodies, were where they wanted to be, since there was nothing to eat and no one to attack. They would withdraw, her two last senseless friends, bored with her. "Get away!" she choked. She went and snapped out the garage lights. In the darkness she could see the dogs' big shadowy shapes slip around the jamb, out against the starlit snow. When she had come out and pulled down the overhead doors, she saw that they were already back, snug in their kennels.

At the top, across the back of the last check, Mr. Banning wrote *Herbert Tracy Banning for deposit only*. He blotted it, laid it with the others. Turning the little pile over, he took the deposit slip and compared the list. Since it was correct, he put checks and slip together in a long envelope and addressed it to his New York bank. Laying the pen on the rack of an old Sheffield tray, he sat back in his chair, thoughtful.

A pad covered with columns of his neat figures informed him that he was slightly better off than he had expected to be. There might not be much margin this year; but really it was remarkable that there was any margin at all.

Part of the difference, he supposed, was not having Virginia's school bills through the winter. Getting herself expelled from Miss Keble's, however regrettable, would seem to have been a very comfortable financial lift. A solid contribution, in fact; both to him, and, little as Guy might suspect it, to Guy. It would not be necessary to bring up the matter of Guy's expenses.

This was Guy's third year at Yale, and he had managed to spend progressively more money. Naturally, he did it without making a splurge. Being ostentatiously rich was something he and his friends regarded with contemptuous distaste; the only possible worse form was being obviously poor. From what Mr. Banning had seen of these young men on rare occasions in New Haven, or when one or two of them came up to visit Guy, he concluded that they were perfectly satisfied if they had, materially, no more than the best of everything in merely practical quantities. This seemed to Mr. Banning reasonable. Philosophy had nothing to do with youth. If you were not a great athlete, or what seemed to be called a Big Man, and so beyond criticism, what buttressed your pride—not less excruciatingly sensitive for being callow—except the perfection of your clothes and possessions? It would be time enough to laugh at this puerile obsession with material things later, when the ego had found a new mainstay in some form of personal accomplishment and might even enjoy not looking like the great man every one could easily learn that you were.

Having by now a fair idea of what it cost Guy to be impeccable in Yale's eyes, Mr. Banning was prepared to add it to the already remarkably large total of Guy's expenses through school and college. Guy's education would probably prove a good investment. Guy would not, naturally, know anything in the scholastic, or even cultural sense; but he would be admirably fitted, through his acquaintances and habits of mind and life to enrich himself. There was no reason to doubt that he would be happy doing it. Since Mr. Banning had never in his own life done anything but reflect, and read in his library, and work in his garden, he was not sure that he was qualified to have an opinion on the virtue or value of Guy's prospects.

Indeed, he doubted if he knew enough about Guy to see clearly where good lay for him in life. He could not possibly guess what it was like to be Guy; or what Guy, in command of his own affairs and able to behave as best pleased him (rather than as his family with its crushing full knowledge of his past expected him to behave), was like. At home you couldn't tell; he deferred to his father partly through habit, partly perhaps because he did not and never had understood the defensive nature of his father's dry, often indulgently ironic speech. The day hadn't yet come when Guy would realize that he himself was much the more formidable of the two; that irony was really a form of embarrassment; and that what his father needed was a little firm handling. Probably, Mr. Banning reflected, he would live to find Guy competently making up his mind for him, patiently seeing that his vagaries didn't do him any real harm. Guy already had the voice and expression; he merely lacked the sharpened eye to see that his father was an aimless old putterer. The patronage of today would be reversed as Guy, turning from his large and successful affairs, found a moment to say: "Father, you know you don't want anything of the sort. It's absurd. I'll arrange to——"

The prospect amused him, and it was only right; for Guy had none of his own disabilities. Without spoiling the effect by trying, Guy could already please people worth pleasing; probably he was learning to command people not worth pleasing. Instead of walling himself up with austere and formal communications, Guy spoke out, if not fluently, positively. His position was altogether in the open and he occupied it, tough spirited, ready to take his chances. Of greater importance than not fearing or envying people more fortunate than himself, Guy would never feel embarrassed and apologetic to people less fortunate or weaker. Never apologetic, Guy could not be imposed on. Mr. Banning was accustomed to being imposed on, and knew that he was. His heart was half on the side of any knave who, having none himself, by begging or fraud tried to get what he could of Mr. Banning's money. In his frequent moments of insight, Mr. Banning could see his life as really one long, half-expressed apology for being born superior, for being kept there by money not earned, for eating when other men went hungry, riding when other men walked, living at idle ease when other men struggled to death. He did not like it much; but any more competent or arrogant attitude he would like less.

Seeing his future master coming into the library now, he shut up the desk, took a silver box from the table and, getting a cigarette from it, offered Guy one. "Would you care for a cocktail?" he asked.

"Virginia!"

She was halfway upstairs, and though she heard her mother step out of the library, she went on while she said, "What?"

"Come down, Virginia. I want to talk to you."

"It's almost dinner time. I have to change."

"Virginia—"

"Can't you ever let me alone?"

Guy had come out, too, now. "Listen, Ginny, the next time you—"

"Oh, shut up, Guy!"

"Virginia!"

The sound of her light footfalls passed along the hall above. Resounding, the door of her room went shut, slammed with all her might.

"For Heaven's sake, Mother, why do you let her get away with it?"

Mr. Banning, standing with his back to the fire, shook his head. "What's to be done?" he asked.

"You wouldn't suggest beating her, would you?"
He looked at his son with frank interest.

"Well," Guy said, "you might take her allowance away."

"That isn't very effective up here. She can't get anything she really wants with money."

"You might promise her something she really wants, if she'd behave herself for a month. Or maybe twenty minutes would be enough."

Mr. Banning smiled. "It seems to me that the last thing she wanted—unless it was your car, which, you notice, she took—was to go to a notorious roadhouse over by Torrington. It seems to be not only a speak-easy but a house of assignation. We thought that it wasn't suitable."

"She must be crazy!"

"No, I don't think it's as simple as that. We're taught that there's no disputing tastes. Only, it happens that almost all the things she wants to do—well! We can't get results by saying, 'Virginia, if you don't obey, you won't be allowed to go to the Congregational Church Supper.'"

Guy was slightly amused. "You might try saying that if she didn't obey, she'd have to go."

"We might," admitted Mr. Banning, "but I think we won't. I don't know whether you've seen Mr. Kean, the new minister there. He appears to be a polite and agreeable young man. I don't think it would be fair to him to send Virginia in a resentful mood. She's no great respecter of places and persons."

"The whole trouble," Guy said, "is that you simply spoil her. She knows by this time that nothing ever happens to her, no matter what she does. That's why she always gets into trouble at school. She's never had to learn to do what she's told and keep still. When she knows nothing is going to happen to her—"

"Now, it seems to me that you're wrong there," Mr. Banning objected. "In point of fact, the most terrible things happen to her all the time."

"Herbert, what on earth do you mean?"

"My dear, I mean that every time she thinks of something she would like to do, her elders prevent her from doing it. What could be worse?"

"Well, she shouldn't want to do such asinine things!"

"Herbert, I don't think that's true at all. It seems to me that she has a remarkable amount of freedom."

Guy, gazing at him, said: "You're always on her side, Father. You'd let her get away with murder if—"

"Dinner is served, M'am."

"Oh, Mary, Virginia isn't down yet. Could we have five minutes?"

"I'm coming," she shouted. She stepped out of the shower, jerked off her rubber cap and slung it into the tub. Snatching a towel, she dried herself ferociously, writhed into step-ins. Coming into her room, she pulled out a drawer and found stockings, flung open the closet and threw on the bed first her blue frock, then slippers. Her stockings on, her frock over her head, she dropped before the dressing table, pulled a comb through her fluffy brownish hair, drove a hairpin in by her left ear to hold it. Working her feet into the slippers, she unstopped a lipstick, smeared her upper lip, passed her lower lip over it. Leaving everything in great confusion, she went out and downstairs, hungry and very pale. It had taken her about four minutes.

In the candle-lighted dining room, her father drew out her chair. "I hear you went for a drive," he said, seating her. "How does Guy's car behave?"

"It's all right."

"Comfortable?"

"Yes."

"He was particularly anxious to know what you thought of it."

A slight, stain-like flush began to appear on Virginia's cheekbones. She lifted her eyes and looked across the table at Guy. "I'm sorry I took your damn car," she said. "I won't do it again."

"Well, all right," said Guy. "It doesn't matter."

Mrs. Banning, starting belatedly at the word "damn," let her lips part to protest, but Mr. Banning said: "Very handsome, Guy. I think we can call the matter closed. What happened at the School Board meeting, Lucile?"

"I want to talk to you about it sometime," she said promptly.

Where Guy got his reasonable decisiveness was easy to see; but the truth was, Mr. Banning found it pleasanter in Lucile. That was; there were known limits to it. If she would consider it weak to be indecisive, she would consider it ill-bred to be assertive; and looking at her, he could guess that that consideration had once more stopped her short of accomplishment.

"As bad as that?" he said, smiling.

"No. I simply want to find out what we can do about a new Medical Examiner. It's really getting out of hand."

"Old Doc Bull cutting up?" asked Guy. "How's his inamorata, by the way?"

"Guy!"

"Oh, heavens, Mother," observed Virginia, her voice reviving, "don't you think I know he sleeps with Miss Cardmaker?"

"Herbert, I really—"

"My dear, Virginia knew all about it, it seems. What is the present difficulty?"

"He simply will not do the work. I think Doctor Verney could find somebody in Sansbury who would come up. The difficulty is what it always is. Mr. Harris and Mr. Lane. Of course, I cannot get on with Mr. Harris. I've always been as pleasant to him as I knew how, but I know he dislikes me and I know he dislikes Mr. Getchell. I've been noticing recently, and I've never known him to agree to anything that Mr. Getchell and I favored. It seems to me real malevolence in a case like this. I mean, for him to insist on keeping an ignorant, careless, indifferent doctor in charge of the school children's health just to be contrary—"

"What happened about your note to the County Health Officer?"

"I had an answer. He said he would bring the complaint to Doctor Bull's attention. Of course that doesn't do any good. Doctor Bull has no interest in public health. He—"

"Or else, too much," Mr. Banning said. "You surely haven't forgotten that his zeal in the

[81]

performance of his duty cost me fifty dollars last week? Larry, by the way, is something only very rich people can afford; it gets clearer and clearer to me."

"Herbert, that fine was simply spite. He knew about my writing to Litchfield. He knew I'd been trying to have something done about the vaccinations at Cold Hill since last September."

"But without success?"

"No. I mean, yes. How could I? I want to take the matter up with Hartford."

"Well, I'll bet he did them today," said Virginia, interested. "I met him coming from around the Cobble this afternoon, when I was going out to Val's. I guess he wouldn't have been at Joel Parry's; I know he wasn't at the Hoyts'; and that awful Mr. Lincoln is away. So he must have been up Cold Hill."

"That doesn't change the fact that he should have done them months ago."

"I'm afraid you'll find it does, though," Mr. Banning said. "As long as his duty wasn't done, you had a slight chance, if you could reach the right people, of getting somebody in lawful authority to write a letter asking him please to do it at his earliest convenience. I'm afraid not much attention will be paid, once it's learned that what you complain about has already been taken care of."

"Herbert, it's hard for me to believe that in this day and age we have to be saddled with that depraved old monster. To leave the health of the whole town officially in his care—"

"My dear, if the town is satisfied with it, what can you do? He isn't our physician. It would be hard to show how his failings could possibly affect us. Consequently I don't know that we have much right to interfere on behalf of people who don't see the need for interference."

"Well, I can assure you that plenty of people do see the need. I think that it would be a very poor attitude for me to take, that because he doesn't affect us, or can't, it's not my concern. I certainly shan't rest until I've seen what can be done with the State Health Department."

"The State Health Department acts in an advisory capacity, Lucile. Strictly advisory. We're very jealous of our small independences in Connecticut. Personally I'm all in favor of as little interference from Hartford as possible; but of course, one drawback to being free is that you have to take care of yourself."

"Well, I wish you'd show me exactly what the law is on the subject. Do you know?"

"Only vaguely, my dear. As a Justice of Peace, I try to keep some track of the Connecticut Code, but there isn't much practical incentive. We so seldom have any cases. However, we can look it up. I'm not sure that I would advise you to press the matter against a general indifference. It's easily misinterpreted as officiousness—the train of pride, the impudence of wealth. If wealth it can be called."

"Are you through, Guy? All right, we'll go and have coffee."

The pantry door swung ajar and Mary said, "Might I speak to you a moment, M'am?"

"Why, yes, Mary." Mrs. Banning turned and went into the pantry.

In the library, Mr. Banning said, "Cigar, son?"

"I guess not, thanks, sir." Guy snapped open a cigarette case. He took a cigarette and Virginia took another.

"I'm afraid not," said Mr. Banning. "I don't want to seem tyrannical, but I've explained to you before that any smoking you do until after your seventeenth birthday will have to be surreptitious. That's not such a great inconvenience for you, is it?"

Virginia threw the cigarette into the fire. "Daddy," she said, "I want to go to Paris. I can, can't I? Val's going. We're going to stay with a French family. Mr. Hoyt stayed with them when he was studying in Paris; and we'd be perfectly all right; and it would hardly cost anything."

"Hardly anything is rather an elastic term."

"I mean, maybe a thousand dollars, for a whole year. Daddy, say I can!"

"Don't be crazy!" said Guy. "What on earth would you do in Paris?"

"I'd learn French, and we could study, and—"

"Good so far," admitted Mr. Banning. "But is it far enough? Perhaps we'd better postpone the hearing to give you time to prepare your case. I don't think your mother would be enough impressed—"

"But you think I should go? You think it's all right? Please, Daddy."

"Now, now, now. I have to see which way the wind is blowing. You can't expect me to go in on the losing side, can you?"

"Daddy, don't joke! Won't you please say yes?"

"Ginny, what good would it do you to hear me say yes, when your mother is so likely to say no?"

"Daddy, I've got to go. I just can't stand it here!"

"When is Val going?"

"In April, unless her father has to go to New Mexico. But he won't have to. She wrote for our reservations."

"My dear, I'm sorry to say it, but there is not the faintest chance of your going in April. I simply won't have the money."

"Daddy! Only ninety dollars! You could send me the rest later. Only ninety dollars, Daddy!"

"Virginia, you may not know it, but with things as they are, ninety dollars is by no means a trifle. If ninety dollars were the end of it, I won't pretend that it couldn't be managed. But, my dear, it's not. The sum you first named wouldn't be a beginning. In matters like this, one thousand dollars always means two and usually three. I absolutely cannot afford to add that way to our expenses at the moment. In a year or two—"

"Listen, Ginny, don't you even know there's a depression on?"

Virginia sat down tense on the edge of a chair. "Daddy, please! Please! I wouldn't ask you if—"

"You might as well ask me for the moon, my dear. I haven't got it. If, in a year or two, things look better, I promise you I'll manage somehow to make it possible for you to spend a year in Paris, if you still want to. You'll be older then, and your mother may not object so much. Now, now; economic necessity is insensible to tears! That's why the poor are always with us."

"Don't be so rotten and selfish, Ginny!" said Guy. "You ought to be ashamed of yourself, sitting here bawling because you can't go on a bat to Paris, when God knows how many million people don't know where their next meal's coming from!"

"Well, son," said Mr. Banning, "that sounds like a social conscience! Is it a permanent improvement, or are you just experimenting with it to add to your sister's troubles?" He came over, drew a handkerchief from his breast pocket and put it in Virginia's hands. "Can't we keep this from your mother? You see, even if she were to consent, we couldn't manage it. No need to have a difference of opinion over what we would or would not do if we could. That's a good girl. You just sit back in that chair out of the light and you'll do——"

"Herbert!"

"Why, Lucile! What is it?"

"Oh, my dear—that poor child! Mary's brother just came in. Mamie's dead."

➤➤➤ TWO ⬅⬅⬅

Even Belle Rogers would not wait until after midnight to learn if or when he left. Walking to his car, there was not a light George Bull could see anywhere; there was no one to see him. Under the dark hill of the barn, in tepid darkness, the cows maintained a vigil in their fashion; some aimlessly standing; some couched philosophic on the concrete. They were not bored; probably they were not sad nor weary. If they heard the mortal gasps of the Devon dying near them, they knew by now that the noise did not mean anything worth attention.

George Bull thought of it, oppressed, for the disgust of sobriety regained, and his body's accumulated need to sleep, took the life out of his wakefulness. Leadenly, he was aware of himself alive, and so, heavy hearted, of death—of when he would no longer be what he now wearily was. The evil destinies of man and the immense triumphs of death, seen so clearly at this bad hour, loaded him down. Discouragement, to feel death's certainty; exasperation, to know the fatuousness of resisting such an adversary—what was the use of temporary evasions or difficult little remedies when death simply came back and came back until it won?—moved him more than any personal dread of extinction, or compassion for those stricken. The stricken, beyond help, were beyond needing help. During the last forty years, fully a hundred human beings had actually died while he watched. He couldn't recall one who gave signs of minding much; they were too sick or too badly hurt to care. If they were conscious enough to know that they were alive, pain blurred their view; they saw no good anywhere. They were not given peace to regret a lost future; they were beyond desiring anything. In its melancholy way, the flesh, maligned mortality, took tender care of its own. It would never let the intolerable be long imposed; the impossible was never required. George Bull thought: "The Bulls are long-lived. I might be here twenty years from now, without surprising any one."

The air he breathed in was raw, but less cold. Clammy, no longer bracing, the bitter windless dark of the valley suggested a wasteland, a country and climate unfitted to support human life. Getting down to them, the bright infrequent street lights of New Winton shone on desertion that could not have been greater had every house stood cold and empty, had every human being lain long dead.

Awakening Saturday morning, he could see how well sleep had served him, how unreal the thoughts of his desolate home-coming had been.

He could see, too, the rain waving in curtains across the hills, the mists hung low. That great disconsolation, that unhappy sense of death and vanity, was doubtless a barometric matter, a mere change in atmospheric pressure.

In the bathtub, George Bull sat in warm water above his waist, soaping impartially his short graying hair, his new shaven face, his big torso. Lying down, he sloshed about, rinsing. He heaved water up in his hands, getting the suds off his head. He wallowed about, grunting and puffing. Sitting up, he spattered water far and wide. It shook gleaming from his shoulders. On his chest and wide arms, the dark hair was spread flat in sleek, bedraggled wisps.

Snorting once more, he regained his voice, cheerful in a mounting sense of his well-being. Below, in the kitchen, Mrs. Cole and Susie Andrews, who were intermittently eating their own breakfasts and preparing his, could hear him begin to sing again, a vibrating bass rumble of *Adeste Fideles*. Triumphant, at the top of his lungs, he handled the awkward English wording with agile malice. It made him think of bitter mornings, Michigan Christmases, maybe fifty years ago; but he was never through being glad that they were over. "—Lo! He abhors not the Vir-r-gin's womb. Ver-er-y Gah-hod; begotten, not crea-a-ted. . . ." He snorted and wallowed again; he emerged, standing on his feet, caroling heartily: "Oh come, let us adore Him! Oh come, let us . . ."

The whole house felt the distinct faint jar of his stepping onto the mat. Working with a towel, he interrupted or embellished his singing with whoops and hoots. Opening the door to go to his bedroom, he could smell the mixed upfloating odors of sausage and pancakes, wood smoke and coffee. The glimpse of rain on the spoiled snow, of soaked tree branches, gave new comfort to the warmth, a new savor to the fine smell of breakfast. He roared with pleasure; he knew plenty of hymns.

Dressed, coming downstairs, his voice preceded him like a herald: "Crown Him with many crowns, The Lamb upon His throne; Hark! how the heavenly anthem drowns. . . ."

He turned back through the hall. His office door was open and in the gloom there he could see Susie dusting, shuffling about in the slippers Mrs. Cole would make her put on instead of her wet shoes as soon as she came in. Susie called thinly: "Morning, Doctor Bull!" and he waved a hand in casual salute. Entering the kitchen, he shouted: "Breakfast! Breakfast! Breakfast! Hello, Aunt Myra! Looking younger every day!"

"Kenneth, where were you last night?"

"He was in Heaven, Aunt Myra. This is Eph's boy, George."

"You've no need to be telling me who you are, shouting around like that! I heard you up in the bathroom. And I'm not so sure Kenneth's in Heaven, much as I hope he may be. Now, sit right down and start your breakfast. Susie doesn't have to go to school today and we have all we can do this morning."

A place had been laid on the cleared end of the kitchen table, and she put a hand on his elbow, impelling him toward it. "Drink your orange juice; and here's your porridge. Where did I put that cream? There. Now, I'll start your cakes. Your coffee will be ready directly— and see you eat plenty before you go out on a day like this."

"Who says I'm going out?"

"Oh. Well, now, let's see. Oh, some one died. That little telephone girl, Helen, I think her name is, told me last night. I was going to leave a note for you, but it went right out of my mind. Susie! Did you hear about any one dying yesterday?"

"I heard Mamie Talbot died, Mrs. Cole."

"Maybe that's it, then."

"Well, I'm damned!" said George Bull. "Died, did she? I thought she'd probably get through. Well, I will have to go out. It's against the law to die around here without a certificate. All we need now's the enabling legislation and we'll live forever."

"George, you stop sitting there blaspheming and scoffing. Here's your cakes and sausage. You eat them. We'll all die in the Lord's good time; and people who go around swearing every other word the way you do will have plenty to answer for, I shouldn't be surprised. There's the syrup, and I'll have some more cakes in a min-ute—"

She stood still, arrested, cocking her head slightly. No sound could be heard in the house and she called out: "Susie! You just keep out of those books of the Doctor's. First thing you know you'll be getting yourself into bad habits. March right out here and begin on the dishes!"

There was a pause, a succession of slight, furtive sounds, and Susie appeared. "I don't ever touch anything of the Doctor's, Mrs. Cole. I was just dusting the bookcases."

"Hm. That's as it may be. It took you a long time. Now, there's no more batter, George, and I'll not mix more this morning. You'll just have to make out with these. I never did see a man eat as much!"

"Got two hundred and fifteen pounds to keep up, Aunt Myra."

"Well, I expect most of it's whisky fat. There's the doorbell. Go and see who it is, Susie."

Susie turned about and shuffled back. There was a sound of the door opening, the murmur of a voice, and Susie called shrilly, "It's the telephone. A man says, will you please hang up the receiver."

*

Virginia Banning pushed her cold bare feet into slippers whose high sides were lined with rabbit fur. Over her pajamas she pulled a flannel bathrobe. Not sitting down, she bent to the dressing-table mirror, tugged the comb twice through her sleep-tangled hair, drove in the single hairpin. Listless, she jabbed her finger over the end of an open lipstick and transferred the scarlet smear to her upper lip. Deepened by animosity and a sort of contempt, her blue eyes gazed hard back at her from the glass. "I look lousy!" she said aloud.

She leaned a moment, supported by her clenched hand on the dressing-table top, held by this consuming, utterly hopeless abhorrence.

[92]

She hated the slight hollows under the drawn, thin-looking skin of her cheeks. Her hair, fluffy without being curly, seemed to her the color of rat's fur. The boy's bathrobe, buttoned across her flat chest, was striped vertically in blue and gray. She had that left from her never-completed fall term at school. It was a regulation garment at Miss Keble's. Severe, practical, it aborted drastically all individual, too-luxurious developments in negligee. "In one of these," she remembered some one saying, "a girl would be safe even rooming with a Yale man. . . ."

Her thought was deflected, for it had been an item in the credulous and absurd general sophistication of the school that youths from Yale were invariably passionate and dangerous. Like so many of the beliefs that made life dramatic and exciting for other girls, this one was spoiled for Virginia. Although she really knew no Yale men except Guy, that was enough. She could see that Yale men were no more than that—just Guy. "God! I'd tear his eyes out!" she said, forgetting even her hatred of her own face in the momentary hotter one for some hypothetical, essentially Guy-like youth putting purposeful hands on her.

Her glance swept from the mirror, met the endless drenching fall of rain over the bare maples beyond the drive. A dissolving mess of snow clung, the white now gray with water, to the lawns. She jerked around, loathing the dismal day as much as she loathed men, for amounting to no more than they did; and her own white face, for looking—she said it through her teeth—like something the cat brought in.

In the hall, she heard her mother's voice, mild and clear from her sitting room: "Virginia?"

"Yes, Mother."

"Are you up, darling?"

"I'm not dressed."

"Well, darling, Val telephoned; but please don't plan to go out there. I may want you to go over to the Talbots' with me this morning."

"Oh, Mother! What for?"

"Virginia, I don't see how you can be so heartless."

"I just can't stand Mrs. Talbot and that awful shack—I mean, if it would do any good—"

"I'm sorry, darling; but if it clears up at all, I think we will really have to go. And get your breakfast right away, dear. Mary has a great deal to do this morning."

Val had telephoned to learn about going to Paris, of course; and, of course, too, there wasn't anything about it. This distracting sense of nothing about anything, the length of minutes and hours of nothing—Virginia thought, screwing her eyes closed and gripping the stair rail: "God, I'll have to go to some rotten school again; I just can't stand it here!" At once she thought further: "If I said I'd go to school and try not to get fired, they'd send me. Why couldn't I have the same money to go to Paris with Val?"

In the dining room a fire was burning. Guy, clad in a tan camel's-hair sweater, knickerbockers, and an extremely old tweed jacket, was not through breakfast. He ate, as he did everything else, with an unconscious assurance. It might not be fair to say that Guy was pleased with himself, in the sense of taking active pleasure in counting over his own good qualities; but at least he didn't worry about himself. He knew by now that he and his more intimate friends were right; or, at any rate, he could easily see that people who differed conspicuously in dress or behavior, in ideals or attitudes, were, as far as his college was concerned, wrong. His gray eyes considered all those in error with a level, complete indifference. He did not know them and never expected to. His face, past adolescence, coming into final form, showed the mold of this ruthless rightness. Virginia supposed some people might think he was good looking. "Hello," she said.

Guy got to his feet, mechanically. "Hoyt girl called you up," he announced.

"I know." Virginia went to the pantry door, pushed it open, and called, "Mary, could I have some coffee?" She came back to the table and sat down.

"Cheerful child," observed Guy. "You ought to—"

"Can't you even let me get some coffee first? And what's there to be cheerful about? Mamie's passing-out party?"

Guy's face showed the delicate, haughty stiffening which indicated outrage. "For Heaven's sake, Ginny, doesn't any one matter to you but yourself?"

"I suppose you mean that you're all broken up about Mamie. I'll bet you don't even have to go over. You'll fool around with your wonderful car all morning."

"At least I have the decency to be sorry."

"That's cheap, I guess. What's it to Mamie? She's dead, isn't she? Who wouldn't rather be dead than living in a hole like New Winton?"

"You sound like a fool!"

"Oh, God, Guy; let me alone, can't you?"

"Well, what have I done?"

"You just go yammering on about what people ought to do and what they ought to feel—who told you? How do you know?"

"Well, what do you want to talk the way you do for?"

"Maybe I don't want to. Maybe you make me. I wish you could hear yourself sometime—'At least I have the decency to be sorry'!"

Guy reddened a little across his firm forehead. He opened his mouth with an icy, drastic animosity, but at the same instant Mary came in and he shut it again. "Morning, Miss Ginny," Mary said. She set down a small silver coffee pot and a covered dish of toast. "Now, just let me boil you a couple of nice eggs—"

"I couldn't eat them, Mary. I only want coffee."

Guy, the edge gone off his anger, said: "Half your trouble is never eating anything—"

"Mary, please don't fix me any eggs."

Her hand shook a little as she lifted the coffee pot, and Guy, observing it, now that the door was closed behind Mary, said: "Look at that! It's just plain starvation. They ought to send you down to Doctor Verney—"

"Guy, for Christ's sake, leave me alone!"

"With pleasure!" He snapped a flame up on a leather-covered lighter, lit a cigarette and got

[96]

to his feet. "Speaking of hearing yourself, I wish you could hear yourself sometime. You can't open your mouth without swearing. If you think that sort of thing is smart, I can tell you it isn't. You sound exactly like a West Haven chippy. I don't care whether you eat anything. If you want to be a living skeleton—" He went past her, out into the hall.

Virginia stared straight before her, at the disordered table, the frilling yellow flames up off the orange embers in the fireplace. Her hand was trembling so that she couldn't pour, and she put down the silver pot. She had her teeth locked together and now she clenched her hands; but it was not going to do her any good. The short, strangling gasps of sobs, unwanted, unendurable, strengthened in spite of her. She pressed her palms over her wet eyes; she bent her head down until it lay on the table. Now came the sudden swing of the pantry door, and Mary's startled voice: "Why, Miss Ginny—"

"Oh, leave me alone!" she wailed. "*Leave me alone!*"

*

Mrs. Talbot had been difficult, of course. First, she would not sleep alone in a house with a dead body; then, she seemed to see it as more Mamie and less corpse. She would not leave Mamie all night alone and sleep in May's house. Harry Weems, coming back with a bottle of gin and some oranges, had solved the problem by saying he would stay with Joe. Much as she disliked it,

May was free to sleep over at Mrs. Talbot's.
Joe didn't care, as long as she got Mrs. Talbot
out of his sight as soon as possible.

Again, Harry had been invaluable. May had
supper to get. Harry made a drink for Mrs. Talbot. Not too far sunk in her misery to feel that
Joe was definitely hostile, Mrs. Talbot couldn't
have been managed without Harry. She kept
saying: "Don't mind me. Don't go to any trouble—" She addressed Harry, but she said it in
Joe's direction, peevish and put-upon. Obviously Joe was unable to go to any trouble, but
he might act as though he would like to, if he
could. Still protesting that she really didn't
want anything and needed no attention, she
drank what Harry prepared for her. After that
she recovered enough to eat a little. The gin and
food joined, mercifully, to stupefy her. She was
soon in danger of going to sleep right there, so
May cleaned up in a hurry and stacked the
dishes. Mrs. Talbot, taken home and helped to
bed, was snoring almost at once, leaving everything to May. The place ought to be straightened up a little, since people would certainly be
coming in tomorrow, so May applied herself to
that. When she had done what she could with the
front room, she hesitated a moment. "I mustn't
be silly," she said, aloud. Turning on the light
in the back bedroom, she went in there.

Of the cruelties of illness, chief might be the
change in disposition, from which Joe, once perpetually smiling, good-humoredly easygoing,
had suffered. He was the same person, and yet
he wasn't. Of the many cruelties of death, there
was one like that. Mamie, living, had been re-

garded as pretty. Living, she had a youthful-
ness, or mere animation, which screened her
resemblance to her mother. May had never noticed it; and she stood, disturbed, for Mamie,
dead, was a little Mrs. Talbot. Her nose looked
slight as a knife. The bony structure of her face
showing through was patterned exactly on Mrs.
Talbot's.

Regarding this phenomenon of a face which
was both Mamie, sick and thin, and some one else
inextricably mingled with her, May continued
to stand, her hands lax, overpowered by discouragement. She had wished, somehow, to arrange
it so that curious people would see Mamie
serenely asleep, not contorted and ravaged. This
way no one could miss the subtle record of her last
struggles, so terrible as they grew more surely
vain, to get air; although unconscious in her
stupor, to keep from drowning in her own
clogged lungs. Any superficial arrangement
would be futile. Whatever was done, Howard
Upjohn would have to do; and immediately May
could guess details of that grim fantastic art—
the work with rouge, the dressing of dead hair—
which simulated peace or dignity in a corpse.

When May finally moved, it was to draw back
the twisted covers. The flannel nightgown had
worked up to wrinkle about Mamie's waist. It
was possible to see, shockingly, the shape of hip
bones through the wasted flesh; the thighs were
shrunk almost to bony pipes; there were no
calves left to the legs. Drawing down the nightgown, May wondered if it would be possible to
dress Mamie. Turning her over, hideous, wasted,
hardly covered, to Howard Upjohn seemed ter-

rible; but she could not see how it was to be helped. She pulled the sheet across Mamie's face, making it lie as straight and smooth as she could, turned out the light.

Mrs. Talbot was still snoring in the front bed-room. There was nothing left to do but wrap herself in the blanket which she had brought over with her and lie down on the broken springs of the couch. May, too, slept. At seven Harry Weems ran over through the rain and woke her up.

Joe said: "Hell! Look at it rain! I bet Louie won't come over."

"He will," promised May. She went to the window, looking out to see if any one were approaching Mrs. Talbot's house. "I'll go and tell him he's got to."

"I'll tell him," said Harry. "I want to go over anyway. Thanks for breakfast. So long, Joe. Be seeing you."

May followed him out through the kitchen to the back door. "Make Louie promise," she said. "And thanks an awful lot, Harry."

"I guess you know I'll do anything I can, May. Listen, some one ought to telephone Doc Bull about coming down. They'll have to have a death certificate for Mamie. Want me to do it?"

"Will you? And you won't forget about Louie?"

Louie came from his barber shop over by the station on Tuesdays and Saturdays to shave Joe. He had started by doing it free. After a month or so, he became, like every one except

Harry, less enthusiastic. May said she thought that he ought to be paid. He hadn't objected, except to remark that a quarter would be enough for both times.

On the whole, it was better to have it arranged that way. In a life like Joe's, Louie's coming to shave him was an event of the first importance. May felt freer about seeing that Louie did come, when it wasn't just a favor. Joe would be feeling depressed enough on a miserable day like this without having to forego Louie. She said, "Joe, I'll have to go back to get Mrs. Talbot some coffee. You don't mind, do you?"

Joe said: "Sure, I mind. But it don't do me any good." He was still surly, oppressed by the weather and the chance that Louie might not come. "Why can't you let some one else do something? I don't see that it's any of your business. Why don't you let her alone?"

"I'll come back as soon as I can, Joe. I just want to wait until Doc Bull gets down and they decide what they're going to do."

"What they ought to do is put her in the nut house over at Middletown," Joe said. "She gets crazier all the time—"

"I meant, about Mamie," May said. "Joe, do you want your bottle again before I go?"

"My God, no!" he exploded. "What do you think I am? The town reservoir?"

To give mere curiosity pause was this ceaseless fall of rain, this dreary, abominable day. To interfere with mere sympathy was Mrs. Talbot herself. Mrs. Talbot had been in miserable want too long. Her poverty approximated a disease; it might be catching. Living on what was called the back street, near the railroad, behind the houses fronting the east of the green, Mrs. Talbot's immediate neighbors were all poor. They struggled to maintain a pinched and difficult self-respect. By keeping their bills small, they managed to pay them, and so to make their poverty their own business. This was the only luxury possible to them; prizing it, they did not practice the sympathetic fellowship of those poor beyond hope in the squalor of big cities. Because it was well known that Mrs. Talbot would borrow, but could never lend herself, or even return, they must exclude her. They could even exclude her with bitterness. Themselves unable to afford that small wastage of borrowed cups of flour or sugar, they could be indignant that Mrs. Talbot should dare to need them when, had she chosen to go without a telephone, used for no practical purpose at all beyond interminable whining conversations with her brother's widow who did housework for the Herrings at Banning's Bridge, she might be that, at least, ahead.

Nobody knew how much money she had been allowed to owe Bates. The clerks would not let her have anything more, but, by appealing to Mr. Bates, she could and did add to the debt. Mr. Bates, cornered, assented at once, trying sadly to stop her explanations; blinking at her as though he hoped that she might change into somebody else and spare him, not the small loss of goods, but the great ordeal of doing what he was a fool to do. His daughter, Geraldine, coming out of the post office, or any one of his clerks, would promptly start what Mr. Bates meekly called, giving him hell; but he had never refused any one credit to buy food. All of Mrs. Talbot's neighbors at some time or another found it necessary to owe Mr. Bates money. Laboriously, they paid it to the last penny. It was hard to see Mrs. Talbot never paying, nor ever likely to.

Mrs. Andrews, peering from a curtained window perhaps a hundred feet away beyond a fragment of picket fence, could not take the risk of visiting Mrs. Talbot. Others, farther along the street, but well aware of what was going on, felt the same. Mrs. Talbot, asked if there were anything they could do, would certainly say yes. She would need things which they could not afford to give. Like Mrs. Andrews, peeping restlessly, they were all ill-at-ease, distressed by their own unkind prudence. The only solace was that May Tupping appeared to be able, or at least, willing, to bear the brunt, to act for all in the role of neighbor. May, they could reflect, got a regular salary from the telephone company. Thus, people who came to Mrs. Talbot would not be the ones nearest at hand.

The first one who did come was Mrs. Jackson. May, looking anxiously out the front window for Doctor Bull's car, saw Mrs. Jackson at the back door of the plain but very neat, brightly red-painted little building which was the New Winton branch of Gosselin Brothers. Mrs. Jackson had a basket covered with newspaper on her arm. In clean white apron and coat, a cap bearing Gosselin's entwined scarlet monogram tilted on his head, her husband, who was the manager, stood in out of the rain, putting up her umbrella for her. By chance seeing this, May could not imagine where Mrs. Jackson was going, as she trudged straight across the back. Mrs. Jackson had gained the road, gone over it carefully through the puddles and softening mud, and May still didn't guess.

The Jacksons weren't New Winton people. Gosselin Brothers simply waved a hand, and up sprang the scarlet store, windows covered with brightly printed strips—*Prunes. Average 55 to lb. 3 lbs. 19c; Fancy Salt Pork lb. 15c*—It was swept and spotless, backed by elaborate refrigerators, blazing with electric light, walled solidly with the profusion of brightly packed goods put down once or twice a week by Gosselin ten-ton trucks. Every item was three or seven or thirteen cents cheaper than the same thing at Bates's or Upjohn's. Mr. Jackson, with his apron, coat and cap fresh every morning, seemed as much part of the fixtures as the refrigerators. What was regarded as the unfairness of Gosselin's competition caused the Jacksons to be let alone socially, as though the people who could not resist trading there wished to pretend that they didn't. The last person in New Winton who might be expected to come was Mrs. Jackson. May, astounded, saw her walk deliberately up the ill-kept cinder path.

Turning, May called: "Mrs. Talbot, Mrs. Jackson is coming in."

News so surprising should certainly draw a response, and getting none, May went to the door of the bedroom. Opening her mouth to re-peat, she stopped, shocked. "Why, Mrs. Talbot, what's the matter?"

There was really no need to ask. May could see that Mrs. Talbot must have decided to let go again. Sitting on the bed, she had brought her feet up, clasped her hands about her knees and laid her forehead against them. The posture, so suggestive of a terrible despair, and so absurd, almost jaunty in its youthful flexibility, irri-tated May nearly as much as it disturbed her. She went and took Mrs. Talbot by the shoulder. "If you don't feel well, you just lie down," she said, "but you can't sit there like that. Mrs. Jackson's coming up the path now."

Thus urged, half forced, by May's impa-tient hand, Mrs. Talbot moved, turning and putting her feet on the floor. "Seems like I can't get any peace," she said with unexpected harsh-ness. "What's that woman want?"

Mrs. Jackson had reached the door and knocked on it. Mrs. Talbot, starting, seemed to weaken. "I don't believe I want to see her, May. I—"

"She won't stay long, Mrs. Talbot. I think she's bringing you some things."

"No, none of them stay. They all get out as quick as they can. I don't have anybody who cares—"

"Now, Mrs. Talbot, that's not true—"

Since nothing could have been truer, May saved herself by rushing out to the door. "Come in, Mrs. Jackson. There, let me take your um-brella."

Mrs. Jackson seemed to be in an anguish of

embarrassment. "Oh, how do you do, Mrs. Tupping," she faltered. "My, isn't it a mean day! I just want to tell Mrs. Talbot how awful sorry Malcolm and I are about her bereavement. I just know how awfully she feels. I just thought I might bring her something. I mean, I know how it is and I thought some things that wouldn't need cooking—"

Agitated, she pulled off the wet newspapers covering the basket. May could see a ham, and at least a dozen cans of various sorts and sizes. Mr. Jackson could get them at cost, of course, but even so that basketful came to money. May found herself almost as embarrassed as Mrs. Jackson. "Oh, that's kind of you—" she said.

"Well, I just thought—my sister-in-law had a little girl die when we lived in Bayonne, New Jersey. At such a time, it just doesn't seem as if you could do anything, and—"

Mrs. Jackson was still floundering, dismayed by the difficulties which she had nervously foreseen. She couldn't quite manage the assured, sympathetic patronage of her less fortunate neighbors. Mrs. Tupping, who was actually nothing but a thin blond girl, came in her civil reserve closer to patronizing Mrs. Jackson. Mrs. Talbot herself hadn't even bothered to put in an appearance. They did not know what to do with Mrs. Jackson, formerly of Bayonne, New Jersey, even when she brought gifts.

Mrs. Jackson, hazily in her own mind envisioning the opportunity of saying to Mrs. Vogel, or Mrs. Ely, or both, that she had just felt that she ought to do something for that poor Mrs.

Talbot over on the back street, saw that it would not mean what she thought. Mrs. Tupping and poor Mrs. Talbot would have known what to do with the Vogels or Elys. They went just a shade under Bates, Ordway, Quimby, Harris, Weems, Upjohn; a shade over, Talbot, Tupping, Clark, Webster, Foster, Andrews. Since no one, by his behavior, gave the faintest sign of considering himself inferior to any one else, these were subtleties you had to recognize by long acquaintance. Mrs. Jackson was not being recognized as anything; no one had taken her in and so given her a level and a place which every one else could understand. The Vogels, the Elys, and Mrs. Fell whose husband owned the meat market were the ones she seemed to be thrown with, but they did not treat her as though the things that interested them could be expected to interest her. They did not ask about her or tell her about themselves. Thus she was greatly confused when she had learned for the first time (months after she had been acting as neighborly as she could) that the Vogels weren't German, in the sense of being born in Europe, the way every one with a foreign-sounding name was in Bayonne. They had been right there for a hundred and fifty years, descendants of the foremen of the old furnace. You had to live here all your life to know, with that perfect assurance, all these things about everybody. There was not one woman in town who called Mrs. Jackson by her Christian name, or offered to share anything but the most superficial and impersonal gossip with her.

May, seeing Mrs. Jackson's disappointment,

though not clearly over what, decided that she wanted appreciation of her generosity. "Mrs. Talbot," she called, "I want to show you the lovely things Mrs. Jackson brought."

Mrs. Talbot groaned, for the first time audible. "Yes, May, I'm coming." She put in her bedraggled appearance, holding the door jamb. "I'm sure it's very kind of you, Mrs. Jackson. I thank you very much."

Mrs. Jackson gathered herself together. "I don't want to intrude at a time like this," she said. "I just wanted to tell you how awfully sorry Malcolm and I—"

"Yes, that's very nice of you," said Mrs. Talbot without conviction.

"I think you'd better lie down again, Mrs. Talbot," suggested May, blushing at the listlessness of the acknowledgment. The sound of a motor coming to a halt outside reached her and she said: "I believe that's Doctor Bull now. You lie down, Mrs. Talbot, and before he goes we'll have him look at you—"

"Well, I will. I don't feel very good, if Mrs. Jackson will excuse me."

"Yes, of course. I just wanted to—"

There was a rap on the door and May went to it.

"Oh," she said, much relieved, "Mrs. Bates. Do come in. Hello, Gerry."

Geraldine Bates carried this basket. "Want me to put the junk out in the kitchen, May?" she asked. She glanced briefly at Mrs. Jackson and nodded. "Oh, how do you do, Mrs. Jackson," said Mrs. Bates, surprised. "Isn't the weather terrible! May, I'll just speak to Mrs. Talbot a moment and we'll go along." She lowered her voice. "Howard been over yet?"

"No, he hasn't, Mrs. Bates. We're still waiting for Doctor Bull."

"My goodness, hasn't he been here at all?"

"Not yet."

"I mean, wasn't he here when it happened?"

"No, he wasn't."

"Well, I do call that dreadful!"

"Oh, my," agreed Mrs. Jackson. "That is terrible, isn't it?"

"Didn't anybody call him, May?"

"He was out all afternoon, Mrs. Bates. I expect he was on another case, and Mrs. Cole had gone to Sansbury."

"Well, why didn't some one try to get Doctor Verney?"

"Doctor Verney won't take any calls up here, except for the Bannings, Mrs. Bates. He always says he simply can't do it."

"Well, it's really an outrage! Doctor Bull hasn't any right to go gadding about when he has a patient as sick as Mamie. It isn't as if it were the first time, either."

"Oh," said Geraldine wearily, "I guess everybody knows he's a bum doctor by now. Keep your hair on, Ma."

"Now, you needn't be so impertinent," Mrs. Bates told her. "Honestly, May, I think something ought to be done to make George Bull realize his responsibilities."

"Yes, I do think you're right," said Mrs. Jackson, attempting to seize an opening. "Mrs. Ely was telling me about the case of that boy at Truro who had diphtheria—"

"There are plenty of cases," said Mrs. Bates flatly. "I suppose nothing can be done now, but there ought to be a law—"

"Sh!" whispered May. "I think he's coming."

"I declare, I wouldn't mind telling him to his face. It's his duty to take care of the sick in this town, and—"

The door opened, admitting Howard Upjohn, his long face very solemn, and Mr. Banning. Mr. Banning said at once: "How do you do, Mrs. Bates. Good morning, May. Ah, good morning, Mrs. Jackson. Good morning, Geraldine." Howard Upjohn said generally, "Morning. 'Lo, May. Doc Bull here yet?"

"Not yet," said May.

"Then we'll just have to wait, I guess. Hermann Vogel said he'd be over and lend me a hand in about twenty minutes. What's keeping the Doc?"

"May," said Mr. Banning, "will you ask Mrs. Talbot if she feels able to see me a moment?"

"Why, of course, Mr. Banning," May nodded. "I'll just ask her—"

The change in atmosphere had become instantly apparent. Every eye, every interest, had transferred to the person who had the means, and it now could be guessed, the intention to pay. After he had gone in, May, withdrawing beyond the door, could hear fragments of Mr. Banning's lowered voice: "Mrs. Talbot . . . our deepest sympathy. I hope you will . . ." He turned presently and said, "May, would you ask Howard to come here a moment?"

Mrs. Talbot had begun abruptly to sniffle, doubtless forgetting that last night her idea had been to revile and abuse the Bannings as the whole cause of her misfortune. Howard Upjohn, entering to stand by the bed, too, was nodding with reflective consideration. May couldn't blame him for being cheered to know that the expenses of burying Mamie would unquestionably be paid. Mrs. Talbot, in a teary unsteadiness of gratitude, got out a few, high, very clearly carried phrases: ". . . don't know how to—" and ". . . never be able to—"

In the front room, Geraldine Bates was looking, with obvious amazement, at the contents of Mrs. Jackson's basket; but Mrs. Jackson and Mrs. Bates were both tense, listening as hard as possible. Mr. Banning was going to pay, and in a reluctant, tortuous way, they both resented it, while both tried not to. To Heaven, the widow's mite perhaps had value; but on this earth, you had to see that the widow was merely absurd. What weighed in the scale of mercy and human happiness were the rich men casting their gifts. Mr. Banning came and with his good, kind money, in one gesture swept away all common difficulties and pulled Mrs. Talbot from the pit. May saw Mrs. Bates looking at Mrs. Jackson, their slight constraint for the moment forgotten. Mrs. Jackson gave quick lip-service to Mr. Banning's virtue: "My, that's mighty nice of him—"

Mrs. Bates, living all her life in the shadow of the Bannings' prestige and high fortunes, said drily: "Well, I think people ought to help according to their means and abilities."

"Come on, Ma," said Geraldine. "Let's go."

On the outer door a heavy hand fell. The door opened then, showing them Doctor Bull's bold red face and massive figure. "Good morning," he said, glancing down at Mrs. Bates and Mrs. Jackson. He put his bag on the table, shrugged off his raincoat and laid it on a chair with his wet hat. "Well, this is too bad, isn't it. Where's Mrs. Talbot?"

"She's in there, talking to Mr. Banning and Mr. Upjohn," Mrs. Bates said.

"Right," nodded Doctor Bull. "Well, May! Tell your husband I'll try to stop in and see him this afternoon." He stood in the bedroom door. His voice boomed. "Hello, Banning. Hello, Howard. Very sorry to hear about this, Mrs. Talbot. I'll just look at her, please. All right, Howard, come along." Carrying his bag he went to the closed door of the back bedroom.

"Why didn't you tell him that stuff you were going to, Ma?" whispered Geraldine.

"Geraldine, you just keep still—"

They all stood waiting, and now Doctor Bull came out again, tucking a stethoscope carelessly into his pocket, proceeding to the table where he pushed things aside. Sitting down, he took his fountain pen and spread out a printed form. Mrs. Bates, reddening, said rather weakly: "Pity you couldn't get here yesterday afternoon. I suppose you might have saved her."

"Not likely," said Doctor Bull, continuing to write. "It's really a self-limiting infection. There are a good many types of the pneumococcus. If it happens to be type one, there's a serum some think helps. I don't believe it. Seventy per cent of the cases recover anyway, so how can you prove the serum did it? Probably you either have

[112]

the stamina to hang on while you develop resistance, or else you haven't. Mamie hadn't. Too puny. Girl like Geraldine would probably pull through fine. Got some meat on her. Well, that's all, I guess. When's the funeral going to be?"

"Why, I don't know—" said Mrs. Bates, worse confused now that George Bull turned his bright, cheerfully contemptuous blue eyes on her.

May came across the room. "Doctor Bull," she said, "do you think you could do anything for Mrs. Talbot? She's so upset, I mean; and—"

"Did she sleep last night?"

"Why, yes."

"How do you know?"

"I was over here."

"Well, then there's nothing to be done now. She'll be all right. She might be better if some of you cleared out. It keeps her worked up. Probably she doesn't feel like doing much, so if you want to help, take her over to your place and give her lunch, Mrs. Bates. You have a car out there."

Mrs. Bates, taken by surprise, hesitated, reddening again with embarrassment, for it was one thing to look in at Mrs. Talbot's, and another to have that dirty creature at your table. With accounts thus so well squared, Doctor Bull grinned cordially. "Or don't, if you don't like the idea. Just trying to suggest some way you could help. Get the body out as soon as you can, Howard. Not a very cheerful thing to have around."

Mr. Banning had come out now. He stood erect and precise, pulling his gloves on. Doctor Bull thrust his big hands into the sleeves of his slicker, humped his shoulders into it, clapped his hat on. "Decided when the funeral's going to be, Banning?"

"Mrs. Talbot wishes to have it Tuesday, Doctor. We'll have to consult the Rector about the time."

"Oh. That's right. Mamie was an Episcopalian, wasn't she? I forgot. The Talbots were always Congregationalists in the old days. I'd have probably gone to the wrong church." He opened the door, stepping out into the rain. Mr. Banning nodded to the women, following him. On the path, he said: "If you'll send your bill to me, Doctor, I'll be glad to settle it."

"All right, Banning," said Doctor Bull with relish. "I'll be glad to have it settled."

*

Upstairs in Upjohn's Hall three rooms looked out, one long window apiece, on the open triangle behind the New Winton station. Each corner room had an extra window, one north, one south. The three shabby varnished doors on the little hall had been lettered in black paint: *Town Clerk; Auditor; Collector of Taxes.* Clarence Upjohn, who had been Town Clerk, no matter what other officials changed around him, for seventeen years, donated the rooms, rent free. A meager sarcasm, living on from the time of Clarence's first offer of them and the lettering of the doors, described the arrangement as City Hall.

Except when the Board of Relief met; or ballots, cast downstairs, were counted; or Clarence was moved to bring over a week or two's work as Clerk—he did the work in the office of Upjohn Brothers' store across the street—to file in the fireproof record cabinets with which the south room was lined, no one bothered about City Hall, or had any reason to come up there. Henry Harris, Collector of Taxes, used the north room designated for him in such merely private affairs as sitting and thinking or to hold confidential interviews and discussions.

The furniture of this room had arrived there only after it had been thrown out somewhere else. There was a tumble-down easy chair, variously ruptured, with bulges of strangulated stuffing, where Henry Harris sat to think. An unsteady table stood under the electric light, a bare bulb hanging on a wire in the center. Two straight-backed wooden chairs had legs of slightly different lengths. In a shabby open bookcase thirteen or fourteen worn volumes of the Connecticut Code sprawled along the top shelf. Below were a few old issues of the State Register & Manual, a couple of reprints of novels ten years past their popularity, an obsolete unabridged dictionary with the binding torn off and a large collection of pulp-paper magazines, mostly without covers. Over the case, not quite in the center, hung a large color print. Obviously it had been turned out, frame and all, in quantity and distributed without charge. A brass plate screwed to the frame bore the words: *Armorial Bearings of State of Connecticut*—the white rococo shield; the three supported grape vines, each dangling four leaves and three purple clusters; the contorted, gold-edged streamer: *Qui Transtulit Sustinet*.

While Henry Harris had been making sure that no one was in any of the other rooms, Lester Dunn, everything else profitlessly examined, stood studying the streamer. "What the hell does that mean?" he inquired.

"Means: who set us up here will take care of us," said Henry Harris, unhurried.

"Oh," agreed Lester Dunn, "I always wondered. There must have been a nice little graft about handing out all those free pictures." Unhurried, too, he transferred his attention to the fly-specked campaign poster on the other wall; the Republican eagles and two large oval photographs with the legend: *Absolute and Unqualified Loyalty to Our Country: Hoover and Curtis*.

"Applesauce!" said Lester Dunn, reflectively.

Henry Harris had lighted the little round oil heater, but he was still busy adjusting the wick, trying to minimize the inevitable stink. Lester moved to the north window, looking out at the rain over the long low roof of the building which housed the New Winton Volunteer Fire Department's truck; over soggy backyards, to the little street beyond and the small houses scattered along it. "Having quite a show at the Talbots'," he remarked. "There's Bates's car, and Banning's, and Doc Bull's. Say, I'll bet it's some wake, if Mrs. Banning is in there with the Doc."

"Don't worry. She wouldn't come out on a day like this. She sent her Herbert."

"What for?"

"Fix it up to bury Mamie. He was over talking to Howard and they picked out a nice medium-priced coffin. Howard's going to do a snappy cut-rate embalming job. Going to order a stone, too. Something in simple good taste."

"There comes Doc Bull now, and Banning right with him. Look just like old pals. When do they bury her?"

"If this weather keeps up, it ought to be thawed out enough to get her in Monday."

"Maybe they could borrow one of those thawing machines from the construction camp."

"The camp's leaving us this coming Friday. I guess they're getting kind of sick of it. I saw Harry Weems slipping one of their men a little something yesterday."

"You see a lot, don't you?"

"Try to keep my eyes open, Lester. Good deal goes on around here when you know where to look."

Lester dropped into the armchair. "Come on," he said. "Let's hear it."

"Listen, don't wreck that! I want it a while yet."

"It was wrecked ten years ago. Come on. What's up?"

"Oh, nothing much. What did you get from Doc Bull for finding out about where Larry dumped the Bannings' junk?"

"Five dollars."

Henry Harris whistled. "With all that in your pants, you probably wouldn't be interested in picking up small change." He sat down and filled his pipe carefully. "Come on!" said Lester.

"Well, it would only amount to about a hundred dollars for you."

"I could use it."

"So could Hermann Vogel or Grant Williams. Maybe Harry Weems would just as soon have it."

"And now I'll tell you. Hermann and Grant are so dumb you don't want them. Harry makes all the money he wants selling liquor. So if you need a constable, I guess, it'll have to be me."

"I don't know. I might be able to influence Harry a little. How would he like a couple of Federal agents in town, do you think?"

"Let's see you get one! All those boys who aren't bought and paid for, if there are any, are running around Bridgeport and Hartford and New Haven with their tongues hanging out. Every time they raid one place two more open up. Think they're going to come way up here to catch the village bootlegger?"

"They get around on a hot enough tip."

"Listen, I haven't said I wouldn't do it. What is it?"

"Just a minute. Did you hear somebody come in downstairs then?"

"No. That was a shutter swinging. What are you so jumpy about? This must be pretty hot."

"I'm not jumpy," Henry Harris said placidly. "I'm just careful. Well, matter of fact, Lester, you're the one I want, all right. I need somebody smart. But try not to be too smart, will you? I can do this without you; you can't do it without me. Now, it's not breaking the law. Absolutely not. You're perfectly safe; and nobody can say anything to you. So how about settling it at a hundred dollars. I'll pay you cash." He got a wallet from his back pocket and began to drop ten-dollar bills on the table. "There you are."

"This must be something," said Lester. "I'm probably a damn fool, but make it a hundred and fifty and I'll do it, short of murder."

"Didn't I tell you it wasn't breaking the law? Matter of fact, it's just doing your sworn duty. Nobody can say a word."

"Sold for one hundred and fifty."

They gazed a moment at each other. "Well, I used to hear in church you hadn't ought to muzzle the ox that treadeth out the corn," said Henry Harris. He counted five more bills, pushed them all across the table.

"I'm just a sucker, I can see that," said Lester. "But all right, shoot. I'll do it."

"You're a smart chap," smiled Henry Harris. "Get your profits in advance every time. Never can tell when something will slip up."

"I'm plenty smart enough to come in when it rains," agreed Lester, "but you're the smartest damn bastard in the county, and I know right now I'm being a boob not to say two hundred."

Henry Harris had been the smartest boy in the New Winton school. His father, Jacob Harris, rewarded him with the begrudged gift of his parental permission; the School Committee arranged about his railroad fares; and Henry Harris became the smartest boy in the then-new High School at Sansbury. He was a feather in New Winton's rustic cap.

Whether or not Henry Harris would have

been the smartest young man at Yale was never determined. Jacob Harris thought that this had gone far enough. In his so thinking, an undoubted part had been played by the fact that Paul Banning's boy was at Yale. Like Jacob Harris, Paul Banning called himself a farmer, but in his case, other men did the farming. Paul Banning's personal approach to the soil was on the trotting tracks of the big eastern fairs. He had bred at least two pacers famous enough for the immortality of those sporting lithographs found in country hotel lobbies and the harness rooms of city stables. He was, of course, a rich man; and so had his father been. Even his grandfather, while he did his own farming, had done it with a simple, patriarchal authority, directing many laborers on the best and biggest farm in New Winton. Jacob Harris was a real farmer, a poor one. Yale was obviously a place for rich men's sons. By this Jacob Harris did not mean to be ordering himself lowly and reverently to all his betters; in his opinion, his betters did not exist. He meant that college was suitable only for such inconsiderable creatures as young Herbert Banning. He didn't believe Herbert Banning could load so much as one hay wagon without dropping dead.

Like many smart people, Henry Harris had always been a realist. The qualities of plainness, poverty unashamed, had their value mainly in his father's mind. Few people, able to be disinterested, saw them as the fine things Jacob Harris said they were. Henry Harris saw better the Banning stables—they had not burned down until after old Paul's death in 1908—stretched beside the green. The building was as long as three barns; and to prove it, carried three graceful cupolas, each vaned with a small gold horse trotting up the wind. A strip of sward as carefully kept as a lawn separated the permanently closed east doors from the road along the green. It was the biggest and, to the small Henry Harris, passing it every day on his way to school, the most beautiful thing in New Winton.

If he were smart enough to see, by some such symbol, how poor was prowess in loading a hay wagon compared to the money to hire all the good loaders you wanted who worked while you sat at ease, he was also smart enough to see, after a while, that Yale was less important to him than Yale had appeared in his hopes and first harsh disappointment. Of course, it was impossible not to feel an envious pang when Herbert Banning came home from college with a boating straw banded in Yale colors on his head; wearing a pale gray suit with narrow trousers and a double-breasted coat elegantly ample and padded on the shoulders; smoking a pipe with a curved stem and Y '04 inlaid in silver on the bowl; but all that took money. Henry Harris guessed that, poor as he would have been at Yale, he would not profit, except perhaps academically. The intelligence that made him a good scholar showed him too that scholarship was rarely of any importance in this world. The adjustment did not mean that he forgave his father or Herbert Banning—the one for thwarting, like the stubborn old jackass he was, the first major ambition of Henry's life; the other, for enjoying as a matter of course what Henry had wanted so passionately and in vain. Here were two accounts to be settled. For the moment he could not pay anything on them, and he did not waste time trying to or wishing that he could. Perhaps one of them was settled when Jacob Harris died without ever enjoying the ease which the prospering Henry, for appearance's sake, would soon have been forced to provide for him. Henry Harris let it go at that; all his energies were given to the problem of making money.

To make money, most young men might have thought it necessary to leave New Winton, where a dollar was seen in its true light—the certificate exchanged for a man's work all day—and where there existed no loose surplus for the gaining or wasting. Such a step is often praised as showing the vision and courage which brings success. Henry Harris had something better than that. He took what was nearest to hand and compelled it to serve him. He answered an advertisement about raising turkeys for profit. Raising them, he made money, exactly as the advertisement said that he would. When he had made a thousand dollars, he persuaded Isaac Quimby to let him buy into Quimby's feed, grain, and coal business. Once in, he began to consume Quimby by insisting on his privilege to reinvest his profits. Eventually they were large enough for him to stop that and begin to take a hand in Sansbury real estate.

This is perfectly simple to see and tell about; but most men, trying it, meet with every possible ill chance. Turkeys can pine and die. Mr. Quimby would have fleeced some presumptuous youths. Others would have plunged ignorantly in Sansbury building lots and lost everything. Doubtless luck is the chief factor, but, dispassionately considered, almost every financially unlucky person is a plain fool to start with. Henry Harris had that cleverness which is the very touch of Midas. He knew how to fatten on other people's efforts. The general method he used could be seen when he first entered village politics. He threw in his lot with the helpless and disorganized Democratic minority.

At the time it was not possible for Democrats to win locally. Henry Harris never expected them to. He meant to live on the Republicans. Other candidates worked hard and worried for the small offices; but not Henry Harris. He was a Democrat. It was considered good policy to let the Democrats have one job. Republican voters might or might not elect this or that Republican candidate, but Henry Harris, the leading Democrat, was always elected.

The next step in this old American story is transferal to a larger town, to a city; to state, then national politics. More than once it has ended only when some Henry Harris became President of the United States. Henry Harris would not be blind to the glitter of the chance, nor deaf to the thunder of opportunity awakening Democrats about 1910. He had all the qualifications. As well as a native, half-knavish wit, his was that careful mean shrewdness by which alone a man can climb, not too visibly soiled, through the sewer-like lower labyrinth of American politics. Henry Harris had, too, the bland, impregnable assurance required to rule on top.

Close-mouthed, sitting smiling on the steps of

Bates's store in his old clothes, it might seem
that sloth had stopped Henry Harris; but he
was a thoughtful man and never an idle one. He
might have reflected that here his time was his
own, his money already ample to buy him everything he saw any reason to want. Out of what
life has, Henry Harris lacked, in fact, only
fame. Sensible though he might be to the violent
pleasures found in overtaking and enjoying her,
the whore, Fame, he did not follow. Musing, far-
sighted and reflective, owing no explanation to
any one, he was apt enough at analogy. Like the
girls at Maggie's in Bridgeport, Fame was at the
end of a trip, inconvenient, tedious, fraught with
expense and anxiety. He had given up Bridgeport, for he could see a bargain; and the short
satisfaction of lewd dalliance, exchanged for a
considerable expenditure of time and money, and
a week of waiting to see if he had got gonorrhoea,
made no bargain. National politics might be
much like a trip to Maggie's.

Henry Harris was smiling now, watching Lester
fold the ten-dollar bills into a pocket book. Henry
Harris's face, saturnine, almost morose in ab-
straction, changed altogether when he smiled.
Seen carelessly, it was a smile of rare, intelligent
warmth. Attracted by it, many people would
never notice or understand the gleam of a puck-
ish, merry spite, an indulgent malevolence in
Henry Harris's dark eyes. The warmth was gen-
uine. It was the inner warmth he felt while he
surveyed the good order of his plans and resources. Reticent, dangerously smiling, he had

[124]

taken loving pains with them. Each little plan was a work of art. He had perfected it; he had subjected it in the privacy of his mind to every sort of test and condition. He would get no surprises when it went into action.

Other people were the surprised ones. As much as success—and here perhaps lay a clue to the compensations of his simple, satisfactory life— Henry Harris could relish that familiar start of first blank surmise, the following quick or slow realization in his victims. Calm, steadily smiling out his unassailable relish, enjoying the belated twistings and fatally late quick-thinkings, he received objections, threats and insults as so much tribute. Knowing it, Henry Harris was modest about it; he never tried to make the fact that he was the smarter man appear in casual conversation. Any one could talk. Most people, if they kept trying, could score small triumphs of repartee. Henry Harris, rarely rejoining, could wait, foretasting the fine jovial day when his enemies themselves would, by their own confounding, speak, even roar, the proofs of his wit.

He said, "Hand me down that last volume of the Connecticut Code, Lester. I'll show you something. I'm fixing up a little surprise for Matthew Herring. He takes such good care of the town money, he probably won't like it, but I doubt if he can help himself."

"Say, what are you going to do?"

"I'm going to try an old Fairfield County dodge, Lester. I don't claim the credit. Down there, they've been doing it for years. They thought it up for the mill town Polacks. Lot of those people don't read English very well, so they never know when taxes are due. When are taxes due in New Winton, Lester?"

"Why, I guess, about March fifteenth."

"Smart lad! And if you haven't paid up on or before that date what happens?"

"Nothing I ever heard of, so long as the town knows you and you pay pretty soon."

Henry Harris fingered the pages of the open volume. "Yes," he said. "That's true. We've been kind of shiftless." He shook his head. "Well, it's never too late to reform. I read here that it happens to be the duty of the Collector of Taxes to swear out warrants promptly for all delinquents. There's a two-dollar fee for him; there's a five-dollar fee for the constable serving the warrant. How many people do you think we might catch napping the morning of March sixteenth?"

"Oh, come to papa!" groaned Lester, falling back in the easy chair. "I knew I was a sucker! But, Henry, I'll have to hand it to you. Why, I bet we could catch a hundred!"

"About what I figured," Henry Harris agreed. "I—" He stopped short, his face stiffening. On the panel of the closed door heavy knuckles had struck suddenly. Lester started with such violence that he stood on his feet while the door swung open.

"Good morning, Henry," said Doctor Bull. "Thought perhaps Clarence was over here. I have a certificate for him. How's tricks, Lester?" His blue eyes, twinkling a little, turned back on Henry Harris. "You don't look too well, Henry. Heart ever bother you? Palpitations?" He put out his hand, closed it over Henry Harris's wrist,

[126]

his finger tips shutting down on the radial artery while he felt for his watch.

Henry Harris jerked his hand away; the corners of his mouth grew firm; he began to smile. "You move pretty quiet for a man your size, George. Is it hard?"

"Professional training, Henry. We try not to go banging around a sick room. Come in sometime and I'll look you over. You're not as young as you were, you know. Little things like a knock on the door shouldn't shake you up."

"I'll probably live."

"Sure, you will. But a time comes when we aren't so spry. Can't do all the things we used to do, Henry."

"Maybe not. Seems like I'm getting a little deaf, sometimes."

"Often happens. It hasn't affected me yet; but I always did have pretty keen hearing. Well, I'll have to see if I can get hold of Clarence. So long."

They could hear his heavy steps in the hall and the brisk thud of his descent on the stairs.

*

The rain continued. All the sky to be seen was the blanket of vapor ceaselessly condensing, in gradual movement just touching the hilltops. Up to meet it a universal mist went off the earth, now colder from its remnants of melting snow than the air. In the little depression at the southeast corner of the New Winton green, a pool widened out. Roads merely gravel surfaced, like

[127]

those at the ends of the green, and the one bi-
secting it from Bates's store east to the station,
were softening. Cars coming off them were spattered high with gray mud. The broad surface
of US6W held here and there flat thin sheets of
water. Presenting a mechanical twitch of windshield wipers, motors moving on it came through
fairly fast, raising clouds of spray. Down across
fields to the west, clear now of snow, hung with
haze, the river ice lay sunk pallid under a half-
foot of water.

At eleven o'clock the up-train got in; great
locomotive gleaming wet, steam merging in the
mist, all the cars dripping dirty water, windows
clouded over, jeweled with drops. Out fell the
mail sacks. In the lighted express car, men, keeping as dry as they could, shoved crates and bun-
dles onto the hand trucks. Forward, the engineer,
goggles in a band across his eyes, shoulder and
left arm covered by a black rubber coat, had his
head out, high in the cab, watching for the conductor's signals. Now the locomotive made a stu-
pendous first effort, wheels slipping on the wet
steel, steam hammering up. The train moved,
groaning at every coupling; the cars began to
slide by. Through the mist, back gleamed the
lighted scarlet markers.

The mail cart, covered with a tarpaulin, was
trundled over to the post office. People had already begun to gather, and most of them had noticed, on the big thermometer outside the door,
that the tinted alcohol had climbed the capillary
bore, crossing fifty. Men, too warm in heavy
coats, women, closing umbrellas as they ap-

proached Bates's counters, expressed themselves:

"Why, it's like spring—"

"Up to Truro, the snow's all gone. Not that there's much here—"

"Wouldn't surprise me if the river went to-night—"

In mud-coated knee boots, an olive slicker and a sodden felt hat, Mr. Snyder, from the construction camp, was talking to Mr. Bates. He wanted to get a tractor. One of the Interstate Light & Power trucks was stuck in the mess of water and deepening mud of the Cobble road. Snyder had been compelled to leave his Ford and walk in, for there was no way of getting past the obstruction.

In Mr. Bates's melancholy opinion, most tractors would be laid up still. Perhaps Weems's wrecking car could make it.

George Weems, consulted, thought that it might be possible. "Harry's pretty handy about that kind of thing," he admitted, "but if you're really stuck on the Cobble road in a thaw like this—"

Faced with this amiable but slightly derisive patronage, Snyder felt bound to explain that the situation was not so dumb as it seemed. He'd seen long ago that the road would be impassable for him in the spring. His plan had been to get all the trucks out of the old barn at the foot of the hill which Mr. Harris had rented them for a garage, and bring them in town at the first sign of a thaw. Who could have foreseen anything like this yesterday?

Snyder had troubles enough and he was close

[129]

to unloading them on New York in a rage. The camp itself, he was finding now, had been built with some regard for snow and cold, but not, apparently, for any such downpour as this. The main bunk house leaked in several places. The site drained all right, but the knoll on which the temporary buildings had been put up, denuded, showed a tendency to erode deeply on all sides. This happened to be important because the latrine shed had been placed at the edge of a particularly precipitous slope into a gully behind. The steady rainwash was already undermining its slight foundations. Oddly enough, this appeared to cheer men who had nothing to do but regard the wet valley. It offered opportunity for ribaldries about themselves tumbling (the most comic situation many of them could imagine) in a heap with their collected excrement, to be washed away together. Snyder was ready to say that this was the last winter construction job he'd ever have anything to do with. He doubted if time saved halfway compensated for the annoyances and expenses. This was the sort of thing somebody who'd never been out of an office in his life thought up; and he, Snyder, was the goat.

Harry Weems appeared then in a yellow slicker. He had been somewhat relieved to discover that Snyder was there for help, not to raise a row about any whisky which Harry might have sold his men. Sure, Harry said, they could try.

He got a set of claw chains, laid them down on the garage floor, and ran the wrecking truck on them; struggled, with Snyder's assistance, to hook them up.

At the door, a horn rang out strident. Guy Banning's car poked its long hood in, crawled neatly past the truck and halted. "Listen, Guy," said Harry, "leave it here, will you? I got to go out for about an hour. We can tackle it after lunch."

"All right. About half-past two?"

"Sure."

Guy Banning fastened the flap and collar of a trench coat, strolling away into the rain.

"Who's that?" asked Snyder. "Don't seem to have seen him before."

"He's down at Yale. Son of the Bannings—in the big place up the end of the green. He's got a sister you've probably seen. Nice-looking kid with a sort of thin face. Drives a Ford coupé around."

"With a red-headed girl?"

"That's right. Mr. Hoyt's daughter."

"Used to see them on the Cobble road. Let's go."

Driving in the rain, Harry Weems said: "Wet on the hill?"

"Wet enough. Listen, do you know the ground up there?"

"I guess so."

"Well, listen, where does that little brook right behind us come out?"

"Damned if I know. Probably down at Bull's Pond. Why?"

"Well, I wondered. Afraid we might be polluting it. You never know in the country who uses what for drinking water."

"Nobody drinks out of brooks around here."

Although the rain had lasted all day Sunday, and looked as if it might last forever, Monday morning was beautifully clear and warm. Virginia Banning, awakening, could feel the changed air on her face—soft, mild and fresh. Lying still, she could see the sunlight on the sodden limbs and ruddy twigs of the maples, and behind them, sky brilliantly blue. At the head of the flag pole by the tennis court, a flag which must be new lifted out, straightening exquisitely sharp and clean stripes; a ripple of vivid red; a swelling and swaying of the blue field with immaculate stars. Larry had apparently decided to consider today Washington's birthday; apparently, too, he was pleased with the world. She could hear the scratch of a rake on a path, and Larry whistling with a clear and sweet skill: *Sometimes I'm happy*—

The danger of dying if she could not go to Paris was suddenly remote; and this irritated her vaguely—as though the vanity of ridiculous existence would not even allow her a quality as solid as prolonged disappointment. She just felt tranquil. Down by the stables, Samson barked, one mild, friendly boom. She would, she decided, get Guy to take her driving.

Throwing off the covers, she sat a moment on the edge of the bed, looking at the bright flag and the marvelous sky. She stood up then; walked barefoot to the bathroom door, and hit the back of her hand against it. Getting no response, she opened it. The door beyond was open too and she could see the sunlight on the floor of Guy's room. He was knotting a necktie in front of the mirror, and he half turned.

"Listen," he said, "you can't get a bath."

"Has that damn electric heater broken down again?"

"No, but wait till you see the water. It's mostly mud."

She turned on a faucet. "It's not so bad."

"Well, it was practically black a minute ago."

"Well, it's not now."

"Let it run a minute and see."

"I am. It's getting better. Take me out in your car this morning, will you?"

"What for?"

"Don't, then."

"Where do you want to go?"

"I don't want to go anywhere. Can't you just drive?"

"I suppose so."

"Well, will you?"

"Maybe. But I'll tell you right now I'm not going to let you drive. You did something to the steering gear when you swiped it Friday."

"Couldn't I even drive it with you there?"

"No."

"Gosh, you're a hog, Guy!" She closed the door, shot the bolt on it, and pulled her pajamas off. He came close to the door and said something, obviously annoyed; but she turned on the shower, satisfied. He was probably mad enough to take her just in order not to let her drive.

Mrs. Banning was glad that it was clear. Leroy Getchell, the Principal of the New Winton school, assisted by Miss Kiernan, who taught the fifth grade, had been working for over three weeks on *Washington's Vision, a Patriotic Pageant*.

Some of the more essential costumes had been rented from a New York firm. Those less essential had been made at home. Into learning lines and rehearsals a good deal of time and effort had gone. Mr. Ingraham, who conducted manual training classes in the basement, had built the set to go on the platform in the assembly hall. Lester Dunn had been persuaded to do the wiring for only what the materials cost him. If it had continued to rain, both attendance and enthusiasm would have suffered.

Beyond underwriting, as she always did, most of the actual costs, Mrs. Banning hadn't really done much about it herself; but she liked things, over which a lot of trouble had been taken, to go well. Mr. Getchell was her strongest ally on the School Committee. Since he was very energetic about such entertainments, she would do everything she could, in loyal exchange for his help in dealing with Henry Harris and his deadlocking combination with Mr. Lane and Mr. Ordway— the one because of a sour and obtuse miserliness; the other because of his liking for his position as representative at Hartford and willingness to arrange any sort of minor deal or compromise with the Democrats to keep it safe. Thus, there might always be three against her. Miss Kimball, the Librarian, could be counted on to do as Mrs. Banning wanted. Mr. Getchell, as Chairman, had two votes; but Henry Harris had cleverly—that was in the guise of being cautious with public money—forced into the rules of procedure a requirement that all financial matters should be approved by at least a two-thirds vote. This completely counteracted the Chairman's advantage, since there were seven votes, and four would never be quite two thirds of seven. Almost any subject of importance either clearly was, or could be so presented as to seem, a matter of finances; so progress, except in directions approved by Henry Harris, was uncertain.

Henry Harris was not interested in entertainments—presumably because there was nothing for him in them. If they had entertainments, it would be on the trifling funds of the Parent-Teacher Association, with Mrs. Banning making up the deficits more or less anonymously. She could not, for instance, have the ice cream sent up from Sansbury charged to herself. That was patronage too direct, and would cause grumbling about what was good enough for the ladies of the association was good enough and so on. The proper procedure was to charge it to the association and inconspicuously contribute to the treasury a sum to cover it.

A person less instinctively generous or less resolute in good works might have washed her hands of the whole affair long ago; but Mrs. Banning felt that difficulties only emphasized duty. Deserting some one who tried as hard as Mr. Getchell to have things go smoothly; or leaving a poor faithful creature like Miss Kimball (her father was Ralph Kimball, the station agent, and a very plain person indeed; making her cultural triumphs the more impressive and deserving of support) unencouraged was just as impossible as failing to support Doctor Wyck's zeal in schooling the scanty, once carelessly low church congregation of St. Matthias's in what he called Catholic Practice.

The entertainment was to take place at two o'clock. Neither Virginia nor Guy was going to be available. Guy couldn't be expected to go, and Virginia would probably have been so bored and rude to both parents and teachers that her absence might be just as well. She had gone driving with Guy, and telephoned from Litchfield that they wouldn't be back for luncheon. Mr. Banning had spent the morning considering his crocuses, likely to be open very shortly if weather like this continued; and helping Larry saturate with boiling water a thoughtfully compounded mixture of loam and rotten leaf mold and sand in the dozen cold frames on the sunny side of the stables. Cheered at the prospects of early planting, he voluntarily said that he would go.

There were at least thirty cars down by the school house, and many people moving about. Mr. Ingraham, Scoutmaster as well as Manual Training Instructor, was running in and out in his uniform, which was a good deal too small for him. This, with the solemnity he showed in exchanging three-fingered salutes with little boys whose similar uniforms were somewhat too big, gave him a slightly idiotic air, but he was very cheerful and enthusiastic. His troop, of all heights and sizes, mostly needing haircuts and busy blowing their noses, looked, if not very military, highly pleased with their work of showing cars where to park and acting as ushers to their indulgent parents. It did seem as though every one were enjoying it, and Mrs. Banning got out of the car contentedly. She even said good afternoon to Mr. Harris, who had put on a starched collar and smiled at her with warmest malevolence, removing his hat. Doctor Wyck, walking down from the rectory, joined her at once, and so did Miss Kimball. Pete Andrews, who must have been sitting in something like tar and wore a thick mat of yellow hair well down his neck under his campaign hat, managed to find them four seats in a row facing the extemporized stage.

Shortly before three o'clock the shades were all pulled down and the curtains dragged apart. Some one had forgotten to turn on the stage lights, but this was hastily remedied and the audience saw, surprised, an illuminated section of forest at the extreme right. Since most of the stage was still in darkness it might be supposed that something else had gone wrong, but, as no consternation arose behind scenes, it was agreeably accepted.

Into the light came now Ronald Fell, a cocked hat on his head, clad in the hypothetical buff and blue of the Continental Army. This was perhaps an anachronism, for where Washington, the Young Surveyor, could have got such a uniform was not clear; but at least every one knew who Ronald was supposed to be. He was immediately followed by the Vogel twins. Their faces had been stained brown and they were closely wrapped in Navajo blankets, indicating clearly that they were Indians. Having, for reasons presently to become apparent, got as far onto the stage as he could, Ronald stopped suddenly, causing the agitated Vogel twins to recoil. With exaggerated feeling, he stretched and yawned. He faced about then and said: "Twenty long and weary miles have we journeyed today, my brothers. Let us lie down here under the pines and sleep, for night has fallen."

Both twins assented to this proposal and they all disposed themselves on the floor, where Ronald fell asleep at once. The Vogel boys, squatting uncomfortably in their blankets, began, after a sibilant prompting from the wings, to explain that never had they seen a white man with the courage and strength of this Washington. Prompted again from the side, Jack Vogel blurted hastily: "But look, he seems to dream——"

Forthwith all the lights went out and there followed a pause, pregnant with rustlings, whispered admonitions and obscure movements. Quite suddenly other lights came on, illuminating, behind a haze of stretched gauze to the left, what could be understood to be a dream or a vision.

Ronald must have got up and gone around in back after it was dark. Somebody could be heard beating a drum in the background while somebody else made a good deal of noise walking up and down. This was explained by Bill Ordway, who, having given the stiffly staring Ronald a résumé of the iniquities of George III, and described the Boston Tea Party and Paul Revere's ride, then informed him that he was assuming command of the Continental Army. Ronald began an acknowledgment, but some one had miscalculated a little and the lights went out, so he stopped. An interval of muffled expostulations followed; there was a great swishing and shuffling and the lights came on again disclosing Molly Ordway and Jane Ely with caps and aprons on, apparently sitting on the floor, while Ronald and Bill, still in his Quaker costume, watched them approvingly. The audience was haltingly informed that Mistress Betsy Ross was engaged in sewing an American flag.

There was a succeeding, somewhat longer, delay, afterwards proving to have been due to the introduction of a painted back-drop representing a snowy forest. In the foreground Ronald was kneeling on one knee looking intently at the ceiling, while two shabby soldiers, readily identified as the Lane boys, observed that the General was asking God's help and things were pretty bad at Valley Forge. After that, Lord Cornwallis (Joe Quimby) was disclosed in a fine scarlet uniform eagerly presenting Ronald with his sword when he learned that the war was over. Bill Ordway next appeared, administering the presidential oath to Ronald. He was followed by Molly Ordway, clothed now in a costume representing Columbia, saying with the greatest composure a piece of poetry about Washington's undying fame and the republic going forward.

Somebody called audibly from behind, "That's all. That's the end." So every one applauded hotly while the performers crowded into the vision part of the stage and bowed their acknowledgments. Mr. Ingraham hissed something, and his boy scouts ran and pulled up the shades. The audience faced about on its chairs and discussed admiringly the dramatic skill displayed by all members of the cast.

In the coat room ice cream was being dished out. Agreeing that all the children did very well, pleased by the simple and innocently festive air —Mr. Getchell's wide smile, Miss Kiernan, pink with modest triumph, saying to Miss Kimball: "Oh, there you are! How did it go?"—Mrs. Banning glanced at the coat room door just in time to see Doctor Bull lumbering out, a plate raised on his big hand. With gross, jovial relish he was scooping up heaped spoonfuls of ice cream.

Though Doctor Bull had, certainly, as good a right to refreshments as any one else, it seemed to Mrs. Banning outrageous that poor Mamie Talbot, dead through his incompetence and neglect, was not yet even buried, while he stood there with no care in the world nor visible weight on his conscience, gobbling ice cream. She looked at him with chill, reproving distaste, while he put the empty plate on the seat of a chair, wiped his mouth, and seemed to consider for a moment, joining the herd of children getting drinks of water out of the porcelain fountain. Mr. Getchell came by then and all the way across the room Mrs. Banning could hear Doctor Bull booming: "Good show, Getchell. You ought to send Molly Ordway down to the Follies."

"Thanks for lunch," Virginia said. "I'll pay you back."

"Forget it," Guy nodded. "Where do you want to go?"

"Not home. We don't have to go home, do we?"

"Well, I don't want to drive all over the map. I have to get back to New Haven tonight, anyway."

The car was parked last in a line, almost in front of the Congregational church. Said to have been built from the same plans first used in New Winton, here in Litchfield greater skill or more liberal funds had been available. The four white pillars of the porch were a lofty, elaborated Corinthian, high enough for serenity which was lost in mere squat quaintness at New Winton. Perfectly restored, painstakingly cared for, it stood to best advantage, half against the north valley, at the fall-away of the Torrington road. Virginia looked at the sunlight slanting on it with distracted pleasure.

"We could swing around Torrington and Winsted to Canaan and come down US7," Guy said generously. He sank into his raccoon skins. "I'll bet you're cold. You ought to have worn your fur coat. This isn't spring."

"Why, it's hot, Guy! I'm not cold. I'm not a bit cold."

"Anyway, that's the lousiest-looking thing—" He indicated the leather jacket. "You ought to throw it away."

"It's all right," she said, subdued and flushing a little. "I don't care how I look. What difference does it make around here?" She turned her blue eyes on him desperately. "Guy, couldn't I—"

"Listen, I said I wouldn't let you drive. If you're going to make a fuss, we'll go home."

"All right," she sighed.

At Canaan, when it was at least as far back one way as the other and Guy had stopped for gasoline, she risked it again. "Guy," she besought him, "just a little, please?"

"Lord!" he groaned. "I suppose you won't be happy till you kill yourself. All right."

Headed south, she drove with zeal reluctantly curbed while Guy watched her as though she were going to meet head-on every approaching car or, if that failed, smash into the next telegraph pole. Through the wide fields beyond the South Canaan church, she turned down into the Housatonic river valley. Here, between the hills, there was no wind and the sun was warm, glittering off the shallow, ice-free river. She was doing a carefully gained fifty miles an hour when they passed West Cornwall, but Guy did not protest. From the high viaduct and great white arch lifting US7 across the river, they could look down on the railroad tracks, the roof of the station, the bare tree tops and shingled back of the original small covered Cornwall bridge far underneath. Virginia, reassured now, sat at alert, unstrained ease, her gloved hands over the lower spokes of the big wheel. She was attuned to the car, as a practiced rider may be to a horse. Knowing nothing of a time when there were no motors, unable to remember when those there were could not be wholly loved and trusted, she shared Guy's special sympathetic feeling for fine machinery. Such cruelties as improper lubrication or careless adjustment would move her with almost the same compunction as the wanton ill treatment of an animal.

Moved grudgingly by the obviousness of this

[142]

right attitude, and by Virginia's resulting competence, to be seen well enough through her calm heavenly pleasure, not in going anywhere nor in the hills and the river valley, but in the perfect performance of a motor as fine as could possibly be built, Guy said: "As a matter of fact, you drive pretty well for a girl. Some women do drive all right if they can keep their minds on it and nothing happens they don't expect—"

"Just a little longer, Guy—"

They swept down under the great bare maples in long alignment through Kent. Virginia crossed the railroad tracks faster than she should have, but after all, somewhat slower than Guy would have crossed them, so he didn't point it out to her. Reaching New Milford, sprawled on the eastern slope in unpicturesque array across the river, he said: "Cut over here and back through Southbury. It's getting late."

Indifferent, or moved to pity by the intensity of her small pleasure, Guy still did not suggest that he drive. Silent, he occupied himself with a pipe which he did not like, but which happened to be a fad among his friends, a revolt against the cigarettes so incessantly smoked by people they did not care to know. He was occupied, too, with the crowded world of his college: how much tutoring he was going to have to invest in to get through his Economics; how much whisky he had better provide for Friday night; whether he could spare a chapel cut to go to a Friday night (the next Friday) dance in New York, and whether, if he could, he could afford to stay the week end; and if he could afford it, whether Marjorie Pitkin were worth the trouble and expense.

Or would he do better to call up the DeFoe girl? He had almost decided, along with several punctilious friends, to drop her, after her tipsy behavior caused almost a scandal at the Junior Prom. However, being seen with her in New York was not the same as being seen with her in New Haven and she would probably let him sleep with her.

He was surprised to find them into New Winton, with the twilight over the green. Virginia relaxed, slumping as though at last tired, at the wheel. "Thanks a lot," she startled him by saying, "I've had a swell time, Guy."

She looked at him, a little tremulous; and so, rather ridiculously, resolved his last difficulty; for he did not care to think of his sister, whose purity or innocence he didn't exaggerate, but who none the less had it in the senses he considered important, in connection with the shamefully attractive and obscenely available DeFoe girl—after all nothing but a slut of good family. Righteousness thus triumphed, probably definitely; and he resolved to call up Marjorie as soon as he got back to New Haven.

Virginia, unconscious of her service to him, wheeled precisely through the gate. Another car was standing on the loop the drive made approaching the side door. "Hoyts'," she said. "They must have been down to that lousy play."

Behind the cedars and the chestnut sapling fence, she stopped the car. The dogs, muzzles down, had been bolting their suppers; and though they both turned, barking and wagging their tails, they did not trust each other enough to leave their separate feeding pans. Larry, smoking a cigarette, perched on the doorstep of his stable quarters. He waved a hand.

Virginia sat still a moment while Guy got out. A white moon, approaching the first quarter, hung half a foot above the long summit of the western hill, and she sighed again, aware of the wonderful stillness of the mild air and the calm vacancy of the impending clear night. She breathed deep then, trying to get together the remnants of a day almost entirely happy to protect herself. Larry had got up and come over negligently. "Val Hoyt's inside with her father looking for you, Virginia," he remarked. "She came down to see if you were around the stables. Told me she was going away some place."

"I know," said Virginia, her tone flattening. "She's going to Paris."

"Nope," said Larry with calm positiveness. "They had some changed plans. Somewhere west. With her father. Somewhere in New Mexico. They were going to be gone two months and they were fixing it up for you to go with them."

Virginia snapped open the car door. "Larry!" she gasped. "They haven't left, have they?"

"Car's still there. But I guess you better hurry. Val said she thought your father was going to let you, if you wanted—"

She started away, running toward the house; and this was too much for the dogs. They left what they hadn't eaten, eagerly overtaking her, bounding and barking.

"Just look at her!" invited Larry, shaking his head. "She don't want to stay home much, I guess. She's sure funny when she gets excited."

Guy automatically gave him one of the freezing blank stares used effectively to annihilate impertinent inferiors at college. Here, it passed harmless over Larry's thick-skinned amiability. "Going to go down to college tonight, Guy?" he asked.

"I am."

"Might as well leave your car out, then. Not much chance of freezing tonight, I guess. Yeah, the Hoyts want to drive down there. He's got a ranch there, or something, hasn't he? I always heard—"

"If you haven't anything else to do," said Guy, "get a rag and wipe this off, will you?"

*

"Thou turnest man to destruction: again thou sayest, Come again, ye children of men. For a thousand years in thy sight—" Doctor Wyck naturally knew it by heart. Against the fresh lawn of his surplice, the rector held in his left hand, forefinger marking the Burial of the Dead, a black leather-bound book, but that was purely formal. Every word out of his mouth had the perfection of familiarity and practice. To Virginia, disinterested, his voice differed not at all from the clean even print in the prayer book—an unnecessarily exquisite one given her on the occasion of her confirmation—which she held idly open. Doctor Wyck even supplied the punctuation. Here, in a psalm, he held over on the caesural colon. His voice surged, paused drily, returned, like a calm sea on a beach:—*thy wrathful indignation—the light of thy countenance*

—the days of our age—apply our hearts unto wisdom—

To bury Mamie to such a strain really seemed absurd.

Virginia, in the prodding pleasure of her own constantly recalled happiness, noticed it at once, with the solemn pronouncement of the preliminary sentences. It was part of her feeling so acutely and joyfully stimulated. Everything had an edge and an interest; every detail was cause enough for some sort of joy. Even perceiving how wrong all this was gave her pleasure. Who could imagine Mamie doing anything so resolute as, though she were dead, yet living? Where on earth would she get the nerve to see God for herself, her eyes beholding, and not another? Mamie, stretched out, shut up in the shrouded coffin, would probably think that they were making fun of her. As it is to the wise, a word to the weak is sufficient. Unless you were proud, strong, well up in life, you had no need to be reminded at such length that you were nothing and went down like grass. Who could doubt it?

Doctor Wyck had launched now on the long, resounding muddle following I Corinthians xv. Virginia, looking at it in print, felt invulnerable even to that awful boredom. She did not want to think about Santa Fe too much, for she had learned that anything thought about eagerly would be bound to disappoint her; but she could at least think of not being in New Winton, or not being in any rotten school. Even that might be risky, however, so she turned back, began to read at random: *Here is to be noted that the office en-*

[147]

suing is not to be used for any unbaptized adults, any who die excommunicate, or who have laid violent hands upon themselves.

She thought: "If I killed myself, would Doctor Wyck make a fuss about having a nice service for me? I'll bet he wouldn't." Exhilarated by her own cynicism regarding Doctor Wyck's attitude, she let her eyes slide away to the atrocious colored glass of the window at the beginning of the nave. It commemorated her great-great-grandparents, who, in 1823, had been largely responsible for erecting the church. A plump, vacant-faced Gabriel seemed to be fanning the Blessed Virgin with an object perhaps visible to the eye of faith as a lily. The Virgin Herself sat absorbed in a patch of dirt with two stones and thirteen—such were the desperate resources of long ago Sunday mornings—blades of grass painted on in superficial black. The mantle, Virginia noted now, was of precisely the blue used for medicine bottles whose contents may be injured by natural light.

The next window—Virginia felt strong enough to bear the boredom of a quick look at it—showed the ox-eyed, curly-bearded apostles giving forth the lots which fell upon Matthias. It stood to the Glory of God and in loving Memory of Paul Banning, twenty-one years Senior Warden of this Church; and of Mathilda, his wife. Virginia had an early, uncertain memory of Mathilda, his wife —by that time, his relict; a small sedentary figure with a black shawl and a distinctive odor, much like a linen closet, which she associated with the phrase—"a very old lady."

By the third window, Doctor Hall, a former

rector, was remembered; but that, Virginia felt, she could not look at. To mix with the pleasures of impending departure, the colored glass brought back the old ache of time slowing to a stop within these walls. The watch on her left wrist, half hidden by her glove, seemed for a dreadful moment to be measuring again the world without end minutes of a child's Sunday morning. Made up of them, the mere hour of a service could seem worship as everlasting as the awful reiteration of the six-winged beasts, the repetitious falling-down of the four and twenty elders. Doctor Wyck's voice reached her ears, proceeding urgently: "Howbeit that was not first which is spiritual, but that which is natural; and afterwards that which is spiritual—"

Virginia shook herself a little, pronouncing: "I am going away from this damn hole. I am going to Santa Fe a week from Monday. It doesn't matter because whatever happens I'm going away a week from Monday."

This was a success, but she felt, almost as bad as boredom, the insupportable compulsion of her desire, the impatience for what would be then to be now, forthwith. Her throat constricted in the agony of having it put off; there was a nervous congestion in her breast; her veins were cloyed with lukewarm blood; her very bones itched through her flesh and she found herself actually praying: *God, make it a week from Monday—*

Howard Upjohn was uncomfortably clad in the clothes he reserved for funerals, complete to dreadful black gloves covering his prominently large hands. When he was younger he had kept also a silk hat. Whether time had finally ruined it, or Howard had simply decided that its shape made him look too much like the symbolic figure of Prohibition in hostile cartoons, he had some-time changed to a derby. This he felt for on the pew seat beside him now. Inconspicuously turn-ing, he worked along until he could step into the side aisle and go briskly back, motioning up his four pall-bearers. To each he presented a pair of dark gray gloves, and waited while they put them on. Apparently the church part of it was over. May Tupping, not quite certain what was to happen next, wished that she knew the time. She had explained to Doris Clark that she might be a little late relieving her; but she didn't want to be. The Divisional Superintendent was supposed to be coming through today. If he happened to come before she got there, he would do nothing about it, but he would naturally notice that she wasn't very punctual. She turned her head a little to see the pall-bearers, who, after several tries, had got stiffly into step, tramping down the aisle. Harry Weems had on a good and expensive blue serge suit. He was paired with Lester Dunn, whose suit, though cut with remarkable jaunti-ness, was appropriately dark, too. Eric Cadbury, who must have been picked up and pressed into service by Howard directly before the ceremony began, was dressed with much less elegance, but being older than any of the others he could con-tribute a certain gravity. The fourth man was Ed Darrow, son of Mrs. Talbot's sister-in-law at Banning's Bridge. Doubtless he only had one good suit, and it happened to be a very light pepper and salt tweed. Sympathetic, May guessed that it was the cause for his face getting redder and redder as he came down.

Mrs. Darrow, sitting on the other side of Mrs. Talbot, looked at Ed with a trusting approval, however; at least, until Howard had got the wheeled conveyance into motion, and the bearers fell in behind, to escort the coffin with its low heap of flowers—all rather shoddy except the sheaf of lilies which had come up from Water-bury, professionally packed and expedited, with the Bannings' card—uncertainly toward the door. Mrs. Darrow then began to weep and lament with annoying facility, causing Mrs. Talbot, heretofore contented with occasional sniffs, to break out, too.

May got them both to their feet and into the aisle with the handful of the congregation. From the far side, Mrs. Banning said quietly, "May," and May stopped. "Larry has the car outside," Mrs. Banning whispered. "You take Mrs. Talbot and Mrs. Darrow down to the cemetery in it, will you? We'll see you there."

They came into the warm sunlight on the steps of the church. Doctor Wyck, who had gone to the sacristy for a cloak and biretta, was waiting for them. Howard and his assistants had just eased the flower-topped coffin into the half-ton truck which served him now that he no longer kept horses, and business did not warrant buying a motor hearse. Mat Small was driving the truck. He was in working clothes, for he had spent the morning with Albert Foster digging the grave and would afterwards fill it in.

May said to Mrs. Talbot: "Mrs. Banning has

been kind enough to offer us her car to go down in—"

Larry Ward, sitting bored at the wheel, in a cap and old chauffeur's uniform, got out reluctantly, waving rather than helping them in. From the clock on the dashboard May could see that it was quarter to twelve; and, glancing across the green to the telephone office, she was dismayed to find that the coupé with the telephone company's round bell-marked seals on the doors was already parked there. The superintendent would undoubtedly wait until twelve and observe her tardiness.

The others had formed a straggling group following Doctor Wyck around the stone side of the church to walk the few hundred yards. Harry Weems and Lester brought up the rear, with Doctor Bull, whose presence had been severely ignored by every one else. There would be no satisfying people on that point, May recognized. If he hadn't come, there would have been a general outraged criticism of his callousness. When he did come, the criticism was to the effect that one wondered how he had the face, considering that he'd done everything he could to kill Mamie. Doctor Bull, however, didn't need her sympathy. Standing well above, and twice as big as, Lester or Harry, he moved with an assurance which was almost blithe. He blinked cheerfully in the warm sunlight; he stared with obvious robust contempt now at Doctor Wyck's wind-stirred vestments and the biretta, now at the roll of fine silver fox fur draped over Mrs. Banning's erect shoulders, concealing her neck, piling high as the lower edge of her neat black hat.

By the cemetery gate, surmounted by a curved iron scroll and small cross, Larry ran the car off the road. May helped Mrs. Talbot and Mrs. Darrow out. The others, waiting for them, let them now lead, following Doctor Wyck and the coffin down the path past the weighty granite and marble monuments, the substantial blocks —Coulthard, Cardmaker, Allen, Bull, Banning —dominating railed plots, most of them already thick with small markers. Among lesser stones, and graves planted with the iron star of the G.A.R. holding a stick and faded tatter of cheap flag left from last Memorial Day, a grave had been dug for Mamie. The turned-up earth was elaborately covered by mats of coarse, bright green imitation grass. Stretched across the pit were the bands of the device for lowering; and laboriously the coffin was placed upon them, the flowers removed and laid to one side where Albert Foster waited patiently, leaning on his shovel.

They were all gathered together now, forming a semicircle—Doctor Bull on one end, the Bannings on the other. Mrs. Talbot and Mrs. Darrow had quieted again. Doctor Wyck's distinct voice was the only sound while they stood, no one looking at any one else, until Howard startled them all by making a motion to Albert Foster.

Albert drove his spade into a heap of dry gravel, plainly brought there for the purpose, since the excavated earth was dark and damp. Shaking off any that was loose, he advanced clumsily, proffering the shovelful. Doctor Wyck took a little, hardly stopping his recitation except for the measure of emphasis. Fastidiously, he dropped it, in lieu of dust or ashes, on the coffin.

May, her attention thus attracted, saw Mrs. Banning moisten her lips. One hand against the fox fur on her breast, she had found a small handkerchief with the other. She brought it inconspicuously first to her mouth, and then, turning her face away, to her eyes. Virginia's arm was through hers and she held it a moment. Suddenly close to tears herself, May thought; she's just imagining if it were Virginia there instead of Mamie. Mr. Banning, composed and serious, slipped a hand under her other arm. Doctor Wyck was reading: "Come, ye blessed children of my Father, receive the kingdom prepared for you from the beginning of the world—"

May looked sadly at Albert with his spade, aware of the possible horrid irony in the words, thinking how unlikely it was that anything remained for Mamie except the earth Albert was waiting to shovel back. Now that she was right up against it, Mrs. Banning could probably feel that, too; and May looked back to see her still holding Virginia's arm, her face still averted and the small handkerchief tight in her gloved fingers.

*

From big wooden drums deposited along the transmission line, wiring crews were drawing sixty-one-strand aluminum steel core wire over the great spans. Six conductors, caught up to the pendent insulator strings; two grounded guard wires; now joined the delicately shaped, strong towers with an airy warp of metal more delicate still. New and untarnished, these spun filaments hung hardly more substantial than so many threads of light, dipping from tower to tower across the valley, mounting the hill in fine shining lines. On the high cross girders men worked hatless, in their shirts. The fields under them were growing green; there were already a few dandelions.

Monday and Tuesday, it was agreed that this could not last; every one who saw Mamie buried commented on it and said so. Wednesday and Thursday, most people said that they had never seen anything like it. By Friday, this spring in the midst of winter became as natural as life in the midst of death. Sunday would be the first day of March; and once it was March, a mere change of name could change what was wrong and amazing for February into what was right for spring.

The light, the length of day, which had lasted ten hours and fifty-five minutes Monday, lasted, Saturday, eleven hours and nine minutes; so any one could see that it was spring. Snowdrops were open everywhere, and Sunday Mr. Banning found two of his purple crocuses out. Behind the stables, the leafless forsythia was about to break in sprays of yellow blossoms. There were buds on the wild goose plums; in a few more days there would obviously be blossoms.

3

At eight o'clock Tuesday morning, Doctor Bull, sitting in the old swivel chair at his office desk, grunted as he bent in the long process of lacing up a pair of hob-nailed knee boots. His shabby old bag stood open on a heap of not read copies of the *Journal of the American Medical Association*. Next to it he had laid out a couple of patent rubber ligatures, a cased scalpel, a hypodermic syringe, a pint bottle of whisky and a bottle containing a chloride of lime solution. Finished with his boots, he checked these articles over and added them to the contents of the bag. Rumbling contentedly: *"Once in the dear dead days beyond recall—"* He pawed through the closet in the corner until he was able to produce a roughly finished oak bludgeon and a forked stick. Taking a fold of his jacket, he wiped the dust off them, laid them beside a pair of worn leather gauntlets. The telephone rang then and he could hear Susie shuffling to answer it. "Hell!" he remarked, stopping his singing, for Harry Weems and Lester were due any minute and he wanted to get up to North Truro fairly early.

Susie shrieked: "Doctor Bull, Mrs. Kimball says Ralph is sick; could you come right away."

"Tell her to wait a moment," he said, shutting up the bag. He went into the hall and took the receiver from her. "Hello," he said. "What's wrong with Ralph? Oh. Take his temperature? Well, how do you know he's feverish? Oh, he says so, does he? Give him a dose of castor oil and make him stay home. If I get back from North Truro early, I'll look in."

He started to hang up, but Doris Clark's voice interrupted: "Oh, Doctor Bull, I have another call for you."

"Who is it?"

"Mr. Ordway."

"Well, all right—" His eyes swung around to find Susie listening anxiously. "Beat it!" he roared. "Oh, hello. What's the trouble?"

"Well, I'll stop in a minute and look at her," he agreed. "I'm trying to get off to North Truro. No, I thought I'd take Lester and Harry and try to clean out some of the snakes up on the ridge. Been so warm a lot of them may be out—" He heard the front door bell and added, "Guess they're here now; but they can wait a minute. I'll be over. Come in, come in!" he shouted, hanging up.

Lester and Harry stood on the steps and he said, "You'll have to wait a while. Molly Ordway's had to get sick. Be right along." Harry had his car at the end of the path. "Might as well get my things in now," Doctor Bull observed, turning back to his office. Out in the hall again with them, he called, "All right, Aunt Myra. I'm leaving."

Mrs. Cole appeared at the door of the kitchen. "Good morning," she said sharply to Lester and Harry. "George, you'd better let those snakes alone. They aren't hurting anybody way up there. You'll probably get yourself bitten."

"They aren't hardly awake yet, Mrs. Cole," Lester said. "This warm spell sort of fools them and they start coming out; but they'll be so stiff they can't hardly move."

"Got to do my duty, Aunt Myra," said George Bull. "Can't be Health Officer if I don't protect the community."

"You'd protect it better if you stayed home

[157]

and tended to your business. You're too old a man to go climbing around cliffs killing harmless creatures."

"These are rattlesnakes, Aunt Myra; we aren't hunting rabbits today."

"Well, I expect they wouldn't harm any one who let them be; and if you're going to be late for dinner, you call me up."

"We'll be all right, Mrs. Cole," Harry Weems promised. "Wait for you in the car, Doc."

They had been waiting ten minutes when he came out the Ordways' door and across the lawn. He got into the car and Lester said: "What's wrong with Molly?"

"Oh, they used to call it spring fever—" He began to fill a pipe while Harry backed the car around. "Everybody's kind of run down in March. I'll bet half her trouble was she didn't feel like going to school today. I gave her a dose of castor oil so she'd have something to do at home."

"She's getting to be a good-looking kid," said Lester. "How old's she?"

"Sixteen, I guess," answered Harry Weems. "Same age, about, as Gerry Bates and Virginia Banning. Looks like they were turning out all girls that year. Matter of fact, Charlotte Slade, too."

"I hear she can be had."

"Maybe so. She looks sort of warm."

"Somebody saw her with Larry Ward parked outside that dance at the Odd Fellows Hall in Sansbury. Had her skirt around her neck."

"Yeah, that somebody would be Grant Williams. He gets more peeking done than any six;

and what he doesn't see he can always say he did."

"I hear Virginia Banning's going to New Mexico with the Hoyts."

"That's right. They're leaving a week from yesterday."

"That Hoyt girl is some kid. I could use her."

"Well, I doubt if you ever will," said Harry Weems, "so don't go brooding about it. Bad for his health, isn't it, Doc?"

"It is. You'd better keep your pants buttoned, Lester. I'm telling you. You fool around much now and you'll work yourself up a good hot rein-fection."

"I'm listening, Doc."

"You better listen unless you want to be back for a catheter party with me every afternoon. By the way, how's my old friend Henry Harris these days. He seems to be lying pretty low."

"Oh, he's around," said Lester.

"Who's going to get done now?"

"It must be a secret," said Lester mildly, "he isn't telling."

At North Truro they turned at the fork where a big sign showed a cowboy on a horse pointing to Robert Newell's Lakeland Lodge and Camps, and went the other way, up the muddy hill road in the warm second-growth woods. Through dense spots of hemlock and pine, the gray rock jutted out—short, sharp cliffs, towering split sections, a jumble of great glacial boulders.

"There we are," observed Harry Weems. "We can get up this end of the ledges easiest. We'll just pull the car into the brush here and go up that side." He jerked on the brake and turned off the motor. George Bull opened his bag, took out the scalpel and syringe cases, the ligatures, and, testing the cork with his thumb, the bottle of chloride of lime, distributing them in his pockets. "That good whisky, Doc?" asked Lester.

"We'll see when we get back," he promised. "Got a sack?"

"May be one on the floor there," said Harry.

"We'll try to get a couple alive. Bates would like them in a box in the store."

"Supposing we find any."

"If they aren't out after a nice week like last week, they're dead already."

Up on the ledges, above the tree tops, the rock was warm in the sun. George Bull, blowing a little, wiped his forehead, glancing down over the wooded slopes to fields in the valley bottom. There was a tone of pale, fresh green over willows along the creek. Cows stood bunched by the fences. Behind the Clark house somebody was hanging out laundry.

Harry Weems had been studying the broken stone shelves, damp shades of moss, blotches of lichen, and the low huckleberry bushes growing from drifts of old leaves and open chestnut burrs. "Listen," he said, "I think the best thing would be for me to get up there and Lester up above and we'll all work along together. Then, if we go slow and look sharp we can cover quite a lot of space. Here's your club, Lester. If we see more than one, we'll stand still and let the others get there. The rock's so warm they may be feeling pretty spry."

At the end of half an hour they had covered the whole southern face without success. "I saw a swell place for them," said Lester. "I'll bet they've got so much sense they know it isn't spring."

"We'll try the upper ones," George Bull said, swinging the oak stick. "They're around here somewhere."

"Wait a second," said Harry, seizing his arm. "What's that?"

"A rattle. Right over there. Hang on, Lester. Let's see him first."

They stood together, looking. "Funny," Harry said. "I bet I could walk right on him but I'm damned if I can see him."

"I see him," George Bull said. "Middle ledge. See the dark lichen? Now, look right down; this side of the little hemlock. See? It's moving. Holy Christmas, there's another."

"I don't see it."

"You better get glasses."

"Sure!" agreed Lester. "There's one, sliding down off the rock. See his head? Come on, let's go."

"Cut down there and come around from the other side, Lester," Doctor Bull said. "You come up this side, Harry. I'll go up above and jump on them."

"You'll what?"

"Get going and I'll show you."

They could see him clambering along the top ledge. When he paused, he took a handkerchief from one pocket and what proved to be a match from another. Striking the match, he set fire to the corner of the twisted cloth. "All right," he roared suddenly, "come on in!" He dropped the burning handkerchief down the side of the ledge. "Get that old black bastard, Lester!"

The drift of dry leaves under the overjutting stone began to frill with little flames from the handkerchief. "Come on, Harry! We've got them by the short hairs. They'll never get home to mother now!"

Up a crevice, onto the stone at his feet came a pitted, fluke-shaped head, the adroit neck swinging. He stamped his hob-nailed heel on it. "One down!" he shouted. Lester was slashing the leaves with his cudgel. From the sunny face of the lower ledge a half dozen snakes were scattering, sliding away frantic, but too stiff and slow. A single courageous, or stupidly amazed, female had coiled, fire behind and enemies on all sides, tail tip twitching up, stub head couched. "Coming at you!" roared Doctor Bull. He leaped from the ledge, both nailed boots and his better than two hundred pounds landing on her before she could move. The thick end of his oak bludgeon rang dull on the stone; he struck again, catching a little one attempting a panic-struck ascent of the crevice. Wheeling, he brought it down with all his force on a thick sliding coil under a huckleberry bush, producing a head, writhing back in anguish. He smashed it against the stone. "Whee!" he shouted. "We'll be coming round the mountain—"

"Doc!" yelled Harry. Some instinct had already warned him; he started to jump. Although the snake in the crevice was not coiled and had to pounce rather than strike, the head easily reached his hand holding the cudgel. Fantastically wide open, the small jaws swung, closing faster than sight on the side of his thumb.

"Hell and damnation!" George Bull roared, in what was both pain and anger. He dropped his stick. His violent left hand grasped the neck, dragging clear a thick, three-foot body. The head was torn from its hold; one fang pulled out of the worn leather of the glove; from the groove of the other a drop or two fell. "Here's one son of Satan who'll never see town!" Regardless of his bitten thumb he caught the writhing body, twitched it belly up and snapped the spine backwards. "Rattle for you, Harry!" He tossed it ten feet over toward him. "Go on, see if you can get a couple alive."

"Aw, never mind," said Lester. "I'll bet we killed ten. We'll bring the rattles in. Did he get you bad?"

"No. Went through the glove." He shook the glove off, regarding the dark puncture in the thick side of the thumb. "Damn neat job, though," he said, shaking it. "He was full of juice." He moved down the ledge. "No need to sit on another." He pulled the scalpel case from his pocket. "Take that out for me, Harry."

Laying the thumb on the stone, his left hand a little awkward, he drove the keen blade point in one line across the puncture; grunting, he crossed it remorsely with another line. Laying down the scalpel he fished out the chloride bottle and the syringe case. "Too bad I didn't know it was going to be for me," he said cheerfully. "Might have got myself some of that serum. Can you figure it out, Harry?"

"This come off?"

"That's it. Fill it up. Needles right there. See how they go?"

"Uh, huh."

Doctor Bull thrust the bloody thumb into his mouth, sucking it while he felt for the ligatures.

[163]

"Here you are, Lester. Take the little one twice around the thumb." He looked critically at his hand. "Daresay we don't need another, but we might as well have it. Unbutton that cuff for me, will you? God damn it, it would have to be my right hand. Let's have it, Harry. We'll give it a couple of shots after I've sucked out a little more."

"Taste good?" asked Lester.

"I've drunk better. All right, I can take care of the rest, thanks. See how many of those sons of bitches we got. Better stamp out that fire too. Think it's still burning under the side. Bring along the rattles."

Down at the car, where Doctor Bull, unassisted, had managed to get a covering bandage around his thumb, Lester produced eight severed rattles. "There's your friend," he said, holding up a seven-ringed one. "I'll bet he wishes he hadn't been so smart."

"I'll bet I wish he hadn't, too. Got a corkscrew, Harry? Two ounces of spiritus frumenti orally as a stimulant seems to be indicated. I'll leave the rest of it to you. Funny thing, though. Back in Michigan fifty years ago everybody believed whisky was the cure for snake bite. First thing to do was get pie-eyed. We're so smart now we know you couldn't do anything worse; but the fact is everybody who did it recovered. Figure that one out."

"Here you are, Doc. How're you going to measure two ounces?"

"Weigh it on my tongue. Here's to science."

Mrs. Cole said: "What did you do to your hand, George?"

"Snake bit me."

"My goodness! Didn't I know it? You can't say I didn't warn you."

"That's right. I can't. How about some lunch?"

"Are you in pain, George?"

"Well, naturally it hurts, if that's what you mean. But I can eat all right if I ever get a chance."

"Lunch will be ready directly. Some people called up. Susie, who called the doctor?"

"Vogels did," shrilled Susie. "And Mr. Fell. And Mrs. Kimball called again."

"Yes, there's plenty of sickness, weather like this. You better stay around and tend to people, George, and let those snakes alone."

"Sure, they all get the pip. What can I do about it?"

"I don't feel very good, either," announced Susie, appearing. "I—"

"Sure; you're getting a bad case of incipient dish-washing. I'd prescribe a couple of whacks on the rump with a shingle."

"No, I ain't. I felt awful sick this morning. I got a pain in my stomach."

"Well, we've got plenty of castor oil."

He brought his bag into the office, but he had scarcely set it down when the telephone rang. Susie cried out: "Doctor Bull's house. Why, yes, he's here. Oh, yes, I'll tell him—" She came to the door, announcing with interest, "Mrs. Vogel says Jack is still awful sick. She says he's got an awful fever. She's put him to bed."

"Tell her I'm having lunch. I'll see about it afterwards."

The car at the first gasoline pump in front of Weems's garage couched low on its hundred-and-forty-two-inch wheelbase. It was sober enough black; but rich and lustrous, with a general silver-like glitter of non-tarnishable metal. On each wide hub cap was embossed a V12. Besides whatever intricate refinements of mechanism, it suggested unconcern about running expenses. Similarly, the model—it was a convertible coupé —suggested driving for pleasure and when the owner chose, not struggling through all weathers, year in and year out. On the silver grill fronting the broad radiator was affixed a round enamel plaque bearing the crossed Aesculapian staffs of the county medical association.

Incommoded by the difficulty of using his sore right hand, Doctor Bull halted his own cheap car at the other gasoline pump. "Some outfit," he said to Mat Small, nodding at it. "I wouldn't mind getting me one of those. Only, what with? Give me six." He stepped out into the afternoon sunlight and walked over. "Hello, Verney," he said. "You certainly look prosperous. Lots of sickness in Sansbury?"

Doctor Verney had just finished paying George Weems. He turned in the deep ample seat, extending a hand. "Good afternoon, Doctor. No, as a matter of fact, everybody's too damn healthy." Laughing, to show that his deploring of such a situation was a pleasantry, his ever so slight ill-ease was apparent and George

Bull grinned. "Snake bit me this morning," he said, raising his right hand. "The snake died." He continued to examine Verney, his blue eyes twinkling. "Who's sick at the Bannings'?"

"Virginia's laid up. Nothing much. I wouldn't be surprised if it were just excitement. She's going on a trip with the Hoyts. Or the weather. A chill. It's not as warm as it looks, really. It's always that way. I'll have more than one case of pneumonia as soon as it turns cold again."

"Yes," agreed George Bull. "I lost a case a week or so ago."

Doctor Verney's features—even; rather handsome in a severe, alertly intelligent way—underwent a small, disconcerted change, showing that Mrs. Banning had told him all about it, or her version of it. "Well," he said, "that's the way it is. The winters are really pretty hard up here—"

He would be glad to get on, George Bull recognized, but his awareness of the fact that he had cut Doctor Bull out on what ought to be Doctor Bull's best-paying patients made him anxious not to add incivility to that injury. George Bull grinned again, enjoying Doctor Verney's delicacy. "Yes," he said, "the spring crop's beginning to come in. I've been running around dealing out castor oil for two days now. Regular epidemic. Every two minutes the telephone rings and somebody doesn't feel so good. Wish I could soak them twenty dollars a visit. That's one of the greatest modern contributions to medical science. Just thinking about it cures half the people who wake up imagining they're sick. Well, I'll have to be getting on. Quite a car, this—" He banged his left fist approvingly on the doortop. "You ought to send a snapshot of it to the editor of the *Journal*. Stop all this belly-aching about starving country physicians."

He grinned again and waved his hand.

Doctor Verney stepped on the starter, but for a minute nothing happened as he had forgotten to turn on the ignition. Absorbed in grinning at this slightly uneasy departure, George Bull realized that some one had come up casually and joined him. "Hello, Henry," he nodded, half turning his head. "There's the kind of car you want. Planning to get one next month?"

Henry Harris's face warmed to his silent smile. "Is that when they begin giving them away?" he asked.

They stood watching it down past the end of the green in silence. "Why, no," George Bull said. "But the taxes ought to be along pretty soon. You aren't going to waste them on civic improvements, are you?"

Steadily smiling, Henry Harris said: "We have to pay the Board of Health, I guess. I always believe in sharing the Lord's bounty with the deserving. It's kind of hard when Herring squeezes the buffalo off every nickel; but if it were left to me, George, I'd see you were rewarded in a way commensurate with your sterling abilities. At present my assets are mostly good will."

"Uh, huh," agreed George Bull. "So are mine, Henry; so are mine. If you ever burn your hand on red-hot money, you can have my professional services gratis." He started to move toward his car. "Oh," he said, stopping, "was there something you wanted to see me about?"

"No, nothing important. The Democrats are having a little meeting tomorrow night. Just discussing our policies, and so on. Wouldn't care to look in, would you?"

"I'd be sort of out of place, wouldn't I?"

"A lot of thinking people are going to vote Democratic this fall, George. I had an idea you were getting on pretty bad terms with the Republicans. Or maybe I should say the Mrs. Bannings. She's doing her best to get you into trouble. And now I hear Emma Bates is going around saying things. That doesn't seem the right way to treat a regular party man."

"Well, Mrs. Banning's been doing her best for a long time, and it doesn't seem any too good, Henry. As for Emma, she's mostly wind. Quimby and Ordway would want something more substantial. The School Committee would have run me out long ago if anything could be worked there. I must have some friends."

"You've got me and Paul Lane. We've always stood up for you. So's Ordway, on occasion. The Bannings don't own the town yet. I'm not saying they haven't influence with their gang of boot-lickers; that's just what I mean. You never know when they may pull a fast one on you. I think you're in the wrong camp, George."

"It's mighty nice of you to be so worried about it, Henry. Now, what were you thinking you'd like to have me do for you?"

"Absolutely nothing. I just hate to see a man knifed in the back. Of course, we'd be glad to have your vote; but we aren't buying them. We're going to get too many free this fall."

"Henry, ingratitude's a terrible sin. I hope you'll never find me guilty of it."

*

Wednesday morning, George Bull's right hand was too sore for him to shave with any comfort. He came downstairs grumpy, and Aunt Myra said at once: "My goodness, George, you look like a tramp! You go to that barber shop and let somebody shave you."

"Let's have some breakfast."

"I'm not ready yet. You can sit down if you want."

"Where's Susie?"

"Oh. Susie. Well, Pete came up with a note from Mrs. Andrews. Susie's sick in bed."

"She would be! Jumping Jupiter, it's a puny bunch we have around here! Man, woman, and child, they haven't the guts of a two-day kitten. All lie in bed and holler for the doctor. Want me to dose them up with a lot of rubbish and tell them how brave they are in their afflictions. Even a spell of nice warm weather's more than they can stand. I know of ten cases lying around feeling weak and wanting somebody to wait on them— eleven, with the Banning girl. They don't feel good; they got a belly ache; they just seem all worn out—"

"Well, it's a good thing those snakes don't bite you often, George. Looks to me as though you got out the wrong side of bed this morning. There are some prunes for you, and don't use all that cream on them. It's got to do your oatmeal and coffee, too—"

"God Almighty! There's the door bell. Can't a man even eat in peace?"

"You better sit still. I'll see who it is."

When she came back, she said: "It's that Ward boy, from the Bannings'."

"What's he want?"

"Wants to see you. He looks kind of peaked. I suppose he isn't feeling well."

"Huh! Why don't they get Verney up? I guess they figure he isn't worth it. Horse doctor will do for him——"

Passing by the back door through his office ten minutes later, George Bull looked into the waiting room. Larry Ward was sitting slumped in a chair by the front window. "All right, come in," George Bull said. "Might as well see you, since you're here. My morning hours are from nine to ten. Don't come banging around at half-past eight next time." He closed the door. "Sit down. Well, you look kind of green. What's the trouble?"

Larry clasped both hands together, swallowing. He shifted in the chair. Finally he said, hushed, "I think I got something, Doc."

"Oh, you do, do you? Well, what have you got?"

Larry gulped again, wordless, and George Bull snorted. "Uh, huh," he agreed. "Well, don't get in a sweat. This isn't the Y.M.C.A. When do you think you got infected?"

"I don't know."

"You don't know? Been fooling with Betty Peters?"

"No, I never——"

"You going to tell me you must have got it

off a toilet? Have to be a minister to manage that. Where did you get it?"

Finally he said, "I guess it must have been Charlotte Slade, Doc. She's the only one—"

"That kid? When did you have intercourse with her?"

"I guess it was a week ago Friday. I felt pretty rotten for a couple of days, now. I—"

"Well, she's certainly starting young. All right. We'll have a short arm inspection. Don't get the wind up; we'll take care of you. Just come over here—"

When he had finished he said, "There's nothing wrong with you. What are you, crazy? Charlotte tell you she had something?"

"You mean, I'm all right, Doc?"

"Sure, you're all right. When you're not, you don't have to wonder about it. I didn't think it was very likely with a kid like that—" He considered Larry, standing stupid in his incredulous relief. "Got any reason to think you weren't the first?"

"Oh, she said I was; but—"

"Well, the odds are you were. Somebody always has to be. Old man Slade's been afraid of God for forty years and so he gets back at life by making the women and children afraid of him. Charlotte isn't old enough to have stopped being scared of him long. Do you mean business?"

"Hell, I don't know, Doc."

"If you don't, stick to girls old enough to know what they're doing. You'll find plenty of them. Once is an accident; might happen to any one. But if it goes on, and by any chance I see her start swelling, this town'll be too hot for you not married to her. That'll be five dollars, just to help you remember. And tell her if she isn't regular this month to come up here and I'll see what we can do."

"All right," Larry said. "But, listen, Doc. Just the same I feel pretty bum. I mean, kind of sickish—"

"That's called the fear of God. Take a dose of castor oil tonight and go to bed early. Generally fixes it up."

Larry grinned uncertainly. "All right," he repeated. "I got to admit I feel some better. I was certainly scared, Doc."

"You were. But you get over it pretty quick. Until the next time. You better think about marrying Charlotte. She can give you all there is, and it might save you plenty of trouble and expense. Nice little kid, in spite of her old man. Beat it."

With Larry gone, he set himself to putting a new dressing on his thumb, reflective; for now that he thought of it, he could remember Charlotte Slade's birth. Or maybe it was the Slade boy, who was killed in a motor accident. When he got there the baby was just about born, with Mrs. Slade yelling as loud as she could, and Slade, who didn't think it was decent to be present, yelling prayers in the front room even louder. On second thought, he decided that it was Charlotte, not the boy. The boy had been born in winter. George Bull guessed that he himself was at least twenty years older, but Slade seemed something left from a long time ago. Old man Slade preserved a sort of mean and comic rusticity which might have been general once in the outlying farms. Even sixteen or seventeen years back there had been little of it left—it was hard to believe that those illiterate, goat-bearded farmers, stubborn and credulous, had ever existed.

Well, they had, all right. Their vanishing was part of the process in which Charlotte Slade, a year or so ago caught up by the heels while he slapped the breath into her, was being seduced by what had once appeared a perpetually fixed brat in rompers. George Bull gazed at his thumb and he thought that he could almost see the proof of age. The first steps in healing looked reluctant. Other people, perhaps, hadn't got around to noticing, but to his own body he was old man Bull, hardly worth the effort. Cresting the swell of inflamed flesh, the angry crust of the still frail blood clot filled the criss-cross slash like a red mark of his certain mortality.

In the hall the telephone rang. Aunt Myra must have been close enough to reach it, for he heard her almost at once screaming into the mouthpiece: "Hello—"

"Tell them I'll be over when I can," he called. "I've got to go down and get shaved. Who is it?"

He could hear her gabbling a form of this information and then she hung up. "Who is it?" he repeated.

"That's Mrs. Bates, George. She wants you to see Geraldine."

"Huh! Changed her tune, has she? Well, we'll let her stew awhile. I've got half a dozen visits to make. Doubt if I get back for lunch."

"I expect I'll go to Sansbury, George. I'll leave an apple pie in the pantry and there's plenty of milk, if you want anything."

"You better hang around and answer the telephone."

"No, I'm going to Sansbury, George. There's a picture I want to see. I'll ask that little girl at the telephone to write down any calls and you can ring her up from wherever you are and ask her. There'll be plenty of sickness, I daresay. Mr. Cole's mother always said a green Christmas makes a full churchyard, and—"

"This isn't Christmas, Aunt Myra."

"Well, I expect it still holds good, whatever it is."

He picked up the five-dollar bill which Larry had laid on the desk and went to the door. "Take this along," he said. "You might see something you want."

"I can manage, thank you, George. I've got my fares and twenty-five cents for the theater. I don't want to be a burden to any one and those people keep sending me the checks. I must say it's very kind of them."

"Don't you worry about them, Aunt Myra. Alfred spent most of his life trying to pay for that insurance." Taking her hand, he pressed the five-dollar bill in it, closing the fingers. "Now don't put it in the stove," he said, "it's money."

Louie, his loose hand working in the lather spread on Doctor Bull's chin, said: "I hear Mr. Jackson's sick—" He tipped his head indicatively toward the wall which concealed Gosselin Brothers' scarlet-fronted store next door. "He come and opened up, but he went home pretty soon. Gus Ferris said he was awful shaky. He was going to get Mrs. Jackson to come over and help Gus, but she hasn't come, so I suppose he must be real sick. I hear you got a lot of patients."

"Quite a few. It looks like a mild form of influenza, whatever that is. I'm damned if I know how to help them. That what you want to know?"

Louie laughed. "Sure," he admitted. "Lot of people ask me. Not contagious, is it?"

"Very likely. It's been spreading around somehow."

"I was over shaving Joe Tupping. He don't feel so good. If I get it from him, I'm going to be mad. I fixed it up to go to New York over this week end."

"Well, I wouldn't worry. It doesn't amount to anything. Come on! Get going! I can't stay here all day." He lay practically prostrate in the chair, staring at the pattern of the once-white-painted, stamped sheet tin which covered the ceiling. Louie, getting through his preliminaries in a burst of activity, smeared down the side of his face and applied his razor.

"What the devil have you got there?" George Bull roared. "A meat ax?"

Louie lifted the razor. "You grow an awful tough beard, Doc. I'll give it a couple more licks." He struck the strop a few times with it. "I hear you're turning Democrat, Doc."

"That's news to me. Didn't hear it from Henry Harris, by any chance, did you?"

"Somebody said something about some row you had with Bates."

"Well, you tell Henry that when I want a row I know how to make one. He doesn't have to think up any for me."

"I thought Mrs. Bates was kind of sore at you."

"That was yesterday. Today she's been ringing me up and wanting me to rush right over and look at Geraldine. Guess we'll have a truce as long as she thinks she needs me. While you're at it, you can just spread that around. But Henry oughtn't to stick his nose in so far. First thing he knows he'll find it pulled off." George Bull clasped and unclasped his left hand. "Come on! Hurry up! I've got to see all these invalids!"

*

Janet Cardmaker, in breeches, boots, and a man's white shirt with the collar open on her thick neck, sat on the kitchen steps in the noon sun. At the corner of her lips a neglected cigarette smoked itself away. The many folded sections of last Sunday's *New York Times* lay on her lap. Occasionally she read a paragraph at random; mainly she looked past the barn and the bare apple trees. A confused, unready touch of spring showed in blotches of new green over the dull, sere, sunny fields; the buds on some bushes were already big and beginning to split. The valley was filled with vague haze in the mild, windless sunlight.

Out in the lot she could see the formidable fawn-colored shoulders of Moloch III, moving with sullen majesty in the radius of the forty feet of thin steel cable which attached his ringed nose to a stake. He was the biggest Jersey bull she had ever seen; he must weigh more than fifteen hundred pounds, and that in a small breed which didn't run to fat. Really, he was too good for this herd; but she hated to sell him at a time when nobody would want to pay anything like what he was worth. It might be better to buy a couple of heifers fit for him, and see what she got. She threw the cigarette down, turning her head and calling, deep voiced, through the kitchen door: "When do we have lunch?"

Mrs. Foster answered, "About twenty minutes, Miss Cardmaker."

"Well, lay another place. Doctor Bull's coming up."

She could hear more distinctly now the sound of a motor which had attracted her attention, changing gears to get up the bad road. She sat still on the steps until it came in sight beyond the barnyard and turned in the gate. George Bull drove it close to the steps and banged the door open.

"You haven't eaten, have you?" she asked.

"They don't give me time."

"We'll have something in about twenty minutes." She stood up. "I hear a snake bit you. Is it all right?"

"Sore as hell. I had to cut it all up. Well, I went and asked for it. Hurts my patients more than it does me, I guess. Moloch looks pretty good out there."

"I guess I'll keep him. Sit down."

She went into the kitchen, presently returning with a couple of the crystal wine glasses beautifully emblazoned with Levi Cardmaker's self-conferred eighteenth-century coat and crest. Setting them on the step, she took a jack knife from her pocket, levered a corkscrew from one side of it, sank it with a muscular twist and drew the cork of the whisky bottle. "This is from Sansbury, on your prescription," she observed, sniffing it. "I guess it's better than Anderson's." She sat down and filled the wine glasses. "What are you so busy about?"

"Healing the sick." He raised the glass and swallowed half of it. "That is pretty good. Oh, a lot of them collapsed when the sun hit them and curled up. They should have stayed under their stones. We'll get a blizzard next week."

"Who's sick?"

"The whole bunch. Regular epidemic. A good many may be just malingering, but Ralph Kimball looks like acute nephritis. We may not see much more of him. Perhaps it has nothing to do with the others. Or they may all be reacting to something like that Spanish 'flu. Stay out of town awhile. It seems to be running around. A cold snap will probably finish it off."

"You don't seem much worried."

"It's their hard luck, not mine. Nothing to be done, except see how it comes out. It takes a lot of forms, this influenza. For all we could do about it, some specially bad sort might start up again any time. Wipe out three quarters of the human race, given a real start."

"No great loss. Speaking of loss, I hear the Talbot girl's death got the gang down on you."

"Some of the women took it to heart. Emma Bates was all set to give me a piece of her mind. Her idea was I should have been there that afternoon."

"What's your idea?"

"That's mine, too," admitted George Bull. "Not that I could have done anything short of an oxygen tent, or some such nonsense they think up to milk the paying customers—but I could certainly have saved myself a lot of dirty looks. Emma was pretty riled. She never did get rid of that piece of mind, so she spent a week chewing it for anybody who'd listen. I could see her at Mamie's funeral wondering whether she couldn't get Doctor Wyck to have me ejected."

"Who else was unhappy?"

"About everybody, I guess. Except Howard Upjohn. He got some cash business—Banning's cash, I don't need to say. And, of course, Mamie. Where she is now, she won't have to be an Episcopalian; or clean up after the Bannings; or give her money to her mother; or wonder whether she'll have a baby if she does."

"Blow over?"

"Sure. That was damn near two weeks ago. Even Emma was calling me up this morning. The real trouble was, I forgot to put on a big show entitled 'The Wonders of Science.'" He lifted the glass and drank thoughtfully. "Funny thing, Janet, to see the change there. When I was first practicing, they kind of thought a doctor was a medicine man. They didn't know what it was all about; he was sort of dabbling in the occult, and anything he did was all right with them. They don't know any more now; but they've been reading the papers and they want some of that, not God knows what out of a bottle. You ought to see Verney's place. Nurses sitting around in uniform making urinalyses. Half a ton of fluoroscopic machines. Verney telling all the women to get undressed for a thorough examination. When he's through, he has a four-page record. Nine

[180]

cases out of ten, he doesn't know a thing he couldn't have found out by feeling a pulse and asking a couple of questions. Talk about the occult! But everybody thinks when he's written down so much he must know something; and the women are purring like cats, wondering if he didn't think they looked pretty good in the raw. That's giving them proper attention. People like the Bannings, who can pay for it, are going to have proper attention or know why not."

"Was Mrs. Banning at the Talbots'?"

"No, just Herbert; but she's on her hind legs as usual. Henry Harris knows she'd like to oust me from Medical Examiner to the School Board, and anything she wants, he seems to make it his special business to see she doesn't get. I guess it annoys her a good deal."

"What's that rat got against the Bannings, George? I've always wondered."

"I don't know. Wish I did; it might be good for a laugh. Maybe it's just politics. Henry can get a lot of people into line voting Democratic for no reason at all except that Banning is a Republican. He was even having a try at me. Fact is, half the people in town know that if they were in Banning's place, they'd think they owned the earth; so that must be what he thinks. They're just going to show him he doesn't. They're going to show him that there isn't enough money in the world to make them stop being contrary damn fools, if they've a mind to be."

Janet laughed briefly, shook another cigarette from a flattened package and thrust it in her mouth. "They make me sick," she said. "The whole lot of them. Kill all you want, George."

"Oh, they aren't so bad, as people go. They're just trying to be free and equal. Fun watching them. I've been right here for forty years and I've never been what you'd call bored."

"You wouldn't have been bored anywhere on earth, so long as they had lots of food, and a little liquor, and a couple of women with their legs open."

George Bull's great laugh boomed out. "Sure," he said, "the simple life!" He lifted the wine glass and emptied it. "Can we eat? I got a lot more patients."

⫸ THREE ⫷

A four by six cut of a photograph taken from the crest of the Cobble showed the great steel towers of the finished transmission line crossing the valley at New Winton. There was also three quarters of a front page column about it. Henry Harris, examining the weekly issue of the Sansbury *Times* while he sat on the steps of Bates's store Thursday morning, observed beneath the cut the minute italics: *Courtesy Interstate Light & Power* and allowed himself to smile. You wouldn't catch Marden wasting money.

Henry Harris's interest, though detached, was personal. No one in New Winton knew it, and no one would be likely to guess from the *Times's* vigorously Republican editorial attitude, but the controlling interest in the paper, and in the Times Print Shop, had long ago joined the host of miscellaneous properties always quietly accumulating in Henry Harris's hands.

Owning the *Times* was really one of Henry Harris's amusements and by far the most expensive one. Not that it actually cost him anything, for the printing plant made up its deficit; but he did sacrifice a possible profit for the pleasure afforded him weekly. Marden, a stumpy, swearing little man, was a fanatically honest and economical manager. Knowing, of course, that it would be good business for Henry Harris to scrap the paper, politics quite aside, Marden's continued assaults on the Democrats, whether in Sansbury, Hartford, or Washington, had a subtle extra note of defiance. He felt that he was tilting, too, at Henry Harris's indulgence. Every paragraph said also: "Put that in your pipe, Mr. Harris. If you don't like it, you know what you can do."

Henry Harris, his warm private smile lighting over the current example of Marden's valor, turned contentedly on to the section headed *New Winton Notes*. These were written by Miss Kimball, and if Marden's exaggerated blustering hadn't been reward enough, Miss Kimball would certainly justify his extravagance. Miss Kimball's importance rested entirely on this little job; it made her feel that she was not merely the underpaid village Librarian, but actually somebody. Probably it contributed the assurance shown when she sided so haughtily with Mrs. Banning against Henry Harris. Not an unkind man, Henry Harris was content to enjoy the irony hard to miss in Miss Kimball's rudeness to the person whose most casual word could knock out the props of her whole self-esteem. The spectacle of her skating with dignity on this (had she only known) thinnest possible ice, tickled him. She did not ever mention Henry Harris, just to pay him for daring to differ with Mrs. Banning. As he did not wish to be mentioned, Miss Kimball was not only funny but perfectly satisfactory. He read: *Mr. Norman Hoyt, the well-known artist, is planning to start on a motor trip to Sante Fe, New Mexico, Monday. He expects to be away for two or three months. Accompanying Mr. Hoyt will be Miss Valeria Hoyt, his daughter; and Miss Virginia Banning, daughter of Mr. and Mrs. Herbert Tracy Banning.* This item was the unquestioned cream of Miss Kimball's news; but immediately under it appeared the line: *Mr. Ralph Kimball is confined to his home by a slight illness.*

Henry Harris chuckled. "Next thing to nepotism," he remarked.

Lester Dunn, letting the store door close behind him and standing still on the step, said: "What the hell are you mumbling about, Henry?"

"Just enjoying the news. Smart girl, Miss Kimball. I hope the *Times* appreciates her. Where are you going?"

"Nowhere."

Henry Harris folded the paper and tucked it in the pocket of his old corduroy coat. He pointed a pipe stem at his car, standing isolated by the pavement edge. "Come on," he said, "I'll take you there."

"What's up?"

"You never can tell." He glanced at Lester. "You don't look so hot. Got a hangover?"

"Oh, I got a damn cold or something. I feel lousy. What's the trouble?"

"No trouble yet. You're probably getting this influenza I hear so much about."

"Bunk. It's something I ate."

Driving slowly down the green, Henry Harris said, "How's Doc Bull's hand?"

"Don't know. I haven't seen him since Tuesday."

"Saw him Tuesday myself. By the way, he didn't say anything to you, did he?"

"No."

"I've got a notion he didn't hear anything that time. But he may think something's up. It would be sort of uncomfortable if he does. More I think of it, the more I'm afraid passion betrayed me, Lester."

"What does that mean?"

"Well, you see the whole business isn't really worth the money. I wouldn't have started it if I hadn't felt the urge to annoy my friend Matthew. He needs to be heated up every little while so he won't mildew. But—" He shook his head thoughtfully.

"Listen, Henry, I'm sorry, but I've spent that money, if you're thinking about a refund and calling it off. Besides what difference does it make if Doc Bull knows? What will he do?"

"Probably nothing. But I like a neat job." He laughed. "You can usually take a chance on big things, Lester; but you have to be awful careful about little ones. Well, we'll try to mop up the spilt milk. Maybe it'll be a lesson to me."

"Lesson about what?"

"Maybe about paying people in advance."

"Watch out!" Lester said.

A glittering black car, going fast, gave them a perfunctory blare of horn and was by. "Doctor Verney," Henry Harris nodded. "Well, I guess

Virginia'd better hurry up and get well if she's going to accompany Mr. Norman Hoyt, the well-known artist, to New Mexico."

"They're an awful lot of people sick in this town. Maybe Doc Bull will be so busy he won't get around to anything, anyway."

"Glad to hear it. What I'm worrying about is his getting around to see the mess the Interstate people left that camp in. I'm going to send Albert Foster up as soon as he gets off the job he's doing for Ordway. I hate to pay somebody else three dollars a day when Albert would do it for two fifty."

"Why didn't you make them clean up themselves?"

"Oh, that Snyder chap was kind of sore. I soaked them pretty hard for rent. That land on the hill isn't worth anything. They could have bought the whole mountain for less. They were late and wanted to get out so I thought I wouldn't bother them."

"What's it to Doc Bull?"

"Nothing, but if he wanted to, he'd probably figure out a way for the Board of Health to fine me. It's right on the edge of the water supply area. After the way he got Banning about the dumping, anything might happen."

"Doc Bull would never bother to go up there. Being Board of Health here's just a racket. Keep your shirt on, Henry. We may make some money yet. Listen, drive over to my place, will you? I got the trots. Been on the can all morning."

"You better take a dose of something and go to bed. We'll never make any money with you laid up. Sure, being Board of Health's a racket;

but you can't expect Doc Bull to run himself ragged for three hundred dollars a year salary."

*

A traveling clock whose silver face could be folded away in its supporting case of pale gray morocco was turned half toward her on the bedside table and Virginia Banning, shifting her head a little on the pillow, could see that it was five minutes of nine. Waiting a moment, concerned, to find out how she felt, she decided that today she was all right. There was perhaps a trace of faintness, a hint of yesterday's bad headache, but both would probably go as soon as she had some coffee. Relieved, she remembered wondering, when she felt so rotten Tuesday and yesterday, if she were really going to be sick. She had not quite dared ask Doctor Verney how long what he called a touch of influenza might last, but her misery had a solid permanence which could easily mean a week or two. The Hoyts wouldn't be able to wait that long.

Brooding on the possible malice of fate so serving her, she had concluded that nothing could be more like life or her luck. You could see in it the dreary pattern of too many remembered anticipations which had somehow come to nothing. In fact, the whole plan had been perilous from the start. Like the first idea of going to Paris, motoring to Santa Fe had an ecstatic desirability which at once jeopardized it, made it inherently improbable. Frowning a little, she could even recall thinking, in feverish extravagance, that probably there was a God. Knowing that she regarded

[188]

him as a lot of nonsense, God was always on the alert to pay her sauciness with the inspired punishments of a loving kindness which did not care if she were really injured and never made any mistake about what could hurt and disappoint her most.

She drew a breath, not wanting even now to tempt Heaven with too scornful a rejection of that possibility, and lifted her head enough to see that the morning was once more clear, the sunlight still warm on the trees. Shifting her head again, something arrested her. She came up sharply on one elbow, staring with a jolt of alarm at her pillow. How it could have got there was a mystery for the moment sinister and appalling, but the stain was undoubtedly blood. Revulsion was eased then by relief. Asleep, she must have suffered a slight nose bleed. Bringing her hand to her face, she could feel blood dried on her nostril and lip.

"God, what a lousy mess!" she said. She threw back the covers and sat up, indignant.

The violence of the motion made her giddy, so she sat a moment, recovering her balance. Finally, standing up, impatient, she made for the bathroom door. Almost there, she was forced to realize in new, dismayed anger that she wasn't completely over her illness. An abrupt tightening cramp stabbed her bowels, a wave of sickness rushed up from them, landing with a painful impact inside her skull. The echo of it jarred, lingering, in her ears.

The handle resisted her. She tugged harder, half in support, trying to make her wrist turn. Something gave suddenly, but it was only the surface of the knob sliding on her palm, now lubricated disgustingly with sweat. Frustrated, she stood an instant trying to master the cramping nausea. Sweat was all over her now, and at once she was aware of cold, like a breeze on her. Down her back, under her arms, across her breast, the skin crawled, quailing from this strong draft. She put a bare foot out uncertainly, interrupting her partial stagger, held the sliding door knob and braced her other hand on the jamb while her body seemed suddenly porous, like weak white ice frozen full of air.

She must get back to bed, and she found herself phrasing it through the hard chatter of her teeth: *But I would rather go to bed*—the word bed was seized by a paroxysmal multiplication, a leaning tower of many million paper-thin but hard sounds soaring past view or reach. Shaken too violently to stand, her legs melted, her icy hands astoundingly failed. She went down on her side, in the weak relief of this surrender anticipating, even as immediately she felt, the cruel remote pain of bone banged on wood. The smooth floor held her face, turned sideways.

Opening, the door seemed only to have been waiting for this. But it was the other door, she realized. The bathroom door had not relented. "Take that damn knob down—" she managed to say. "You can't get in—"

Seeing that it was her mother, Virginia made at once an effort to get up. She would never convince any one that she was all right and able to go; even what she said was crazy. Shutting her eyes, she forced an order into the words: "I meant, the door, not the knob—"

Picked up, she could feel her own lightness and it amazed her; she weighed nothing. She could have floated on the ringing air. "Virginia, darling—"

"Leave me alone," she whispered automatically. "I just slipped—"

The bed mounted and met her shoulders and numb buttocks and light legs with a soft, intolerable jar. "Oh, my God, my head—" she moaned. "Mother, my head aches—"

She got her chill wet hands to her forehead, palms grinding her eyebrows. She rolled her face into the pillow. In this hammer of pain she could hear another voice—it was Mary—crying: "Oh, the poor lamb! There, now—you go on, M'am. There, Miss Ginny—"

"Hello," Virginia murmured, perplexed by the positiveness with which she could recognize Doctor Verney by his hands, by touch and a distinctive washed smell. His grave oval face and intent brown eyes moved, smiling. "Hello, Ginny. What have you been up to?"

"I just sort of fainted, I guess—" But fainting, she saw at once, did not in the least describe it. "Have I been asleep?"

"I guess you have. How do you feel?"

"I'm all right. My head hurt so damn much; but not now."

"Well, we'll fix you up in a hurry. Let's see the tongue. Now, wide open. That's it. All right."

"Am I going to be well. I mean, Monday. Am I—"

"I don't know why not! Only you mustn't keep

getting out of bed. A little fever can weaken you a lot. Know that now, don't you?"

"I had a nose bleed."

"That's a nuisance; but at least it doesn't hurt much, does it? You stay in bed today and tomorrow. Saturday you ought to be all right. What would you like to eat?"

"Nothing."

"How about some ice cream?"

"No. But I'd like some water ice. I'd like some lemon water ice if they could get some."

"All right. Ice cream would give you a little nourishment; but if you don't feel like it, don't eat it."

"It's too thick. I don't want it."

"All right. Here's a thermometer. Don't eat that." He put out a hand, bringing into view a gold wrist watch. His fingers closed on her wrist. Virginia, interested, saw that the watch bore an amazing long thin second-hand which made the whole round of the dial rapidly. Moved to comment on it, the thermometer halted her, so she made a vague circular motion with her finger.

"That's right," he agreed, smiling. "It's supposed to be easier to see. Got it for my birthday."

*

Her head, crowned by a preposterous black bonnet, was tilted reflectively to the side. She kept pursing her lips, making while she did it, George Bull knew, small decisive clicks with her tongue. She walked right past the path up to the house. George Bull, leaving his car by the roadside, said, "Whoa! Where are you bound, Aunt Myra?"

Stopping short on the gravel along the old lilac hedge, she turned, blinking. "Oh, George! My, you startled me! Well, I've been to see Susie. I just wanted to see for myself how sick she was."

"She'll be all right."

"Maybe she will, and maybe she won't. I'm not setting myself up against you, George, but I can tell you one thing. I know now what's wrong with that girl, and likely with all these other people."

"You do, do you? Well, I wish I did."

"Now, don't you go laughing at me. When I was stopping with Mr. Cole's sister in New Haven, I learned all I need to about that. They had it in every other house. That little niece of mine, what's her name, had it. It all came just the same way. Now, George, what Susie's got's typhoid fever, sure as you're alive."

"Don't you believe it, Aunt Myra. This is Susie who's sick, not that niece of yours."

"It won't do you any good, telling me not to believe it. I know. It's from drinking dirty water. Back whenever it was the water ran all dirty, I just said to myself: 'Myra, you watch out!' "

"Just a little mud, Aunt Myra. You can drink all you want of it."

"Well, George, I don't believe you can. They had doctors in New Haven as good as you are, and they said that's what it was. That was in the year 1901. I remember."

"Typhoid fever is a disease caused by a specific organism, bacillus typhosus, Aunt Myra. Doesn't grow on trees. That organism has to be in the water. It can be clear water or muddy water; that hasn't anything to do with it."

"Maybe you're right, George. I don't know

anything about all that. But what Susie's got is typhoid fever. I can smell, George. I know what it smells like."

"You can what?"

"A person has a smell, George. It's not a subject I'm going to discuss, but I'd know that smell anywhere."

"Listen, Aunt Myra; you can't have typhoid fever without getting it from some one! Now, nobody around here has had it. In forty years, there hasn't been a single case in this village. Matter of fact, it isn't easy to find a case anywhere nowadays!"

"Don't you go shouting at me, George. People might think you weren't so sure of what you're talking about, getting all excited that way. Now, you can call it anything you've a mind to. What concerns me is that Susie won't be off her bed for six weeks, supposing the Lord spares her; so I'm just going on up the road to see if one of those Baxter girls wants to come in, meanwhile."

"Lot of foolishness! You wait a couple of days—"

"Now, George, with all these people sick, there's no sense in waiting. Everybody'll be wanting help. You go look in the water for some of those things, if you think they're there."

"You can't see them by just looking in the water, Aunt Myra. You—"

"Well, then; what makes anybody think there are any, I'd like to know."

"You'd have to make a microscopic examination for evidence of fecal pollution—"

"Land sakes, then; why don't you take down

[194]

that microscope you have sitting year in and year out on that closet shelf and use it?"

"It's quite a trick, Aunt Myra. Not much in my line."

"Well, I haven't any time to stand here arguing. If you can't find out yourself, it seems to me you'd better take my word. Now, I'll be back to fix lunch directly."

Grinning a little, he watched her depart. "That's a good one," he thought. "How would I know it was there if I couldn't see it? Why, I'd send my specimens to Torrington and let a lot of girls do it for me."

It would be girls, probably. Some little wench, as likely as not called Doctor What-is-it! It certainly seemed that women had a natural aptitude for bacteriology—or maybe one naturally evolved. If you watched one of them so much as flaming a platinum loop to fish in a test tube you got the point. They were effortlessly adept at the delicate scratching of culture surfaces, the casual quick trick of heat fixation without spoiling the smear or cracking the slide. Slight shoulders hunched in a familiar minute absorption; the clean narrow fingers faintly scarred, in patient practiced movement; absorbed faces with a light gleam of sweat— men did it, not often so neatly, as a meticulous, irksome means to some experimental end; but these young women knew how to treat it as an end in itself. The implanted tradition of fine needlework had found an unforeseen outlet.

In his office, Doctor Bull set down his bag.

"Typhoid!" he thought. "That would be quite a show! Certainly make all the castor oil I've dished out not such a good idea!"

He searched slowly along the line of books until he found the faded letters: W. Budd—*Typhoid Fever, its mode of spreading and prevention.* London. 1873. That was a great book in the old days; probably still was. Of course, treatment kept changing. It wasn't so long ago that Johns Hopkins, giving out the gospel, was starving patients as near death as not on the milk diet. Last he'd heard, they were yipping for forty-five hundred calories. Of course, they might have changed their minds again by now.

George Bull couldn't, personally, recall ever treating a typhoid case. Probably they'd been shown a few on the trips to the Detroit hospital when he was at school, and you certainly heard plenty about the theory of it, but as for the real thing— He flipped open the pages of Budd at random and read: . . . *exhibited in turn all the most characteristic marks of the disorder . . . spontaneous and obstinate diarrhoea, tympanitis, dry tongue, low delirium, and other typhoid symptoms, together with* (*towards the end of the second week*) *the now well-known eruption of rose-colored spots . . .*

Well! The disease didn't change; it was only the doctors. To have one of those smart young women would be kind of a help. He guessed they used the colon bacillus for an indicator of polluted water. Whether you could see it without staining and a lot of special tricks, he certainly didn't know. Probably not; and how would be recognize it if he did see it? The answer was, he wouldn't. "No sense bothering," he said aloud.

From the top shelf in the closet he dragged down the case. Age and dust had darkened the varnished surfaces; he soiled his hands as he pushed back the catch. He brought out the microscope and set it on his desk.

"Humph!" he said, half amused, for he could remember buying it at a state medical convention fully twenty-five years ago. He and a physician from Waterbury had spent a jovial afternoon in a saloon, and somehow it all ended in getting the microscope. His companion had noticed it in a pawn shop window. It bore the name of famous German makers; at the time it had been the very last word, and nothing was wrong with it but a first objective missing from the nose-piece. That, according to his companion, could either be replaced at small cost by writing to the makers, or not bothered about. In bacteriological research it was of no great value anyway. George Bull grinned, for he supposed that he must have represented himself as anxious to do such work; or perhaps, even, as already deeply and learnedly engaged in it.

Dipping a swab of cotton in alcohol, George Bull wiped the eye-piece and cleaned the stage. The illuminating mirror was badly clouded. The rack and pinion of the coarse adjustment seemed to have stuck, but finally he made it turn. Not wanting to use his right thumb, the graduated screw head of the fine adjustment resisted him even longer. Taking a handkerchief, he cleaned the condenser and the two objectives. With one eye closed, the other squinting in, he could see that plenty of dust remained. Particles of it, four hundred and forty times enlarged, littered the stage between the reflected enormous branches of his own bent eyelashes.

"Hell!" he said aloud. "This isn't getting me anywhere!"

He straightened up. He took the book that he had laid down and leaning back began to read again. There was one thing about it, he reflected, there wasn't one of them who couldn't be displaying prodromal symptoms. Shutting the book once more, he reached for his bag, snapped it open. Arising, he began to gather together what he needed. "Maybe one hunch is as good as another," he said.

Jerking his car to a halt in front of the Kimball house, he walked up the path. It was Miss Kimball who opened the door and he said: "I want to see your father. I'll go right up."

Disconcerted, she stammered: "Oh, well, I think he's asleep. Wouldn't later—"

"I'll wake him up."

He brushed past her, leaving her staring, outraged, as he mounted the stairs. In the upper hall he pushed open the door of the sick room.

"How're you feeling, Ralph?" he asked. "We'll have a little light in here." He went and pulled up the drawn shade. "This isn't going to bother you any." He set his bag on the table. From it he produced an iodine bottle, some swabs and a syringe which he held up and shook. The door moved now and he saw Miss Kimball.

Still affronted, she said with a thin dignity: "Would you be kind enough to tell me what you are planning to do?"

"I will. I want to make a blood test. Come on, Ralph. Brace up."

Sitting on the edge of the bed, he shoved back the loose sleeve of the night shirt. Unscrewing the cap of the iodine bottle, he pressed a swab over the mouth, daubed a wide smear on the pallid blue line of the median basilic vein below the elbow joint.

"There's an alcohol burner," he said to Miss Kimball, "and here's a match. Take the cap off and light it. No, bring it here where I can reach it! Now you'd better look the other way or get out. One or the other. Don't go keeling over as soon as you see blood."

He tightened the tourniquet which he had been adjusting, waited while the veins engorged, flamed the needle and jabbed it through the iodine-painted skin. "All right, Ralph," he said, "that didn't hurt you any—"

Glancing at the graduations in the glass, he pinched it off at fifteen cubic centimeters, freeing the needle. "That's it." He took the stained swab, smearing the arm again. "I'll be in tomorrow," he told Miss Kimball. "We may be getting somewhere. How we'll like it when we get there, I don't know. Pull that shade down again if the light bothers him."

Stirring on the bed, Ralph Kimball said hoarsely: "Feeling kind of bum, George. None of that stuff you gave me seems to do much good—"

"Well, that's the way with most of the stuff we give," George Bull answered. "Sometimes it helps; usually it doesn't."

To Miss Kimball, still looking at him with stiff distaste, he said: "Be pretty careful about washing your hands when you've been in here—" He considered her cheerfully and added, "Be a good idea to see that you sterilize the bed pan and contents before disposing. Lysol's as good as anything else. If the feces aren't fluid, stir 'em up well."

The pin at the low "V" of the ironed-down collar George Bull recognized as St. Luke's. She looked up from the desk, showing him, under the cap and rumpled reddish hair, large brown faintly oblique eyes in a demure short face. George Bull thought: "I could use that!" He said: "I'm Doctor Bull, from New Winton. I want to see Doctor Verney on an urgent matter."

"Yes, Doctor Bull—" Her voice had the automatic, submissive respect for physicians learned in the exact discipline of her hospital. "Doctor Verney is at luncheon; but I'll tell him, at once." She arose, adding, "Won't you sit down?"

He stood, however, watching a moment the trim departing shift of her narrow shoulders, the precise desirable stir of her small buttocks under the immaculate uniform. "Ho, hum!" he grunted, and looked out the reception room window.

Over the long lawns, down the four leisurely spaced rows of great elms, flat on the narrow asphalt surface of the road known as Stockade Street—humbler Sansbury called it Millionaire's Row—sunlight fell pale and chill from a sky becoming overcast. There was an air of well-to-do, but not rich nor fashionable, respectability in the bad architecture of the ample houses. The clumping of shrubbery, the generous spacing of the trees—each flagged sidewalk was forty feet from the edges of the asphalt road—seemed more suburban than rural. All was vaguely old-fashioned, the work of prosperous years in the '90s when Sansbury had been a quiet, informal summer resort for a few New York families who joined with the modestly monied best local people in friendly community.

Presently deaths and changed tastes had ended it. To present-day eyes, Sansbury was left the poorer, for several fine old houses had been replaced by bad, bigger ones. Stockade Street lost actual continuity with its long past. It gained only an immense boulder to which was fastened a bronze plate marking the site of the seventeenth-century blockhouse, and an atrocious memorial library constructed of cobble stones.

Across the street, toward the end, George Bull could just see the slate roofs, the dank red brick breaking out in eruptions of heavy woodwork—objectless bay windows, a small tower, graceless oversized verandas—of what had once been the Ross place. It was hard to believe, but he could remember making long drives down in a buggy, entertaining seriously the idea of marrying Maud Ross—or, he guessed he ought to say, marrying the First National Bank of Sansbury.

Maud had been a blankly plain, perhaps a little pop-eyed, girl with her mess of hair bundled up off a neck tightly protected by shirtwaist collars. Despite the material soundness of the scheme, it hadn't been possible to act very enthusiastic about her. Maud would certainly be pretty cold mutton, and though he finally forced himself to make a proposal, it was rejected. He could remember Maud unreally saying that she had never guessed that his sentiments were of That Sort. She would long ago have felt bound to tell him that she was not Free; she had an Understanding with Another. This absurd untruth merely added to the constraints of the situation. George's listlessness had been, perhaps by a very narrow margin, too marked. Frigidly aghast at her own doubtless uncertain idea of human copulation, she would have to be pressed to the ordeal harder than George could make himself press her. The decision had, in all likelihood, been a hard and unhappy one; for certainly, her fabrications properly discounted, it looked as though he must be her man, or she'd have no man at all—the suddenly recalled measures of that old tune went through his mind with a ghostly gay sweetness. He turned about to see the nurse coming back, her short face sweetly sensual, her pert flanks shifting. "To bed! To bed!" he thought, his appetite willingly tickled again. "Doctor Verney will be right out, Doctor Bull. Won't you wait in his office?"

On the walls here, visible from the armchair in which he seated himself, were three framed diplomas in cumbersome Latin—Harvard, Johns Hopkins, Vienna—George Bull guessed that the Vienna one was nothing much—six months fooling around with psychoanalysis or something. "Huh!" he thought. "All the fixings!"

Doctor Verney came now through the door at the end. "Glad to see you, Doctor. Something up?" He went and closed the door to the reception room. "Have a cigar."

"All right." George Bull took it from the held-out mahogany case. "Nothing wrong with them, is there?"

Doctor Verney laughed. "Not that I know of.

I generally stick to cigarettes during the day. I like a cigar after dinner." He sat down behind the massive, polished desk. "All right, shoot!"

"Well, first of all, tell me something about the Banning girl's case. Just what do you make of it?"

Doctor Verney, he saw, was embarrassed. He picked up a paper weight, balanced it, set it down. Then he picked it up again. "Why, Doctor, I really don't make much of it. The patient's general condition is a little below par, and any trifling infection hits her harder than some people. It's grippe, or influenza—loose term, but what else can you say? Temperature about one hundred and two; rather slow pulse. Headache. Coated tongue. Bowels are loose with a certain amount of griping. No appetite. We've got her in bed and I think if she stays quiet there for a few days she'll be perfectly well."

"Uh, huh. Now, I have eleven cases a good deal like that. Some of them seem sicker than others; a few have additional symptoms. They've all come on since Monday. I'm not satisfied with the diagnosis. Are you?"

"Yes, on the whole, I am. What's your theory?"

Doctor Bull bent and opened his bag on the floor beside him. "Want to try an experiment?" he asked, looking up. "I have a sample of blood here. Drew it in a syringe with a little citrate solution. I guess you have the facilities to see if you can grow anything from it. I'd be interested."

"We could do it, all right. But what are you looking for?"

"Bacillus typhosus. In view of the Banning girl, I thought you might like to find out."

Doctor Verney set down the paper weight with an uncontrolled bump. "Have you any reason to suspect such a thing?"

"Well, I don't know that I have any you'd admit, Verney. Your style isn't mine; I'm just an old horse doctor, you know. I have to work on hunches. In this case, I don't mind telling you that I first thought of it when my aunt told me it was typhoid. I've been thinking about it a lot since, and damned if I don't pretty well believe the old lady's right."

Doctor Verney relaxed a little. "It's a hard diagnosis for a layman, Bull." He smiled, recovering the paper weight.

"Most doctors have some trouble with the early stages, too, I guess. Not much to choose. Sure you couldn't be fooled?"

"I don't mean to imply that. Short of rose spots, I could very easily miss it. It simply looks like a long shot to me—unless you can lay your finger on a probable source of infection. Can you?"

"Well, I can use my head. Most things are out. There's no general distribution of milk. There hasn't been anything like a church supper. No flies. The cases are all in town, which means that there aren't any among people who have their own water supply."

"That's good reasoning," admitted Doctor Verney. "But after all, it doesn't show anything about the water. Unless there have been cases in the vicinity I really can't believe— Well, I have

[204]

a lot of respect for the opinion of a man of your experience; you probably know more about real, practical medicine than most of us young fellows will ever learn—"

"I wouldn't be surprised," agreed Doctor Bull. He could see the small disconcerted blink of Doctor Verney's eyes, and laughed. "You mustn't think I don't appreciate your sentiment," he said. "It just so happens that, barring bone setting, a few surgical tricks, and some push and pull obstetrics for women too soft to turn the corner, I've found out there's no such thing as practical medicine. Glad to hand on the torch."

"Oh, it seems to me we do some good—"

"Well, if you're not interested in my aunt's idea, I can go to Torrington."

"No, no. I'd be glad to try it. There's a perfectly good ten per cent bile solution out in the lab right now. We'll fix it up and incubate it. We could get some agar plate smears tomorrow and see if we have anything."

He pressed a button on his desk. When the door opened, he said, "Oh, Miss Stanley, I want to do a blood culture. We'll use that bile solution. I think there's plenty left. Put two hundred cubic centimeters in an Erlenmeyer flask. Add ten of this specimen of Doctor Bull's and shoot it in the incubator."

"Yes, Doctor Verney."

She went on past the desk to the closed door beyond the one open into the consulting room. George Bull got a glimpse of sinks, shelves and a long table crowded with bottles and tube racks. "I was born thirty years too soon," he observed.

The door closed after Miss Stanley and he added: "You must find it quite a strain keeping chaste around here."

"Oh, no," Doctor Verney protested. "She's a nice girl, Bull. Comes from a fine family."

"Uh, huh. Well, much obliged."

"I'll let you know tomorrow."

*

All Friday morning the cold west wind came bitter across the hills, poured hard and furious down the valley from North Truro. Off the worn bare earth of the playground beside the New Winton school, whirls of dust lifted and drove away. On high, this pale gritty haze trailed over the cemetery and rolled repeatedly past St. Matthias's Church before dispersing.

May Tupping wrapped her old coat tight against the vicious edge of the gale. She bent into it as she came across the green at noon, her face turned aside, her eyes half closed, stung to exasperation by that roaring, senseless violence. Every few minutes bleakly covered by the journeying clouds, the sun was brilliant, but without comfort. The bare trees groaned in their crotches; a shutter banged; a sheet of newspaper had glued itself, flapping, about the legs of the soldier on the monument.

In the telephone office, Doris had a good fire. May struggled into this unstirred warmth, her cheeks whipped to color, her eyes watering from the last hard assault of the wind down the small sunless veranda.

"Hello," said Doris, yawning.

"Oh, that's the most awful wind! And after it was so nice—"

"That freak weather couldn't last long. How's Joe's cold?"

"He feels pretty bad today."

"That's tough. Well, I'll be getting on. Oh, say, listen! The damnedest thing happened. About an hour ago, Mrs. Talbot called up and when I asked her for a number, she said she didn't want any number. She just wanted to know if anybody was here. She said she was kind of scared, because there was a man out on the road who kept looking at her. Honestly, May, she sounded goofy. Then, another thing she said was, I shouldn't tell Doc Bull because if he knew about it he was going to come down and kill her. After that she tried to ring up twice more, but I'd heard all I wanted to. I just disconnected. She hasn't paid her bill for two months, I know, so we're supposed to refuse her service Saturday, anyway."

"I know," said May. "She hasn't any money. I don't know what on earth is going to happen to her. I suppose they'll have to send her somewhere."

"Well, I should think they would. But, anyway, I wouldn't bother about her line if I were you. It'll just give you the creeps, May. I'm not fooling."

Sitting alone before the switchboard, May reflected that the worst part of Mrs. Talbot's trouble was how little any of it was Mrs. Talbot's fault. Her husband was dead. So were her son and her daughter. The same amazing clean sweep had been made of her relatives. Fifteen or twenty years ago there had been quantities of Millers up on Cold Hill and almost as many Darrows. Now she was the only Miller left. Of her father's sister's children there was none left—Jed Darrow's widow and son couldn't help even if they wanted to. Bill Talbot had two brothers. Both of them had been in the Navy, and both of them were taken, dead, from a submarine which had lain three weeks, fatally injured, in the mud off New London. Mrs. Talbot was perhaps forty, and certainly looked nearer sixty. She hadn't any money, and no means of getting any. Plainly she was a sick woman; she might even, as Doris suggested, be really crazy. When you got a case like that, you could see what a help it was to be able to believe all partial evil, universal good, or to feel sure that God was punishing Mrs. Talbot for offenses so cunning that He alone saw them. Your reason might revolt at it, but at least it would give the speculative mind some peace. A possible security was implied. A little plan, which would make it impossible for such a torrent of disasters to touch you, was indicated—*I have been young and now am old, yet have I not seen the righteous foresaken, nor his seed begging bread.*

There had been a lull, but now came a quick flurry of calls: for different stores; two for Doctor Bull, which Mrs. Cole answered; one to ask what time it was. The laborious progress of May's thought was interrupted; but, in any event, she knew by now that thought would not get her anywhere. She might half see several points that would look true; or at least, look more likely to

[208]

be true than several others; but how could she tell, knowing so little?

She remembered thinking—she had probably been fifteen or sixteen, and had doubtless just begun to half see points—that what she wanted was an education. Miss Coulthard, at school, had been interested in her and they even made an effort to get a scholarship at Mt. Holyoke, but some one else got it. This was, of course, a disappointment; for she had seen, amazed, page after page of college catalogues ranked solid with numbered course after course—three courses in Provençal; fourteen courses in physics; two half courses in the Kantian philosophy; French literature from Ronsard to Rousseau; three lectures a week for half a year on the history of Portugal. Seeing really nothing that she did not long to know all about, she would have done anything to go there. Or perhaps she should say anything she could. She couldn't manage algebra.

Not quite crushed, although Miss Coulthard lost interest in her, she turned to the books in the New Winton library. When some one presented the library with the set of thirty-odd volumes containing all that was best in the world's literature, it seemed to May at least a godsend. While she might never be really educated, in the sense that Miss Coulthard with her Vassar degree was, she would soon be well-informed. What she had expected, she couldn't imagine; but she saw presently that even when she had finished all the volumes she would not know anything in particular. She got, when she got anything for her patience, entertainment, not instruction.

Facing such problems—surely the real meat of

great minds—as why the Bannings should be rich, while Mrs. Talbot was destitute; or why, when they were both out together, similarly armed, on a similar errand, it was Joe who was shot and not Harry Weems, she had nothing to fall back on except the promptings of common sense. You had, if common sense was your only resource, nothing remotely resembling any of the conflicting conclusions of the philosophers. She had read as much of a translation of Plato as seemed to fall into the class of best literature several times, thinking at first that because of her ignorance she had not understood, and in a minute she might see its relation to the realities of existence; she saw instead that it really had none. It was pure wisdom, untouched by common sense.

Left to herself, and to what she could see of the universe, real and ideal were lost together in an indifference so colossal, so utterly indifferent, that there was no defining it. This immense mindlessness knew no reasons, had no schemes; there was no cause for it. Where could it begin, and why should it end? There was even an error in personifying the universe as It, saying: How could It either plan or prevent Mrs. Talbot's misfortunes? How could It care? "Only, I care," May thought. "I think it's terrible. It oughtn't to be that way."

"This is the Sansbury operator. One-one, please, New Winton."

Making the connection, May could hear Doctor Bull's voice, irritable, blare on the transmit-

ter promptly. He must have been in the hall on
the way out.

"Sansbury calling, Doctor Bull."

Doctor Bull roared again, "Hello, hello—Operator, who the hell is ringing me?"

"One moment, please—"

"Hello? Doctor Bull? Doctor Bull, Doctor
Verney is calling. I'll connect you."

"Oh. That you, Verney? Hello. Got something?"

"I'm sorry to tell you that we certainly have."
Doctor Verney's voice was clipped and urgent.
"There's no doubt about it at all. Your hunch is
absolutely correct. Doctor Moses happened to be
over from Torrington and I've had him check up
on it. He's just out of school and he's fresher on
it than I am. Naturally, I haven't done any work
with that particular bacillus and I hoped I might
be mistaken. I'll be coming right up. If I can help
you in any way—I mean I suppose we ought to
collect specimens all around and get them to
Torrington—"

"Well, come on then—"

May let go the key. Doctor Verney's agreeable
tones and clear, educated accent always impressed
her. Talking to you, he wouldn't make you feel
so surely that he regarded your life or death as a
matter of no importance, and considered you a
fool to be roared at for bothering him about it.
Whatever the present matter might be, she could
see that he was genuinely concerned, ready to go
to any trouble to do all he could.

In the light of such a spirit, she wondered, as
she had before, if it might not be possible to have

him look at Joe some time. If Harry drove them down to the hospital, surely Doctor Verney would not refuse to see Joe just because he had been Doctor Bull's patient—the line lamps lit up together as the receivers were replaced. May pulled the plugs. As soon as Joe's cold was better, she would get Harry to do it.

*

A low-hung central chandelier with a bead fringe and six stained glass panels framed in ornate, antique bronze poured light on the bare amber oak of Bates's dining-room table. There were five of them gathered around it, counting Doctor Bull himself. Matthew Herring, susceptible to chills, had left his black overcoat on, merely unbuttoning it and sitting back with his long legs crossed. His reflective, intelligent regard appeared fixed on the large framed picture of the Coliseum across the room, but nothing ever trapped him into the inattention of frank boredom. No matter how far away, he would be instantly back with quiet and concise objections to protect the town treasury. He knew all about special meetings.

Isaac Quimby, Second Selectman, had a cold. His round, pugnacious old nose was sore and red from the applications of a damp handkerchief. Behind his silver-rimmed glasses, his eyes glowered. His irritable misery was, of course, aggravated by the fact that it was his latest enemy, Robert Newell, Third Selectman, who was holding matters up. He wasn't, however, sick enough to make him easy to handle—that was, anxious for nothing but to agree and get home. George Bull, considering his own sore bandaged thumb, shrugged. He wasn't feeling any too happy himself, and it wouldn't be surprising if he and Isaac had words before the evening was over. Isaac was yearning for trouble. Sarcastically, Clarence Upjohn had put his finger on that when Quimby grumbled something about getting on; time enough to wait for Newell if it came to voting. "Why don't you just go home?" Clarence said. "If there's any voting, we'll count you against whatever it is."

Quimby and Clarence Upjohn had been intimate friends for twenty years. Their quarrel, when it came, began over a matter of officers in the local Grange, but what made it irreparable was actually a piece of Henry Harris's work. Clarence, recognizing it, had been stung into pointing out that Isaac didn't have a mind of his own; he was simply Henry Harris's errand boy. There was too much truth in it for Isaac to take the charge calmly; he had to put himself in the detested position of insisting that Henry Harris's ideas were his own. At least he could that way avoid admitting that Henry had outmaneuvered him into a practical direction and control of what had once been Quimby's business.

The way Henry always turned up with reason on his side was remarkable. In that case it had been about gasoline. Quimby's trucks had for years got their gas from the pumps outside Upjohn's store. Henry, taking a tighter and tighter grip on the business, soon decided to stop that. They used enough gas to put in a tank and private pump of their own. Clarence could see reason; all he really wanted was for Isaac to admit that he was doing it because Henry Harris was making him do it. This feud lasted perhaps a year while they cut each other on all public occasions. Howard Upjohn then managed a reconciliation, a formal shaking-hands. Now, each held back the sharper edge of his hostility until the other was no longer present.

George Bull had never been able to decide whether it was simply the fine tart flavor of this ruined relationship which Henry liked; or whether it was actually all part of a long patient scheme to disrupt the Republicans beyond repair. Henry, he realized, had probably been right the other day. The word Republican couldn't stretch much farther when it included Banning and the scoffingly named Better Element; Bates and the Upjohns; Isaac Quimby and Ordway; and Robert Newell. No amount of oil-pouring by Bates, meek and neutral, could form a film wide enough to keep such an expanse smooth. George Bull supposed that he ought to include himself; he'd always voted Republican.

Bates, jumping up in an agitation of relief— he could feel the room already charged with ill temper and fear for the outbreak—said: "That sounds like Robert, now. Come on in," he called.

Clarence had opened his minute book on the table and put on his glasses. "Well, Newell," he said, looking up over them, "I hope we haven't kept you waiting. We came as quick as we could. Now let's give it a name. What is it, Walter? Special Meeting of Selectmen in Council, Friday, March sixth—called by whom?"

"Just put your coat on the chair there, Robert," Bates said. "Sorry we had to bring you all the way down from North Truro. Why, if the meeting will now come to order; why, Doc Bull asked me to call you together to discuss a matter of public health. I guess that's all I know about it. You might as well go ahead and say whatever it is, Doc."

"For God's sake!" said Newell. He pulled out a chair indignantly, with a sort of expressed contempt for its lightness, holding it, erect and angry. "What's the idea, Doc? Why can't you wait until tomorrow?"

Newell's mouth snapped shut under the short-cropped black mustache. The natural belligerent stare of his brown eyes widened. Had a drink or two, George Bull decided. There was a distinctive note of bold, unnecessary hardness about Newell. Although he had been born in Truro, he went West as a boy, spent several years in Idaho. Back with him he brought a probably spurious western air—a suggestion of whisky, of violent horses violently treated, of boots and ropes and whips (not confirmed, a rumor concerned the use of one of the whips on his wife). He was known to patronize and believed to promote the cockfights secretly held at a village just across the New York state line.

As owner and manager of Lakeland Lodge & Camps, up on Quail Pond, beyond North Truro, he was, as New Winton counted things, an economic factor. During the course of the summer he would require supplies for as many as five hundred guests, in transient lots of fifty or sixty—girls in knickerbockers and silk stockings; men who wore cheap colored polo shirts with invariable cigars in their mouths. George Bull, summoned professionally from time to time, could testify that those who wanted it got plenty to drink at the Lodge. Now and then, he had reason to believe that couples sharing a cabin were not married to each other. Around the barber shop, Lester Dunn had made it more or less the fashion to call the camp Tail Lake, but Lester's mind ran along those lines. George Bull, in a somewhat better position to know, didn't believe that any more out of the way went on there than most places. What talk there was could be traced largely to Lester's imagination and Quimby's quarrel with Newell over horse feed and ice. It was Quimby who barked out now: "Sit down, young fellow! We've wasted plenty of time already. You hear the business first and tell us what you think afterwards."

Newell's thick lip curled a little under the cropped mustache, but he said merely: "Another county heard from! All right, Doc."

"This won't take long," George Bull said. "Doctor Verney has been up from Sansbury this afternoon with me. As some of you know"—he jerked his head toward Bates—"we've been taking blood specimens. Thirteen in all. They're over at Torrington now. In that sense, we haven't a complete confirmation, and won't have until tomorrow or the next day; but Doctor Verney made a culture yesterday, and I don't think there's any reasonable doubt about the situation. Probably every one of those tests is going to show the same thing, so we may as well say right now that what we've got's a first-rate typhoid fever epidemic."

He turned his glance down the table, inspecting them. In the silence Matthew Herring said quietly: "Dear me, Doctor, that's really terrible! Are you quite sure?"

Ignoring this, since the others were still staring simply, George Bull raised his voice. "Now, let's not waste time. Doctor Verney agrees with me that the most sensible immediate measure would be to arrange tomorrow for general inoculations. We can't do much about what's already started, but we can at least try to prevent any spread from established cases. I suppose the inoculations can't be made obligatory, but we ought at least to make them free of charge. We'll have the telephone exchange ring up all numbers and explain. I want every one in town, and particularly the school children—everybody who doesn't show any febrile symptoms, that is—to be ready to take a first injection tomorrow morning. Better do it down at the school. Somebody can get hold of Getchell and have him arrange it. Tomorrow's Saturday and there won't be any classes, but the buses had better collect the children as usual. I hope to have the vaccine here—at least enough to start—within the next hour or so. If you'll just vote an appropriation to cover it, that'll take care of that. Now, we have one other job—"

Pausing, he looked at Matthew Herring, who, somewhat to his surprise, simply nodded. He might, after all, have foreseen that. Herring could be pretty stingy with the town money, but he had enough intelligence to— Isaac Quimby said sharply: "Hold your horses, Doc. There may be some of us who don't believe much in sticking children full of those bugs at the public expense. Myself, I've heard it's a lot of nonsense, anyway. I wouldn't have any child of mine——"

"I don't know that I hold with it either, George," said Clarence Upjohn, poising his pen. "All this vaccinating stuff—I know Howard darn near lost his arm when they were doing it to him for smallpox back in——"

"All right, we'll vote about that later. You'll have to do what I say, so I won't waste time arguing with you. You've got one vote, Isaac. I think Newell and Walter Bates have sense enough to back me up, so you can use it any way you like. The other matter is this. I want to find a place we can use for a hospital. It doesn't have to be much; but a certain number of cases can't be properly nursed at home. Verney's afraid that the Sansbury hospital's too small to spare any nurses, but we can get some from Torrington all right. The Evarts house is the best place I can think of. See if you can get old Jethro to let you use it, Walter. If you can't, we'll just use it anyway."

He looked directly at Bates, who was sitting forward in his chair, the light fairly on his pale face, his lips busy with his shaggy mustache ends. "I will, George." He swallowed, and meekly taking the opening, said, "I suppose you mean then —well, that is, I suppose that that's what Geraldine's got?"

"Well, I'm afraid so. I didn't tell you this afternoon because I wanted to get it settled here before it was being passed all around town. Sorry if it's a shock; but you know the way Emma gabs, I guess."

Isaac Quimby, halted for a moment, said now:

"Look here, George, you take a pretty high hand, it appears to me. I'm not agreeing to any of that needle stuff. Especially I'm not when you can't show me yet any proof that this is more than some idea you and Verney cooked up. Said yourself you wouldn't know until—"

"Ah, don't be a driveling idiot; or if you are, try not to show it!" Robert Newell's loud and cruel voice leaped negligently at him. "You vote no; and I vote yes, so we can go home now and let Walter do what he's told. This doesn't seem to concern Truro much, so I haven't any more to say." He stood up.

"Maybe you haven't," rasped out Quimby, infuriated, "but let me tell you the township of New Winton may have something to say when you try to start up your whorehouse next summer. Maybe you'll have something to say to the State Police. You better start getting it ready—"

"Listen, Grandpa, don't make me mad. Why, you superannuated little runt, I might forget you had a foot in the grave and knock your face in. You'd better go home to bed."

"That's a fine idea," agreed Clarence. "The rest of us can settle the details—"

"Now, let's all calm down," Matthew Herring said. "I have a few questions I'd like you to answer, Doctor, before any one goes home. Am I right in believing that there must be a source of infection for an outbreak of this sort?"

"You are."

"Has that been located?"

"Yes, by process of deduction. Samples of the water are over at Torrington for bacteriological examination. The typhoid bacillus doesn't live

[219]

long in ordinary water, but there are more robust organisms which indicate pollution satisfactorily. I imagine they'll find some. If they don't, we'll have to look for something else; but nothing else seems indicated. That reminds me that when Isaac began his objections, I wanted to add that it would be just as well not to drink the water without boiling it. We'll see that people are warned about that."

"I see. Yes, that would seem wise. You inspect the reservoir pretty regularly, don't you, Doctor?"

"Why, yes. I keep an eye on it."

"In spite of that, then, the water has been contaminated in some way?"

"In my opinion."

"I see. This must have been a recent thing, then?"

"Well, it's hard to say. There have been plenty of cases in which the organisms have remained alive all winter, frozen in ice. You can't tell."

"I see. By the way, when did you last make an inspection?"

"Why, I really couldn't say, Herring. Not for some time. There isn't much to inspect. It's well fenced and posted. That's about the most you can do. The Water Board has to look out for the mains and valves. If Eric Cadbury sees anything, I go up and look it over. Nobody's around there. No reason to——"

"Yet somebody must have been. Am I correct?"

"Well, if that's your way of saying that dung from a person harboring the typhoid bacillus has got into the water, you are."

[220]

"How about the construction camp? That's in that general direction, isn't it?"

"It's quite a way back. I don't think it could have any connection, as far as the camp itself is concerned. Some of the men might go wandering around."

"Well, come on, come on," said Robert Newell. "Grandpa and I want to get home."

"One more question, Doctor. Did you ever inspect the camp? I mean, are you in a position to say definitely that there could be no connection?"

"You heard me say it, Herring."

"You haven't answered my question, Doctor."

"Hm," grunted Clarence. "Aren't you supposed, as Board of Health, to sort of check up on that, George?"

"I don't know that I am. They got out last Friday. The property belongs to Henry Harris, and I'll go up some time and see that he has it cleaned up, if it needs it. We generally give them a little time. As a matter of fact, I guess you're Tree Warden, Newell. Seems to me it might come under the head of fire prevention—I mean, getting the buildings out of there."

"Well, I don't see it that way, Doc."

"Then, in fact," said Matthew Herring, studying the Coliseum, "you never did at any time inspect the camp or its sanitary arrangements, Doctor?"

"That's right, I never did."

"Suppose, then, we inspect it tomorrow?"

"Who is we?"

"You and I. Walter if he cares to come. Perhaps Eric Cadbury, on behalf of the Water Board."

"I won't have any time tomorrow."

"Perhaps Walter and I could look at it. Or would you rather have somebody from the State Health Department?"

"But, Matthew," Walter Bates said, "why couldn't we wait until Doc Bull could go?"

"Yes. Why the pressing hurry, Herring?"

"I've got this to say—" Quimby had got to his feet. "It appears to me that there may be some responsibility here. Wouldn't be surprised if Herring were trying to get at that. You were in hurry enough yourself, Doc, about all this injection business. I'm not going to sit around here tonight, but maybe we'd better find out just why, if it's true, Doc Bull didn't bother to do any of these things."

"You're kind of out of temper, Isaac," suggested Clarence. "I don't think Matthew meant any such thing. Nobody but yourself seems to suit you tonight—"

Matthew Herring looked back from the Coliseum. His drawn, sober face was still composed, and he spoke evenly, without emphasis. "I'm afraid that that's what I did mean. Some of you don't seem to have grasped the situation. I think Doctor Bull will agree that typhoid fever in epidemic proportions is a disaster of the first magnitude. He won't question my right to want a complete explanation. If there is any blame to be assigned, we must assign it. Public health may need more attention than we have been giving it."

"Than you have been giving it is right!" George Bull said. "You don't give it any. When something like this happens, you go yowling for help and who's to blame? Herring, you're at lib-

[222]

erty to investigate what you please, when you want to. All we need from you is your signature on the authorizations for expenses. I hope you won't impede matters any more than you can help."

*

Doctor Verney said: "Back again, Mary." He put his hat, and driving gloves tossed into it, on the table.

"Let me take your coat, sir. Mrs. Banning is in her sitting room, if you'll go right up—" He slipped out of the heavy black fur-lined coat and she took it. "Oh—this is Miss Valentine, Mary. She's going to be the night nurse—"

"Yes, Doctor Verney. How do you do, M'am."

"I'll want to give you and Edith the first injections before I go. We must be as careful as we can. You don't object to taking it, do you?"

"No, indeed, sir. We'll be ready whenever you want."

"Good. We'll go up, Miss Valentine. Mary, will you ask Larry to get Miss Valentine's luggage out of the rumble seat—"

Mr. Banning was standing by the fire in the sitting room upstairs and Mrs. Banning arose. "Mrs. Banning, this is Miss Valentine. And Mr. Banning—"

Mrs. Banning said: "I'm afraid you've had a terrible trip, Miss Valentine. Of course you've had supper?"

"Yes, Mrs. Banning. Doctor Verney took care of me."

"Perhaps some coffee after that cold drive. Let me have some sent up—"

"You're very kind. If it's no trouble. But—"

"Of course it's no trouble." She lifted the round ear piece from the hook beside the small enameled telephone box: "Mary—oh, Edith. May we have some coffee, please." She hung up the ear-piece, turning back. "I've put Miss Stanley in Guy's room— Doctor Verney, how are you going to get on without her? I feel so guilty about letting you leave her here—but I thought I'd put Miss Valentine in the west room; it would be fairly quiet and there won't be sun in the morning. I'll show you now. Larry will have your things there. Miss Stanley's with Virginia. I think that cot has been set up—"

"It has, my dear," said Mr. Banning. "You sit down. I'll show Miss Valentine her room—"

She remained standing, though, turning again to Doctor Verney, and he said: "Mrs. Banning, I don't want you to worry. The reason that I want Miss Stanley to be here, and that I was anxious to get Miss Valentine, is simply that it's mainly a nursing problem and they're both extremely intelligent. The point is to keep the patient as comfortable as possible and to see that complications don't get a chance to start—" The phrasing, he felt was excusable; but what he meant was, to see that complications, when they started, would not be overlooked or misinterpreted.

Mrs. Banning's expression changed, in a kind of disciplined obedience as she forced her anxiety to yield a little ("everything is being done—"); but her eyes remained on him, half-pleading for a more absolute and of course impossible reassurance. She stood with her remarkable, unconscious light erectness—you could guess the years of chiding and reproof, when a child, when a girl at school—*Don't slouch; a young woman's posture is the real test of her appearance; Lucile, hold your head up!* Finally it succeeded. At forty, it was part of her; even her disquiet had a reserved, inbred politeness. Her distress of mind expressed itself in hardly perceptible small nervous tremors. A great anguish of anxiety broke her speech into short, distracted sentences, but each one finished and precise. In a sense, pride had her on the accustomed rack. Habit, so patiently formed, gave her no choice but steeling herself against any giving-way, which might be necessary or even permissible for others. As she accepted without question the privileges, she accepted too the exact obligations of being born a New Haven Brooks. Vulgar reliefs were closed to her. Without perfect success, but with all her heart, she held to a tradition, not in the easy right of an established aristocracy, but, if possible, prouder for being less public—the deliberate ascetic superiority of the dying Puritan strains. Make the willful body do right! Make the doubtful heart fear nothing!

Doctor Verney said: "Typhoid fever, properly cared for, is very rarely a grave matter, Mrs. Banning."

Mr. Banning, leaving Miss Valentine, had gone downstairs; for her luggage hadn't yet appeared. Coming from the room shown her, Miss Valentine was walking up the hall when she saw the door at the far end open and a white uniform step out. "Why, Peg!" Miss Stanley said, "you certainly got here!"

"Three-twenty train from town, by the skin of my teeth. Doctor Verney drove me up from Sansbury."

"Don't touch me, darling. I'm all germy. How are you?"

"Fine. I've got loads to tell you about every one." She lowered her voice. "Laura, what a lovely house!"

"They're awfully nice people. You'll like it."

"How's the patient?"

"Pretty sick, poor kid. She's got a hundred and four right this minute. You'll have baths all night, I expect. I just finished one. My dear, she's so thin you could weep. Ask the doctor to come in when he can, will you?"

Mr. Banning was coming upstairs now. He had one of Miss Valentine's suitcases in either hand. "There you are," he said. "Larry seems to be laid up. Everything considered, I think we'd better have him looked at."

2

Into the sunless north light of the Principal's office Saturday morning broke the dim scurry of running feet on the worn hard earth of the playground as some game went by the windows. Shouts preceded, squeals and protests followed, the occasional muffled thud of a kicked football.

"All right, Ingraham," Doctor Bull called. "Let's have another batch. Might tell the rest they'll feel better if they don't go running around before they come in." He arranged a score of sealed glass ampules on the table, glanced at Miss Kiernan, who was doubtfully moistening a cotton swab with iodine. "How're you coming, Verney?"

From the next room, Doctor Verney answered: "All right, Doctor. I think we'll have plenty. I just dropped out one child. She's running quite a temperature—"

Beyond the other door a fresh line of children, forming in hushed, half-apprehensive silence, stretched a little way down the hall; all their left arms bare; their faces indecisive—afraid that it was going to hurt; intimidated by the formidable figure of Doctor Bull at the table. By way of relief, some one pushed some one else, produced an exaggerated protest, a few nervous giggles.

"You stop that, Marty!" Miss Kiernan said. "This isn't any time to rough-house. John, is every one here?"

"Except Pete Vogel. He's sick, Miss Kiernan."

"Where's Bess Parry?"

"Oh. Well, I saw her."

"I know," some one volunteered. "Her father came for her. Said he ain't going to let Doc Bull do anything to her. He went to see Mr. Getchell."

"Quiet! Now, the doctor's ready for you and I want you to come in one at a time. I'll put this on your arm. You'll go to Doctor Bull and get your injection, and out by the other door to Miss Coulthard, who will—"

"I won't let anybody stick me. No, sir! I—"

"Marty Fell! A big boy like you afraid of a little pin prick! Why, even little Jane isn't afraid. Are you, Jane?"

"No, Miss Kiernan. I'm not a bit afraid."

"Teacher's pet!" called some one.

"All right, Albert. I heard you. We'll see about that later."

From the door of the assembly room at the center of the hall, voices sounded. ". . . and what's more, I'm going to see he don't. You mistook me, Mr. Getchell. I ain't got nothing against this inoculation stuff. Needn't think I'm a fool—"

Mr. Getchell came in sight, his neat dark clothes and carefully cut upright, graying hair given an immediate amazing contrast by Joel Parry shuffling beside him. Joel had on a round wool hat of the sort which could be pulled down in severe weather to cover the ears and neck, leaving an oval opening for the face. From under the old mackinaw, dull and stiff with dirt, came the loose, soiled blue legs of a suit of overalls, tucked and buckled into short heavy rubber galoshes. One hand clutched the arm of his tow-headed, now tearful, daughter Bess; the other rose in incomplete gestures toward Mr. Getchell. "Doc Bull took care of my boy, Joel," he said. "I'll see he don't lay a finger on Bess. This Doctor Verney, now, can do it, if he wants."

Mr. Getchell, observing the line of children, dropped his voice. "Of course, that can be arranged, if you prefer, Mr. Parry—"

"Doc Bull ain't any doctor," continued Joel. He raised his voice, for he was more pleased than not to have even this audience. "He don't know what he's doing half the time. Never has known.

Near as I can hear, the whole thing's his fault anyway."

Mr. Getchell was trying to hurry him, almost impelled to touch the filthy sleeve of the mackinaw, but Joel was in no hurry. "I see Mr. Herring and Eric Cadbury and Walter Bates up the hill this morning trying to find what he did about that camp place. Huh! He did nothing. He just gads about with that Board of Health sign in his car, too busy looking for ways to fine honest men money! Leave his real job waiting for him to do, and he don't do it. Not he! He—"

Out the door past Miss Kiernan with the iodine bottle and the head of the line of children, Doctor Bull came now, a white coat hanging open from his wide shoulders. "Hello, Joel!" he said. "Didn't hear you mention me, did I?"

Both Joel and Mr. Getchell stopped, so he came up to them. Joel, startled, but now cowed, said, "I reckon you did."

"Maybe I missed some. Want to say it again?"

"Don't mind if I do. I was just mentioning to Mr. Getchell here how it would be a good thing for this town if you lived somewhere else. You ain't no doctor for human beings. I got to laugh every time I see that Board of Health sign. Huh!"

"Sure, that's a laugh for you," agreed George Bull. "Now, how about a laugh for me? See how you look this way!"

He put out his right hand, heedless of the bandaged thumb, and took Joel by the mackinaw collar, twitching him irresistibly about. With his left hand, he caught up the slack in the seat of the overalls. Grunting a little, and redder in the face, yet not seriously disturbed by Joel's squirms and shouts, he carried him suspended from these two points up the hall. The center door to the playground he kicked open, held it against the automatic closing device with his knee, and tossed Joel out. Waiting, while Joel staggered to his feet, he roared: "I wouldn't come in again, if I were you. We're pretty busy here this morning."

Mr. Getchell, stunned by so sudden and successful a resort to the very violence which it was half his work to keep the children from attempting on each other, grew pink; as though he feared that his charges had caught him in part of his lie about real adult behavior. They, speechless as the Principal, every face turned, most mouths open, made neither move nor sound. To greet Doctor Bull returning was only Bess Parry's solitary doleful wail.

"All right, Getchell," Doctor Bull said, clasping his bandaged right thumb a moment. "That'll settle that difficulty, I think. Take the child in to Doctor Verney with my compliments."

*

The heavy mahogany secretary-desk had been made by Aaron Chapin of East Windsor, in 1774. On the wall adjoining, a plain small frame enclosed Chapin's bill, and Jonathan Brooks's copy of his own stiff letter accompanying payment, but characterizing the charge as excessive. Judge Brooks had no way of knowing that in his great-great-granddaughter's day Aaron Chapin's best work would be worth some fifty times the price so unwillingly paid for it.

The closed writing flap was decorated with three concave shells, topping the solid embossed blocks of the front. Walter Bates put out a finger, fitted the tip into the delicate fluting of the nearest shell, ran it pleasurably up and down. Noticing then what he was doing, he jerked his hand away, guilty, looking to see who had observed him. No one had. Biting his mustache, he glanced quickly up and down the packed shelves of books covering the opposite wall. Uncrossing his legs, he crossed them the other way, nodding in unrequested agreement with Matthew Herring, and considered the fire a moment. Finding nothing there, he lifted his eyes to admire the rare color lithograph of *Ivanhoe, The Connecticut Whirlwind: Property of Paul Banning, Esq.*, furiously pacing past a fading judges' stand on an age-stained track.

"You see, there's no doubt about it," Matthew Herring said. "The latrines were placed above this gully. We followed it down for perhaps a quarter of a mile, and, of course, it does empty into one of the brooks feeding the reservoir."

"Of course," said Eric Cadbury, "I'll say this. In summer I don't think it would be a brook itself. It was just when all that rain came, it simply washed right down."

"Granting that," said Matthew Herring, "the fact was that Doctor Bull never made any kind of an inspection. He said frankly that he hadn't bothered. That seems to me pretty close to criminal negligence. How would it look to the Grand Jury, Eric?"

Eric Cadbury smiled. "You can't tell," he admitted. "I haven't been a Grand Juror very long, after all; but as near as I can see, you can always fix up an indictment if you're willing to swap. You can usually find something the others want, and just hold out on it until they agree to scratch your back. I'd be willing to try if you help me make a summary."

Mr. Banning, sitting with his hands clasped, had not spoken at all. Now he shook his head. "I think that any court would and should throw the indictment out," he said. "The errors in judgment statute would take care of Doctor Bull. Unless his duty regarding the inspection of the reservoir is defined exactly—say, he is to make four inspections a year, and you can show that he only made three—you haven't any case. You can legislate duty, but not supererogation. It all goes to pieces as soon as he says that in his judgment the reservoir didn't need inspecting."

"Well, you know more about law than I do," Eric Cadbury said. "It depends some on the judge you get. Old Cochrane, now—"

"Exactly. Get Judge Cochrane, and the Supreme Court will automatically reverse him. Not two in ten of his rulings are allowed. It would be really funny, if it weren't so scandalous."

"We'll try, anyway," Matthew Herring said patiently. "You're a little too finicky, Herbert. In abating a nuisance, the point is, to abate it. If we can indict him, I think we ought to—even if the court throws it out, or the higher court reverses it. He'd have something to worry about at any rate."

"I'm all against it," Mr. Banning said. "The

people—some of them—who ought to be indicted are sitting right here in this room. Doctor Bull's negligence may be inexcusable, but it's our negligence that's criminal. I don't think any one here has had much doubt about Doctor Bull's indifference—and, very probably, incompetence—for the last twenty years. I can't see anything but the grossest injustice, after letting it slide so long, in now trying to engineer matters to have his medical license revoked. He's an old man, now—"

"Well, who said anything about his license?" demanded Eric Cadbury. "Haven't we a right to protect ourselves and our children? Mr. Banning, your own daughter is lying sick upstairs. Now, what about it?"

"I haven't forgotten Virginia," Mr. Banning said. "Perhaps, if it would help her, I'd have more taste for vengeance—I think that's the word, Matthew. As for the other matter, Eric; you ought to realize that if Doctor Bull is indicted and convicted, he won't be allowed to practice medicine either here or anywhere else. That's what Matthew is planning on, I think."

"It is. Exactly." Matthew Herring nodded. "The sentiment doesn't seem to be very popular today; but what a man sows, let him reap! I don't think I'm vengeful, Herbert. It's impersonal. I think that I may be allowed to say that. You and Walter here might have personal reasons, but I haven't. I've watched for years now a general let-down under the guise of mercy, and not casting the first stone. It's a mistake. It's doing to others what you hope they will do to you if at any time you decide to take advantage of the situation. That can go on until there are no duties, no standards, no responsibilities left. I think that we were better off when a man was expected to do right, and people were shocked if he didn't. Today, a man seems to be expected to do wrong; and it's considered rather ingenuous to be shocked."

"Well, I don't know about all that," Eric Cadbury said, "but it sounds good. It seems to me the case is whether Doc Bull ought to be allowed to get away with taking his salary and not doing his job. I don't know who expects what, but unless you're a Tammany Democrat in New York City, I guess you more or less expect to be out of a job if they catch you not doing it in any big way."

"I think you'll find the ayes have it, Herbert," Matthew Herring said. "Now, as you say, there's a good chance that we can't successfully indict. The other course seems to me to lie this way. What can we do about persuading the County Health Officer to remove him?"

Eric Cadbury, his eyes puckered up shrewdly, said: "Hold on. That's the wrong end of the stick. If you want to get at him, you'd better get at the eighteen hundred a year the School Committee pays him to be Medical Examiner."

"We'll get at that," Matthew Herring said. "It so happens that he has a certain support on the School Committee. I don't plan to treat with it, because it would simply boil down to some sort of political deal with the Democrats. As long as Mr. Harris controls the Democratic policies, any decent or honest relationship is obviously impossible. I want to get at it another way."

"Go on, Matthew," said Mr. Banning. "I'm not consistent enough to object now. For some reason, I don't mind cutting half a man's throat. It's just cutting the whole thing that stops me."

"What you want, Herbert," Matthew Herring said, "is not to get blood on your hands, I'm afraid. I mean, because you don't like blood, not because you intend to fool anybody. Now, Doctor Lefferts has always tacitly supported Doctor Bull, and he will support him to the last ditch. It's just a professional matter. Making common cause against the laymen. What we have to look for is the last ditch and continue the discussion there."

"Yes. Lucile made some experiments. She discovered that there wasn't a great deal to be done."

"Well, the strength of Doctor Lefferts's position lies in the fact that a complaint or so carries no weight. You can shrug it off. You imply that every one is perfectly satisfied—except a few cranks nothing can satisfy. The medical profession understands that. It's been suffering from a few cranks for centuries. But I think if you could show that every one was dissatisfied, Doctor Lefferts wouldn't lose a minute in throwing Doctor Bull overboard. Now, Walter——"

Mr. Bates jerked his finger away from the scalloped shell. "I'm listening," he said quickly.

"What would you think of calling a town meeting, say next Saturday—that's the fourteenth. I want to have several resolutions presented for adoption—to the general effect that Doctor Bull has been grossly negligent and incompetent, and is unfit to hold his office. If we could get two or three hundred signatures, and send the resolutions along with a petition signed by all the town officers, to Doctor Lefferts, I think Lefferts would remove him."

"I don't doubt he would," Eric Cadbury admitted, "but how about the School Committee?"

"That's a matter for the Board of Education. The District Superintendent would be within his rights, and I know him well enough to be able to say he would exercise his rights, in objecting to the employment of any unfit person in connection with the Connecticut public schools. A man dismissed from a medical office for carelessness and incompetence would certainly come in the class of unfit persons. What the School Committee agreed on or didn't agree on wouldn't matter. Doctor Bull would simply be removed from the field of discussion."

"Say, that's pretty neat!" Eric Cadbury said.

"Any objections, Herbert?"

"I have none."

Walter Bates said uneasily, "Yes, but don't you think maybe we ought to wait until later? I mean—"

"You mean," said Mr. Banning, "that Doctor Bull is the only doctor in town. Probably he is better than none, so let's be sure we have some one else before we annoy him too greatly. I'm not very happy about this, Matthew."

"The State Health Department would step in if necessary," Matthew Herring said. "There's no reason to worry about that. As a matter of fact, I've spoken to Doctor Verney about the chance of getting some physician who could come in to help, at least temporarily; and he gave me the name of a Doctor Moses in Torrington. I didn't explain the situation to him, but it seems that there'd be no difficulty. I don't mean to imply that any of this is going to make any one very happy, Herbert. I'd suggest that you sacrifice your happiness in the common cause."

"You score," admitted Mr. Banning, smiling briefly. "You aren't planning to go all the way home for luncheon, are you? Better stay here. I'm expecting Doctor Verney. He's been busy helping Doctor Bull with the inoculations."

"Well, we'll be going," Eric Cadbury said. "I'm sure you're with us, Mr. Banning."

"I can't be anywhere else, it seems. Yes, of course. You have my support for what it's worth. How's Geraldine today, Walter?"

"She's pretty sick, I'm afraid." He hesitated. "I know what you mean," he said unexpectedly. "I mean, if it would do any good. It seems kind of late somehow. That's what takes the heart out of you when you start going for somebody. Well —still, something ought to be done, I suppose. I mean, that's why I think Matthew and Eric are probably right—" He faltered again. "Well," he added, turning his hat around, "good-by, then—"

*

All Saturday morning it had been getting clearer and clearer that Joe was too sick to be left alone. When he awakened, which was quite early, he seemed so much better, with hardly any fever, that May almost persuaded herself that what Joe had was, after all, a cold and nothing more. Perhaps giving him breakfast was a mistake, for twenty minutes after he had eaten what he could, he threw it all up. Instead of then feeling better, he became, not gradually, but suddenly delirious, spoke vaguely of the heat, made clear and insistently voiced but fantastic references to what appeared to be some sort of game of cards.

To see a person thus swiftly and hectically let go the real world and, obviously very sick, take up some passionate and incoherent business in a realm abutting on insanity, would disquiet any one. May, appalled, could guess that this was no cold. With a cold, Joe, bad-tempered and ill, spent most of his time complaining. As long as he could protest, had the heart and energy to kick against his state, there would be, she realized now, nothing much wrong with him. Confronting him here was, or appeared to be, an emergency in which he was not the captious, easy winner. Drowning men do not complain of the great anguish caused by salt water flooding the bronchi.

Driven to do something, May did try to get Doctor Bull; but Doris was telling every one who called that he was at the school, and wouldn't be free until after lunch. Doris was keeping a list of calls and during the afternoon some one would get around. For May's benefit, she added: "Doctor Verney got some Doctor Moses from Torrington to fix it up to drive over and help. They want to stick everybody who isn't sick with this stuff. Honestly, May, I'm scared to death; and I'm not the only one, I can tell you! Everybody's going to get it, I think. You can die of it, you know——"

It was no exaggeration. Doris was scared to death. Appealing to her to watch Joe for a while would be useless. With so many people sick, and so many more who were probably going to be, there was no one available, even if May could pay. Those who weren't sick themselves, or almost frantic nursing their own relatives, would probably want more than money to expose themselves. Friends could be asked to do favors; but you couldn't ask them to do favors which might prove so deadly, favors which lasted six hours every afternoon.

Only half hearing what Doris was agitatedly chattering on about, May saw that this afternoon at least she would have to try it. Harry Weems would be the only possible hope. She had decided that almost at once, but, even at this difficult moment, she hesitated, for she didn't really know how contagious it was. If Harry refused, she couldn't blame him; it was simply that, after all Harry had done, she hated the idea of crowning her requests with one which he might regard as too much.

This, of course, was the major point but it did not exclude another—a petty, surely irrelevant and contemptible, small one. If she asked Doris to ring up Harry, Doris, though not present in space, would crowd her in spirit. Doris would not be too alarmed by the situation to find time to enjoy her own ideas about this Harry and May business. Doris had done it too often before. Without ever saying a word, she could manage to imply that she knew there was more to it than met eyes less expert than hers.

What made Doris think so, beyond the prompt suspicions of a personal sensuality always on some sexual quest, it would be impossible to tell. That something had, something which Doris considered definite and conclusive, could be judged from the abruptness with which she took May into her confidence. Doris was anything but indiscreet. The unmistakable implication was that Doris knew that May was now on her side of the fence, and could be trusted to keep her mouth shut. Without asking May for any compensating information, she freely admitted her to secrets of such overwhelming local importance as that she had twice had abortions performed as a result of Robert Newell's attentions to her.

"There's a man in Waterbury," she said. "It doesn't amount to anything." She sounded as though she thought that May might have a necessary personal interest in the matter and needed reassurance.

To speak up, to make Doris realize that May was by no means on her side of the fence, and that the relation to Harry could not have been more innocent—common sense really ought to show Doris that; how in Heaven's name could Harry have found an opportunity to sleep with her?—seemed impossible. To say anything, she would first have to admit that she understood what Doris thought. As a result, she never did say anything. Flushing a little, she listened with a tense, wordless revulsion to secrets which she did not want to know, and some of which—such as the fact that Mr. Newell paid his attentions indiscriminately both to Doris and Clara—really disgusted and outraged her.

Shrinking so regularly from this subtle contamination—not that she meant to blame Doris, or even Mr. Newell; nor that she presumed to condemn what she knew nothing about. She just didn't know, any more than she seemed to know about social or economic justice; or God in Heaven; or people going to church on earth— she had reached a point now where, even worried almost sick about Joe, and so distracted that she could scarcely speak, she was able to consider and quail from possible thoughts of Doris's.

"Doris," she said. "Listen, see if you can get Harry Weems, will you? I just can't leave Joe alone this afternoon. If he could spare an hour—"

Amazed, immediately made penitent, she saw that she might have wronged Doris in her own mind as much as Doris had ever wronged her. Perhaps Doris's fear had after all somehow purged her; perhaps the quality of mercy, the openness to human appeal, so much readier always in sinners than in the saints, prompted Doris. She said: "Listen, May. I know you're in an awful jam. If you can get Harry or someone to watch him while I have lunch, I'll come back on the switchboard this afternoon. You can just stay home."

The impossibility of saying anything reduced May. "All right," she agreed, weeping, and hung up.

*

Starting awake in bed, George Bull flung out a hand which knocked the receiver of the extension telephone from its hook. Groping, he found it on the bedside table, dragged the telephone over. In the deep darkness, the telephone operator said, "Peters calling you, Doctor Bull—"

It was one of the Clark girls speaking, so it was past midnight. He sought the chain of the lamp and jerked it, getting a shaded flood of painful yellow light. He ran a hand over his eyes, through his mussed, upended hair. Now he could see his watch, and it was quarter to three.

"Well?"

Pa Peters, quavering comically, said, "Doc, you better come down. Sal's awful sick. She—"

"What the hell do you mean, awful sick?" he answered. "She's only eight months gone."

Some one took the telephone away, protesting, "Aw, you old fool, let me—" This stronger voice was Jeff Peters, and he said, "Hello! Doc! Listen, come down right away, can you? She's pretty near unconscious. She can't see any-thing—"

"If she's unconscious, how do you know she can't see anything?"

"She went blind about eleven o'clock, Doc; only it was dark in her room and she wasn't sure. She had a kind of convulsion—"

"Lord God!" George Bull roared. "She would! All right, I'll be down. Heat some water. Soak some rags in it—hot as she can stand it. Wrap 'em around her belly—" He slammed the receiver back, thrust his legs over the side of the bed and stood up.

"Huh!" he said, fumbling for his clothes. "Now we're in for it!"

He wondered suddenly how much, if any, morphine he had downstairs. His right hand, sore when he went to bed, was sorer now. Man-handling Joel hadn't done it any good. He interrupted the lacing of his shoes to shake it, grunting; exasperated to have any use of his body impaired. Whether Sal Peters's heart could stand it would be something else again. A little of Verney's fooling with urinalysis would have been a help. Catch Verney letting a pregnancy get far without the scientific fixings! George Bull thought: "I guess I've seen pretty near fifteen hundred of them in my time!" The fact was, though, that sometimes you'd think nature was conspiring with science. In rough and readier days it seemed to him that what they didn't do hurt them remarkably little. Once you equipped yourself to look for all kinds of trouble, the patients obliged you by having it.

Overhead in the darkened driveway, the white moon, shrinking toward the last quarter hung high behind the great bare elm tops. The cold engine was hard to start and he must have made quite a racket, for glancing over at the house, he saw Aunt Myra's capped head in her bedroom window, thrust out silent, without remark or gesture. The car finally clear of the garage, the throttle well open, he left it, crossed the hard sod and called up to her: "Peters. You go to bed."

"Now, George," she said, "why don't you wait a minute and I'll get you some coffee. It wouldn't take any time."

"I've got to run. Go to sleep."

Driving, he turned down toward the bridge road corner. Behind him arose a hard, rhythmic pulse, racing louder along the night. Past him, flashing through the successive barren pools of arc-light came a solitary motor—a whine of tires, a rush of torn air. Twin red taillights and a glow cast up on a North Carolina number plate dipped away down US6W. "Long way from home," George Bull said.

He turned left toward the bridge, past the cemetery, past the extended rectangle of the school, lightless and lonely, a glint of moonlight on the gold cupola. The road down the river from the bridge was dirt, and badly rutted. His headlights, watery, picked out the sagging rails of the fence; the hemlocks hung, half undermined at the brink of the worn bank. On his right the underbrush opened suddenly at the bend, a wide swathe cleared to a mark, and fairly fronting him was set the widespread quadruple steel footing of a transmission line tower. Affixed to a cross bar shone back at him an enameled sign, scarlet skull and crossed femurs—*Danger of Death 220,000 volts*. A ruined stone wall began, ran with him through the brush a thousand yards and ended. The dying trees of an overgrown orchard, a lost hedge of lilac before the open foundations of a vanished farm house, went by. Rounding the rocky outthrust of the hill he came carefully down, rumbled on a narrow wooden bridge. Up on the other side he could see a light through the saplings. He turned into the barnyard of the Peters's farm and shut off his engine.

Pa Peters hobbled from chair to chair, gabbling this and that, his thin hair shining in the lamplight. His son Jeff was sulky, but concerned, too.

[244]

Pregnancy was a woman's hard luck; eclampsia was a condition past his understanding; but blindness was easy to understand and no one could encounter it unmoved. The outlook, George Bull saw at once, couldn't have been worse. Sal Peters was a heavy woman and between her fat and the advanced distention of her breasts it was impossible even to hear the weak heart without turning her over. She managed to down what was probably too little of an infusion of digitalis; and, considering her kidneys, the convulsions had better be met with morphine, not chloroform. The results were not encouraging and by five o'clock it was plain that she was going to get rid of the fetus. There was a chance that, this once done, she would show an improvement. Since she lost a good deal of blood in the process, she seemed to improve; but at six the convulsions started again. At half-past six, she was dead.

The person most upset about it seemed to be Betty Peters, perhaps more because of her own long history of sexual miseries—she had begun at fifteen by spending a night with a group of men from Sansbury in a tobacco barn—than because of affection for her sister-in-law. Overcome by the bloody, painful nastiness of life, or the gradual loss of it, seen now in the close room for six night hours, she proceeded to have hysterics.

In no mood for patience, Jeff yelled: "Shut up, you lousy whore, before I kill you!" Pa danced around in a senile ecstasy of alarm, squealing. The best way out seemed to be to give both Pa and Jeff sleeping tablets. A fractional shot of the remaining morphine did for Betty.

Thus, by half-past seven, George Bull could leave them; three variously drugged, one dead; the house shut up, bleak and gray under the cold blue morning sky. Crossing the bridge into New Winton, he could hear the bells of St. Matthias's ringing briefly for Holy Communion.

The sun, just over the thin woods crowning the Cobble, had reached the green—a bright flood across its windy, wintry desertion. Rounding the corner, George Bull was in time to see Miss Kimball, pinched and breakfastless, entering the doors of St. Matthias's, her solitary shadow preceding her. Doctor Wyck came out of the rectory then, clad in a black cassock, and crossed the lawn diagonally between the maples to the sacristy door.

In front of Weems's garage a man in a slate-colored uniform, with black leather leggings, ammunition-filled cartridge belt and heavy revolver, and the triangular yellow shoulder tab of the State Police, stood astride his halted motorcycle. His face was red with cold around the goggles; his ears crimson against the edges of his cap. The wooden shutters of Bates's store were in place, covering the windows; the doors locked, the steps deserted.

New Winton would always look like this on Sunday morning, but to George Bull, knowing in how many houses people were sick, there seemed to be a stupefied paralysis, a cowering indoors as though the plague were abroad. The steady cold wind eddied noisily around his car;

he rattled on up the wide white expanse of concrete.

A little smoke swirled off the lip of the chimney in back of the Bull house. That must mean that Aunt Myra had a fire going, and he was helped by the promise of breakfast. Halting the car before the open door of the barn, he got out. His eye caught, he went to the threshold then. From the floor, just inside, he bent and picked up the bright object. It was a long clean bread knife.

Holding it, perplexed to account for its presence, he was attracted by a muffled, groaning sound. He walked forward at once to the first of the old, shadowed stalls. "Well, I'll be damned!" he said aloud. "Come out of there!"

The figure huddled on the dusty boards in the corner against the splintered, cob-webbed manger made no move, so he went in. "What's the trouble, Mrs. Talbot?" he said. He drew her to her feet, and, compellingly, out into the better light. "That yours?" he asked, pointing to the knife, put down beside his bag. "You'd better not carry things like that around. You'll hurt yourself."

Her mouth, twisted as though she had bitten a lemon; her eyes, angry and injured under the tangle of hair imperfectly pinned up, smeared now with cobwebs, made her look like one of those fantastic, miserably sinister women whose surfeit of misfortunes might once have started the idea that she had some to spare, could visit them on others. An earlier New England, in social and religious self-defense, had sometimes felt that hanging such people was its disagreeable duty. To remove her cheaply and forever from human society no means existed but interring her in the ground. Now, at Middletown, the State of Connecticut had a tomb for incurable witches. Impersonally patient, the state provided for their disappearance with a certainty never reached by the haphazard methods of a magistrate or a crowd. One could hide from the rope or evade the hunters; the state's lethal process was old age and decay.

George Bull didn't pretend to the experience or diagnostic skill which would entitle him to an opinion. If he had to make a guess, he'd say it was a depressive phase of a mild manic-depressive psychosis. Perhaps no more than a cyclothymic case, coming and going; but all the odds were that it would come oftener and go more reluctantly. He didn't believe that she was or would be actually dangerous. The knife probably had to do with some notion of defense, not of attack—some half-hearted effort to repair the exhausting helplessness felt from a general psycho-motor retardation. More contemptuous than not of the unwieldy jargon of this uncertain science, he said, "Well, one thing about it; you must be pretty cold."

"Get in," he added, opening the car door. "I think you'd better go home now."

She simply stood still looking back at him, so he bundled her in. Going back, he got his bag, opened it and pulled out a half-pint flask of whisky. Unscrewing the metal cup cap he filled it. "Drink it!" he said to her.

Plainly she was unwilling. She backed away feebly on the seat, and he said: "All right, don't. I'm not going to argue with you."

Regarding the poured whisky a moment, he swallowed it himself, screwed back the cap, snapped the bag shut. Going around to get in the other side, he saw her struggling with the door handle, intent on getting out. Reaching across, he knocked her hand down.

They were rounding the corner to go along the east side of the green when, with stealth and an unexpected, or accidental, competence, she did get the door open. George Bull roared, grabbing at her; but the cloth he caught tore away in his hand, the door swung wide, and she banged against it, falling.

Veering almost off the road, George Bull drew his brake. Mrs. Talbot lay perhaps ten feet behind. They had been traveling slowly and she demonstrated how little she had been hurt by scrambling now to her feet. Turning, she scurried across the road, over the path, and down past the library. Since she was headed for home, George Bull decided that she was probably going there. Seeing that any sort of pursuit would only make her more frantic, he sat at the wheel, shaking his sore thumb, watching. Stumbling along the back fence, past woodsheds and antiquated outhouses, she had got as far as the Tuppings'. There she suddenly turned in, darting out of sight. Unexpectedly clear in the Sunday morning stillness, George Bull could hear her beating on the back door.

"Hell and damnation!" he exploded. Stamp-

[249]

ing on the self-starter, he got the stalled engine started again, swept with a low-geared roar down the back street to the Tuppings' gate.

May, her hair pulled back and knotted behind, was as white as the long hem of nightgown showing below the skimpy bathrobe tied around her. She opened the door only a little; but, grasping the edge, George Bull moved it back, out of her paralyzed hands, closed it behind him. He could see now the cause of May's horror. Mrs. Talbot, though certainly hurt in no serious way, had taken most of the skin off her cheekbone and the left side of her forehead. Blood, flowing, reached her chin in wet scarlet trickles. George Bull almost recoiled himself before the shocking result.

He said: "She's all right. Jumped out of the car, but it's just a little skin off. Found her hiding up in my barn and started to drive her home. Got any hot water? Well, cold will do; in a basin. Bring it here and I'll fix her up. Get some clothes on, will you? I want to take her over to her place and lock her up. We'll try to get Mrs. Darrow from Banning's Bridge. When Verney comes up, we'll see what can be done. It isn't safe to leave her around."

Probably exhausted by her escapade, Mrs. Talbot made now no protest or resistance. "You shouldn't get out of a car until it stops," he said. "But you're all right this time."

Pressed to sit down on a chair by the table, she remained lax, her back rounded in a weak flexion, her hands dropped open on her lap, her bloody face bent forward, chin on breast.

A little water slopped over the edge of the shallow basin as May set it down. "Make some coffee," George Bull said. "We'll try some on her when I get her patched up—" He glanced at May and added, "Brace up! Nothing to cry about!"

"I'm not," May said.

"What's the trouble? Up all night?"

She nodded. Finding her voice again, she said: "But what am I going to do? I can't take care of him. He can't stay by himself—"

"I'll look at him in a minute. Go and make that coffee."

When she came back with the coffee pot and a cup, clad now in a gray jersey dress, he was affixing the adhesive tape to hold in place the upper patch on Mrs. Talbot's face. "That's better," he nodded. "Get a couple more cups and we'll all have some. Don't worry, we'll get Joe off your hands."

"I don't want him off my hands. I just want—"

"Huh!" George Bull said. "Unless you can hire two nurses, like the Bannings, I guess you haven't much choice in the matter. Go on; get those cups. I haven't had any breakfast."

*

As well as one hundred and eleven children, eighty-seven adults, most of whom lived in houses where there was already a case, had each received Saturday five hundred millions of typhoid bacilli in polyvalent strains sensitized with serum from highly immune horses. Monday, they all took a thousand million more. Wednesday they got a last thousand million.

This would presumably arrest the spread by infection from new sources; but on Wednesday there were thirty-nine unquestioned cases and six or seven highly likely ones. Tuesday afternoon, which was ominously early in the course of the disease, Ralph Kimball died.

The solitary state policeman seen by George Bull astride his motorcycle in front of Weems's garage Sunday morning, had been re-enforced. Above and below New Winton, US6W was half closed with a barrier where motor traffic was requested to proceed straight through. In New Winton the state of siege and emergency had reached a high point Monday. The sickness, not respecting person or position, in prostrating forty people had picked several in simple ways indispensable to ordinary life. Worst hit was the railroad. It was noon Monday before the Chief Train Dispatcher understood that at New Winton there was no one in the railroad's employ able to get out of bed. Signals were consequently not placed. Early trains, milk coming down, mail coming up, halted, put out flagmen and torpedoes, finally telephoned the Danbury yards for enlightenment. The resulting tie-up took half the day to straighten out. A head-on collision and a dozen derailed cars could hardly have done more.

Monday, Helen Upjohn came down with typhoid. Since Geraldine was sick already, and those two were the ones experienced in handling the post office work, even on its much-belated arrival the mail remained in the bags. Walter

Bates was a long while in resuming his titular office of Postmaster, for he was engaged, as First Selectman, in interviewing Jethro Evarts.

Jethro, though he had not lived in the house since his wife died, refused to allow it to be used. Remote, almost impregnable in his complete deafness and partial blindness, his refusal had at first been absolute; then, conditioned by a demand for rent. At that point Doctor Bull, who had come with Walter Bates, departed. He went and broke in the door, started Grant Williams and Harry Weems and Howard Upjohn working on the furnace. Mr. Bates stayed to reason, finally convincing Jethro's sister, with whom Jethro lived. While the old man watched her suspiciously, not able to hear what she was saying, she told Walter, all right, to use it anyway; and there was no need to pay Jethro anything. She would see that he didn't get out, so he would never know about it. When Jethro pushed his pad over for her to write down what it was, she scribbled *Nothing that concerns you.*

Arriving triumphant, with this irregular permission, Mr. Bates found the house wide open, Mrs. Foster and Mrs. Baxter on their knees scrubbing floors, all the furniture jammed in one room, and three nurses from the Torrington hospital making up a variety of cots. In the cellar Howard could be heard banging and hammering around the furnace; Harry Weems and Grant were unloading a Ford truck on the lawn; from another truck Eben Quimby was uproariously dumping a load of coal down a chute. Parked in the overgrown drive was Doctor Verney's shining car.

Seeing that the key entrusted to him was not really needed, Mr. Bates decided not to bother them. He still had all the mail to sort.

Tuesday, nineteen patients had been moved in. One was Helen Webster and May stayed on the switchboard until half-past ten that night. At six the next morning, Doris, coming to relieve her sister, found Clara so sick that it was necessary to telephone her father to come down and bring her home—she couldn't possibly drive the car back to Truro. Until the telephone company could arrange for relief, May and Doris would work on twelve-hour shifts. Wednesday morning, the Reverend Doctor Wyck, who had intended to bury Ralph Kimball that afternoon—Howard didn't consider it prudent to embalm him, so they had to be prompt about it—took to his bed. At the Evarts house, Doctor Verney, stopping a moment on his way to the Bannings', was joined in anxious conference with Doctor Bull over Larry Ward, sunk in what gave every sign of being a fatal coma. His case had chosen to complicate itself with pleurisy.

Just before noon, Henry Harris, leaning against the door jamb of the post office, was reading his way patiently through the New York *Times*, in no hurry to reach the editorials. The news was done with, the rectangles of advertising grew bigger, but sometimes space enough was left for a column or so of something, and Henry Harris scanned whatever it was.

On page eleven he was rewarded. The word, New Winton, in nine-point surprised him. This smallest possible headline topped an inch and a quarter paragraph inserted at the bottom of the second, almost filled column of a minor political story. *Typhoid at New Winton Traced to Water.*

Henry Harris began to smile, warming. *New Winton, Conn., March 11th. An outbreak of typhoid fever in the village of New Winton, Litchfield County, was being investigated by the State Department of Health and local authorities today. The Department said that twenty-six cases of the disease and one death had been reported. The investigation, officials said, had disclosed that all patients had drunk water from the local reservoir, made turbid by recent rains.*

"Short and sweet," he thought; unreasonably delighted by the empty, perfunctory sentences; the figures no longer current; the mean obscurity of place. Aloud, he said, "That'll teach us, I guess!"

Chuckling, he hesitated a moment, for really to appreciate it one had to see the whole page, the rambling political hand-out, the fluently sketched group of pert, slight girls with their long legs and flaring panties enriched by Puerto Rican needlework for $2.97; but, after all, who would appreciate it but himself? With his finger nail he detached the small oblong of print, turned and went into the post office. Borrowing a thumb tack from the lower corner of an official notice, he pinned his story in the center of the worn board.

*

Leaving the Evarts house Friday afternoon, George Bull felt a weariness not very familiar to

[255]

him. To be tired and sleepy, comfortably ready to lie down and repair the great expenditures of an energy great too, outlasting at any time or task most other men's, was his ordinary sensation. Now, in a profound sad wakefulness, he did not want to sleep so much as to sit still, not to be bothered. The constant coming and going in the bright lights and bare rooms of this improvised, uncomfortable hospital; the repeated consideration of this case or that (each one febrile, disheveled; most of them entering or well into a typical helpless stupor) exasperated him with the impossibility of doing anything quickly. He was fitted for sudden prodigies of strength; not for standing still, bearing the little world on his back. This thing could go on forever. Larry Ward had not been dead four hours when they were putting Lester Dunn into the bed thus given them.

His right thumb, which had almost stopped bothering him yesterday, throbbed again now, used too violently for something. His left arm ached to the bone in outward sign of the immense inner disturbance caused by those two and a half billion injected bacilli. That invasion, he supposed, might account for his state of mind. The whole system, which could neither explain nor be explained to, felt a mechanical panic of revulsion, not knowing what next. On his mind weighed the simple physical foreboding of resources heavily taxed and reserves depleted.

He sat a few minutes in his car without troubling to start the engine. The late afternoon, windless, showed a low, long pile-up of thick clouds, bright with the sunset hidden behind the hills. These towering colored mounds reflected down a strong falsely warm glow over the whole valley. Around the green, the shapes of houses, most of them white, a few with yellow windows, stood lucid and distinct between the trees. The surface of US6W, for the moment entirely empty, took on a faint lemon color; the dead whiteness of the Congregational church was relieved; it looked soft as chalk up the deserted green. New Winton, wrapped in this wan radiance, did not rest him. He thought: "By God, I'm getting old; and this is all I've ever had!"

George Bull turned the ignition key, pushed in his gears. Holding the clutch, he began to coast gradually down the slope of the drive. Let in, his engine resisted a moment, braking him, but he had enough momentum to force it over and the cylinders fired. Drawing along the green, he saw the sign before the telephone exchange light up. He remembered that he wanted to see May Tupping. He pulled the car a little off the road and leaving the engine running went slowly up the path.

May was alone. An open book, which she had been holding up to the switchboard light, she laid on her lap, turning her head. "I've just had a call for you, Doctor Bull," she said. "Mrs. Vogel—"

"I wanted to see you a moment," he answered. In his own mind, his news lost all importance. To the weary mind what difference did it make? In few enough years it was all the same. He said, "It's hard to understand some of these things, but there's a febrile condition we call subsultus tendinum—amounts to a sort of picking at the

[257]

bed-clothes. Often it's not a good sign by any means; but in Joe's case, I don't think it's a bad one. He seems to have as mild a case as any one over there."

She looked at him, the book closed now, in alert, frightened attention. "No, no," Doctor Bull said. "No cause to act up. Can't you even see what it means? Doctor Verney agrees with me that it's remarkable; but such things are always happening. Probably, getting up a resistance, the body gets up a surplus. Whatever's been wrong with Joe's spine must have got something good for it. The nervous reaction seems to be re-established in his arms. It works on all the tests Verney could think up. Of course, he's got next to no muscles left in his arms, but when he gets well, they'll pick up. Thought it might cheer you to know the probabilities."

She had come to her feet slowly, as though automatically impelled; perhaps with the thoughtless plan of going to see Joe herself. George Bull could see the glitter of her eyes as they filled with tears. She sat down again then, facing away from him toward the switchboard. The book fell, and stooping sharply, she recovered it.

"Well, that's medical science for you," he said. "Ring Aunt Myra when you get around to it. Tell her I won't be home to supper. And tell any one who calls up that I'll come when I can, and not before."

Back at the car, he turned it about, to go over to the Vogels'; but when he reached the corner, he drove on by, continuing to the end of the green. Turning right, he crossed the railroad, bumped away from New Winton between the lower fields. At the fork he changed gears, crawling loud and slow, his headlights rising, tipping along the fence ahead of him in the dusk, up the hill to Janet's.

The long mound of the barn, the upright cylindrical masses of the twin silos, were solid and dark against the shrouded valley, the black wall of the western hills. In the western sky a pure cold last radiance, the color of sea water in a glass, remained. Lights were on up the slope in the Rogers' cottage and in the kitchen windows of the Cardmaker house. Above the near crest of the Cobble—and, in perspective, hardly higher, the summit of Cold Hill—the eastern night was patterned brightly by the spring constellations; the rising train of the Bear; in serene splendor, the great yellow star Arcturus on the valley's edge.

George Bull stood a moment regarding it, for Boötes was one constellation he could remember. Mechanically he said: "Canst thou bring forth Mazzaroth in his season? or canst thou guide Arcturus with his sons?" God, by his mighty works, convinceth Job of ignorance, and of imbecility!

The Reverend Ephraim Bull used them too. Standing in the darkness of a Michigan road, he found strange testimony to the truth of scripture in teaching little George to recognize the eternal stars recommended to Job; and to the awfulness of God's creation, when the light of this Arcturus, moving a hundred and eighty-six thousand miles a second, took forty years to arrive.

"And so what?" said George Bull, heavily; for he could see well enough what bad sense and worse logic the old man had once terrified him into considering wisdom.

There was a sound now of the kitchen door opening and Janet stood against the light. Her deep, arresting voice called calmly, "Who's there?"

George Bull approached and she said, "I thought it was your car. What's wrong?"

"Just thinking," he said. "Got anything to eat?"

"Come on."

Closing the door after him, she said, "Sit down, George. You look about all in."

"Guess I am. Fooling around our hospital all afternoon. We've got nineteen of the cases there. Helps some, but a lot of others are too sick to move, even if we had room."

"I hear Ralph Kimball died."

"That's right. Yesterday we lost Larry Ward. Well, there'll be more. That's a kind of fate for you! We have about forty-three or -four cases. The mortality is about seventeen per cent—this is a virulent strain all right, so it won't be any less than average. Consequently we're going to have seven or eight deaths. That's perfectly certain. Only question is, who'll they be?"

"Want a drink?"

"I guess not. Got myself shot full of vaccine. Doesn't go so well."

"I'll heat you up a tin of beef broth. Mrs. Foster roasted a couple of chickens this afternoon. Want one of them?"

[260]

"Fine."

Without arising, he worked his shoulders out of his coat. Janet had got a can of soup from the pantry. She snapped the switches of the electric range and found a can opener. "What's this about a town meeting tomorrow?" she asked.

"Hadn't heard, but, I guess, nothing about it. Never is."

"You'd better go to it, George."

"Why?"

"You ought to keep an eye on these people you're so fond of. It's going to be about you this time."

"What about me?"

"They're trying to run you out, George. They mean business. Harold told me. Cadbury and Herring have been going around all week lining people up. Haven't you noticed anything?"

"Nothing that worries me. Sure, a few soreheads. Had a set-to with Joel Parry last Saturday. Tuesday we were arranging to have Mrs. Talbot sent over to Middletown and that old jackass Clarence was objecting. We had a couple of words."

"What I hear sounds like a panic. Watch out, George."

"Sure, but who can help that? My God, you'd think it was the bubonic plague, to see some of them carrying on. Probably eighty out of a hundred typhoid cases will get well without any treatment or cold baths or nonsense. At least fifteen will die anyway. That means you might have five to fool with. If you don't happen to kill them, perhaps you'll cure them. Verney was showing me all the figures. Huh! It's funny what a point of view does for you. An old horse doctor like me looks at them and all he can see is that medical science is perfectly useless in ninety-five out of every hundred cases. When Verney sees them, he thinks the other five show how wonderful whatever tricks happen to be in style are."

"Still getting on with him?"

"Sure. He's helped a lot. Of course, he's upset over the Banning girl. Sort of embarrassed about missing the diagnosis. When he's as old as I am, he won't mind so much; but now he thinks it's a personal affront to his modern equipment and all those degrees of his. What are people going to think of him? When he realizes they aren't going to think of him at all until they decide they're dying, he'll take it easier."

*

Lifting the receiver, he said: "Doctor Verney speaking."

"Doctor, this is Miss Stanley."

"Yes, Miss Stanley."

"Doctor, I hate to trouble you, but Miss Valentine agrees with me that we'd better make sure. About twenty minutes ago, the patient made a very sudden return to normal temperature, entirely clear-headed. There is a slight rise in respiration. She says her stomach hurts her. Now, she hasn't been alone at all, not even a minute since noon, so I'm sure we haven't missed anything. And there hasn't been any sign of vomiting or hiccoughing. But the decline in temperature followed a two point rise about six. I—"

"Right. I'm coming. Have you said anything to Mrs. Banning?"

"No, I haven't. I'm using an extension telephone, Doctor. I didn't want to—"

"Quite right. Don't."

The black car came down the exactly edged gray gravel into Stockade Street with a long sighing expiration of twelve cylinders in clocklike firing order. At the end the lights blinked in jeweled sequence: green, yellow, red. Doctor Verney touched his horn and passed unhesitatingly. Pulled to a sudden noiseless crawl by the confused traffic of Railroad Street, the horn rose up again, fretting at cars looking for a chance to park near the motion picture theater, cars putting erratically out from the curb in front of lighted stores. Under the black and white striped, upended lances of the railroad gates, he took a soft swaying jolt, drew away down to the bridge like the wind. The cantilever fencing of beams rippled by. Snapped to the upper filaments, his strong headlights rose from the road, jumping a hundred feet ahead. Against the dark they found a small metal shield on a short steel upright; CONN. US6W. An exactly perpendicular concrete-footed post pointed three rigid arms north: *New Winton 13—Litchfield 34—Winsted 49.*

On the outside lane a Ford truck seemed to come to a halt. He heard the working roar of its engine a second. In the mirror he could see its weak headlights retiring, jerked swiftly backwards as he slid over again.

Halting his car quietly in the circle of Bannings' drive, he came up to the side door without haste, fifteen minutes from Sansbury. To Mary, admitting him, he said: "Good evening. Tell Mrs. Banning I just wanted to look in a minute."

In the shaded light of the sick room, Miss Stanley produced for him a white gown from the bathroom. While he was fastening the buttons Virginia said, stirring a little, "Oh, hello."

Miss Stanley tilted her head, slightly raising her eyebrow. "Yes, I see," he agreed. "It's been about three quarters of an hour?" She nodded. Miss Valentine, coming from Guy's room, appeared in the bathroom door. Doctor Verney drew up a chair by the bed. "Feeling better?" he asked.

"I feel all right." She turned her head on the pillow and the shaded light caught shining on her chin and cheek bones. Her blue eyes regarded him, clear, enormously large above the concave lines of her cheeks. "Have I been sick long?" she said.

"Not very long."

"How long?"

"Oh, several days." Taking her wrist, he looked at the protruding emaciated point of the styloid process. Pretending to busy himself with the pulse, he counted the respirations through fifteen seconds.

"Have they gone yet?" Virginia said.

He smiled at the nurses. "Why, you don't want them to go, do you?"

"I don't mean them. I mean has Val gone? She has. I know. They were going Saturday. She told me today is Friday."

"Don't you mind that. Wouldn't you rather go to Paris?"

"Yes. But how can I?"

"Your father told me that he was going to send you and Guy this summer."

"I don't want to go with Guy. I won't have any fun. He'll just be mean to me."

"I don't believe he will. You'll have a wonderful time." He glanced at the windows. "I've had them closed for some time," Miss Stanley said. "It's about eighty-one." She came and turned back the covers.

"I don't want that rotten thermometer," Virginia said with sudden energy. "I don't like it. Why can't you—"

"Now, Ginny! We aren't going to take your temperature. They tell me your stomach hurts you. I just want to look at it and we'll see if we can fix it up."

"It doesn't hurt any more."

"Well, it might start hurting again. We'd better see, hadn't we?"

"No."

He made a gesture to Miss Stanley. "There, there, dear," she said, "you must do what the doctor says if you want to get well. You know that, don't you? Now, you mustn't cry. You aren't going to cry, are you? It isn't going to hurt the least bit. I promise you it's not—"

"I don't want people's hands all over me. I don't want people looking at me. I don't—"

"Peg—" said Miss Stanley. Miss Valentine took a handkerchief from the pile on the table. Shaking out a fold, she came and wiped Virginia's cheeks, remaining there, ready to prevent any movement. Virginia made none. The tears continued quietly, overflowing at her eyes' outer corners. "Why doesn't he get through?" she whispered finally. "Why won't he stop now—"

"Through in just a minute, Ginny," Doctor Verney said. "We just want to be sure. There. That's all. Everything's fine."

Miss Valentine covered her up again. To Miss Stanley, by the bathroom door, he said: "Not a sign. I'm sure it's all right. We might as well take a leucocyte count, but I'm positive there's been no perforation. We'll let her alone for a few minutes until she calms down."

"I was practically sure there wasn't," Miss Stanley said. "I really hated to call you. But—"

"I'd rather come out on twenty false alarms than miss the real thing by many hours. I think we'd better try feeding her more, if she can take it."

"I've been awfully worried about that, Doctor."

"See what you can do, even if you have to make it every hour. She's got to get some nourishment. I'll be in some time tomorrow morning, of course."

"You must be perfectly exhausted. I suppose old Mrs. Buck is still getting you up every other night."

"Poor old soul! I'm afraid she hasn't got much longer. You can reach me at the office until nine tomorrow. I'll be down at the Evarts place here for a while after that."

"Why don't you take a day off? I'm worried about you, too."

He smiled. "I'm pretty tough. I'll try to get Moses over Sunday or Monday; but I can't leave Doctor Bull to handle the whole business alone."

*

George Bull took the cup of hot soup, blew on it a moment while he watched the fire over the cup's rim. Sucking in a little, he grunted, "That's good."

Janet came out of the pantry with the chicken on a plate. "You can just pull it apart," she said. "Be careful. It's stuffed. I guess you could use a spoon for that."

"Fine. Give it here." He held out the empty cup to her.

"Matter of fact," he said, splitting off a leg from the chicken, "it's a lot of nonsense. Banning wants to make me the goat. Suppose he does? I don't care whether I'm Board of Health or not; but I'm damned if I'll give them the satisfaction of resigning. Let 'em do what they can. I'd like to see how much it is. I'd like to see them show it was my fault."

"Whose fault was it?"

He sank his teeth in, ripping most of the meat from the drumstick, and he was engaged a minute chewing it. "Whose fault's an earthquake?" he said finally. "If I'd gone wandering around the hill, I might have made them put their latrines somewhere else." Upending the chicken, he dug out a tablespoonful of dressing and put it in his mouth. "And I might not have," he added with difficulty. "God alone knows how much dung a man gets down with his food every day." He twitched off the other leg. "Little more usually does no harm. It seems even possible that most of the traces of fecal pollution found in our water samples have nothing to do with the typhoid. Few of Joel Parry's cows wandering around loose could drop a couple of flops and give just the same effect. I'm not saying I have any better idea. I'm just saying it's practically impossible. The most they could have had was a carrier, and carriers generally don't infect that way. Verney's been looking it up. If they don't think I'm smart enough, let them ask him—"

"They're not going to ask anybody, George. Sometimes you don't show very good sense. They may say it's bad judgment, but even if it's really just bad luck, the result's the same. They say to themselves, 'We've been paying him money for years to see things like this don't happen to us.' They pay you so little money, you might think they understood that the whole pack of them weren't worth a great deal. But they don't understand that. They think taking care of them is a great honor, as well as your natural job, so why should you be wanting money, too?"

Raising the legless chicken, George Bull got his teeth into the breast. "That's a fact," he agreed, when he could. "Most of them aren't worth much, anyway you look at them. They haven't had a real man in town since old Paul Banning died. Most of them are just a bunch of

Miss Kimballs. Well, Connecticut's going to hell, that's about the size of it. Course, if I were young, I'd probably see it was a fine way to go—as much or more fun. Only I'm old. If I were fixing it, I'd have things the way they were thirty years ago."

He got out another spoonful of dressing, detached the wish-bone and nipped the meat off it. Discarding it, he added: "New Winton was a place to live, then; not something a road went through. You didn't have a bunch of bums rushing by all the time, with cowboys like Newell herding them up on Quail Pond. Look at the mills down at Sansbury and the Polacks! Time was when Sansbury was a white man's town. Look at the Roman Catholic convent there, or whatever they made of the Jenny place! What the hell are these monks and priors and novenas of the Little Flower doing in New England? Same with a lot of these Jew artists, like Lincoln over in the Cobb place. Jumping Jesus, what's he mean by calling himself Lincoln? Early American house! Why doesn't he go restore himself a synagogue in Jerusalem?"

He set aside the plate with the chicken's largely cleared skeleton.

"Huh!" he said, wiping his mouth. "I guess my sentiments are pretty wholesome at bottom! If Mrs. Banning could hear me, she might forgive me my trespasses. Got a glass of milk?"

"I ought to have. The cows keep turning it out and it's hardly worth selling nowadays." When she came back from the icebox, she said, "I'll warm it up for you. What you need's a good night's sleep, George. You'd better be feeling spry tomorrow; you may have your hands full with the fine old native stock."

"Sure. They're a bunch of bastards too."

*

At nine o'clock, Mary, knocking gently on the open library door, said, "Mr. Banning. Excuse me, sir, but would you see Bert Ward?"

"Of course," he said, getting up.

At the end of the hall, by the closed door, two men stood, their hats off, their hair laid flat in identical pattern, shining under the light with some oily dressing, one yellow, one black. Their overcoat collars were turned up, their gloveless hands were red. The blond one said: "I guess you remember me, Mr. Banning. I'm Bert Ward. I got your telegram."

"Of course, I remember you, Bert." Mr. Banning put out his hand and took Bert's icy one.

"Oh—" Bert said. "Mr. Banning, this is my friend, Mr. Yedinak. He drove me up in his car. I hoped you wouldn't mind if I brought him in."

"Of course not. How do you do?"

"Very pleased to meet you. I tell Bert he be cold. I just got a open car. 1924 Peerless. Ha, ha. Well, it got here."

"Anton works at Remington Arms with me."

"Have you had supper?"

"Yeah, we got a hot dog at Sansbury."

"Wouldn't you like something more?"

"No, we had more than one. Ha, ha. I had four."

"Come into the library. There's a fire there. Sure you wouldn't like some coffee?"

"Well—"

"Or something to drink?"

"Ha, ha. How about it, Bert?"

"Mary, if you'll take these coats please—and some whisky in the library."

"Boy, does that fire look good!" Anton Yedinak said. "Say, some horse," he added, looking at the lithograph. "Some stepper. I'd bet on him!"

"Bert's uncle used to drive him," Mr. Banning said. "That was long ago. Bert, I don't need to tell you how badly we felt about Larry—"

"That's all right, Mr. Banning. I was awful sorry to hear it. I said to Anton, I guess I'd better come up—"

Some instant change had transformed Anton Yedinak's face. The life and agitation went out of it, replaced completely by a dolorous, gentle, Slavic melancholy. He sighed audibly; he nodded his head several times in agreement. "I tell him I drive him up," he said. "Then we drive back. Don't miss any work that way."

"I guess you're surprised I don't stay to see him buried," said Bert uneasily, "but you see, Mr. Banning, I can't get time off that way. Too many people in Bridgeport would like my job, I guess—"

"Thank you, Mary," Mr. Banning said. "That will be all right. Won't you help yourself, Mr. Yedinak? Why, no, Bert. I can quite understand. I'm sure Larry would too. When times are so hard—"

He stopped, pressingly aware in his own familiar private way of the warm library, the fine

[271]

furniture, the bright unnecessary fire. How deep, how terrible, how smugly jeering, the insolence of sitting here and telling Bert and young Yedinak that times were hard, or that he quite understood the need to leave one's dead brother and at once repeat the freezing trip in the wreck of somebody's discarded car in order to be at a Bridgeport factory when the whistle blew. Then that solemn appeal to what Larry would understand! Did he mean to imply that Larry, in some better, happier world— Next he would be saying that the strife was o'er, the battle won!

To cover this excruciating shy shame—his impotence, when circumstances required him to reach people, saying or acting with simple ease the common word or part which made the contact human—he knew that he had only the mask of his composed face—a formal expression of reserve, with its implied detestable calm of superiority, its heatless charity, its exact politeness. Of course, the mask had its uses. Faced with it, he would be a brave man as well as a rude one who could still remember to say the things which Mr. Banning himself felt to be pertinent. Certainly Bert would not be the Nathan to pipe up—*There were two men in one city; the one rich, and the other poor* . . . Probably Bert saw nothing wanting in Larry's lonely death down at the Evarts house. He would not expect the Bannings to think of taking as good and expensive care of Larry as they would of Virginia. It was enough that they would have been glad, if Larry had managed to survive, to re-employ him, kindly overlooking the inconvenience he had caused them. What a comfort and economy to realize that beggars may not be choosers!

"Times are hard, I know," Mr. Banning repeated. He had the stoicism to do what must be done—the alternative to nothing—however drily and badly. "The arrangements had better be as simple as possible—"

Knowing well enough that Bert would pay for them, if he could, only with the greatest difficulty, he was searching for some way not too arrogantly patronizing—

"I've got a little money saved," Bert said.

This miserable business simply could not go on, and Mr. Banning said, "Bert, Larry has been with us a good many years. I don't like to feel that we can't have any share in this. If you'd care to trust the arrangements to me, I'd like to be able to express in some tangible way our grief. I know, of course, in a matter like this, that you yourself would want to—"

Bert looked up at him quickly, brief and shamefaced. "Well, the truth is, Mr. Banning, I really haven't any money. I mean, I have about forty-one dollars in the savings bank. I would certainly be glad to use that; but I guess it wouldn't go far. I know it seems kind of— Well, Mr. Banning, it's mighty kind of you—"

Anton Yedinak, it could be seen, was also impressed by Mr. Banning's goodness. He nodded his head several times with what might have been spiritual applause. He looked into his whisky glass with a kind of holy joy at man's humanity to man.

[273]

3

By nine o'clock Saturday morning, parked cars lined all the irregular open triangle surrounding the broken and empty horse trough behind the station. They were backed in side by side, a tight rank along the platforms. End to end, they stretched in shabby procession to the apex, and then out the short street between Upjohns' store and the Hall to the boundaries of the green. The open space was filled with the violent bright sunlight of a windy morning in the hills. Into Upjohns' Hall, a straggling constant stream of people moved unhurried through the double doors left open.

The sunlight, in a strong shaft following them, reached part of the way down the central aisle between approximately straight rows of Howard's light, folding chairs. This glow on the floor brought out a gloom in the rest of the big room. The neutral light from the high, narrow side windows fell soberly on standing groups of men, on circles of neighbors and relatives seated and turning to talk across the rows. The mixed chatter of a hundred voices in twenty small conversations rose now to a general unintelligible babble; sank next, letting single speakers, often women, come out clearly for a phrase or two—protest, prophecy, instruction.

"I hear he . . ."

". . . tried six times to get him. Mrs. Vogel told me . . ."

"Now, I got nothing against George. Don't misunderstand me. But . . ."

"Yes, and what's that going to get us? Answer me that . . ."

"I know both my boys are sick, and that's plenty for me to know . . ."

"Just the same, I can tell you . . ."

An outbreak of bold laughter brought a partial silence, for every one, however confused or at odds, was serious. The indignant turning of a few heads found that it was Robert Newell, coming down the aisle with a hard tread of riding boots. His callous, full-blooded face twitched with amusement at something Charles Ordway had said. Arrogantly, white teeth gleaming under his cropped mustache, gloved fists put into his breeches pockets, Robert Newell noticed the pause, appraised it with frank contemptuous pleasure. Mr. Ordway was embarrassed. Either he had not meant to be humorous or had not meant to have any one know that he was.

Mrs. Bates, seated, called sharply to him: "You seem greatly entertained, Charles. How's Molly this morning?"

Robert Newell was out of her range, striding toward the most important of the standing groups, gathered at the end of the narrow platform around Matthew Herring in his black overcoat and Walter Bates. Mrs. Bates and Mrs. Vogel beside her, and Mrs. Jackson, contentedly between Mrs. Vogel and Mrs. Ely, all stared after him. Mrs. Jackson said, "He don't seem very considerate—"

Malcolm's being sick was a high price, but

maybe it was worth it; for Mrs. Vogel, instead of accepting her remark in silence, answered: "I could tell you things about him, Helen. You'd hardly believe his brass walking in here in front of decent people that way——"

Mrs. Vogel would tell her, too, as soon as they had reasonable privacy. You might think that she and Mrs. Ely had needed to know the results of some such test. When Malcolm could come down with typhoid, as Mrs. Vogel's boys and Mrs. Ely's brother had, it would seem that, though from Bayonne, New Jersey, the Jacksons had indeed eyes, hands, organs, dimensions, senses, affections, passions; and so all contact with them need not end after the half-furtive purchase of Gosselin Brothers' cut-price groceries.

If Mrs. Jackson had thought at first that she had as good a right to test and weigh Mrs. Vogel and Mrs. Ely, loneliness had tempered that presumption. It was hard to live, month in and month out, with only your good rights to comfort you. Given some inkling of the social state, Mrs. Jackson was content, too, to be set down a little lower than she first liked. She would not risk offending her two friends by any vain attempt at the more considerable conquest of Mrs. Bates. It was better the way it was, for Mrs. Bates simply wouldn't have her; yet, once sure that Mrs. Jackson was not going to mistake her subtle place, Mrs. Bates was perfectly cordial and civil. All was at last harmony.

"When I was a girl in Bayonne," Mrs. Jackson said, "there used to be a man who lived right across the street from us who——"

Mrs. Vogel had turned her bright sharp gaze on

her, and lowering her voice, Mrs. Jackson went easily on about that scandalous man and those fascinating days.

Against the plain door jamb and the white clap-boards of the adjoining wall, Harry Weems stood in the windy sunlight, bareheaded, a cigarette cupped in a hand red-knuckled with cold. He said: "Been to see Joe?"

May stepped aside to let the people behind her pass. "I was just there."

"How is he?"

"They're always better in the morning a nurse told me. He feels pretty sick; but, I mean, he knows things. He said to me right away: 'Look at that.' He began moving his hand on the bed. Harry, it's true! They don't know what did it, but something did. He's all over that. The nurse says the muscles are too weak for him to move it much; but he does move it. He feels things in it, I mean. He—"

"For gosh sakes! Say, when did this happen?"

"Oh, I forgot you didn't know. Doc Bull told me last night. I mean, and Doctor Verney thinks so, too, he said. Oh, Harry, it's awful! I feel so happy and everybody—"

"Hey, hey! Hang onto it!" He took her arm, drawing her farther aside. She got a crumpled handkerchief from her coat pocket. "I know," she said. "Isn't it crazy—"

"Not so you'd notice it! Gosh, May, you'll never know how much of a relief it would be to me—" He regarded her with an intent, red-faced awkwardness as bad as her own. None of the phrases he wanted would come to him; for all easy, ordinary conversation dealt with things which might be worse; or were not so bad; or were pretty good.

"Yes, I know, Harry," she said. "All you've done—I know he's going to be all right. I didn't get off the switchboard until twelve last night, so I couldn't see. I would have told you, but honestly, I was afraid to. I mean, it's so silly, but I hadn't seen myself and I thought, if there were any mistake. I mean, I even thought it might be sort of bad luck—I wasn't supposed to see him this morning, but I told the nurse—"

Behind her, Henry Harris's warm, inevitably sardonic voice said: "You let me talk to Harry just a minute, will you, May?"

"See you later," Harry told her. "I want to go and see him as soon as they'll let me. Maybe we could when we get out of here—"

"All right," she said, confusedly glad that he had got this artless relief, and that, next meeting, they could both take it for granted, with no need to find any right words.

Inside, she took the first empty seat. The man next to her said, "Good morning, Mrs. Tupping."

Relieved, she saw that it was Mr. Kean, the Congregational minister. "Good morning," she answered. "It seems so dark in here after standing in the sun. I didn't see you."

Mr. Kean was not a native of New Winton, and she was under no obligation to tell him about Joe; to let him see, with everyone so worried and unhappy, her own indecent jubilation. He said at once: "How's your husband?" But she could an-

[278]

swer adequately: "He seems to be better, thank you."

Down in front Walter Bates had mounted the platform. Seating himself, he got the old mallet he used for a gavel from the drawer in the small table. Hitting with it several times, he called: "Harry! Harry Weems! Will you please close those doors?"

*

"Land sakes, George! Why don't you tell me when you're going to be away all night?"

"Didn't know I was."

"Well, have you had breakfast?"

"I have."

"Where were you? I didn't hear your car come in."

"Had a little tire trouble."

"George, what's wrong with you? You act so funny."

"I'm probably going to kill somebody when I find him. Nothing unusual about that, is there?"

"My goodness, I believe you're crazy!"

"If I find the skunk who slashed four tires on my car last night, it'll be some time before he's able to do it again. Now I think of it, Joel goes around that way sometimes. Well, we'll see."

"George, you're too old a man to go getting in fights. Sakes alive, what kind of a way to talk is that? Where was your car, that any one could go doing things to tires?"

"Up in Cardmaker's barnyard."

"Now, George, I've kept silent a long time;

and it's not for me to tell a grown man what he ought to know. But I never heard of good coming from wickedness—well, I won't say more; but it seems like it might be a lesson to you. Now, I guess you could drink some hot coffee, couldn't you?"

"Never mind the coffee. They're having some kind of meeting over at Upjohns' and I'd like to look in on it."

"Now, George, I know all about that, and it's no place for you. You'd just go losing your temper and saying things. That little Baxter girl came around here this morning, and said her father wouldn't let her work here any more. Seems some people think you let all this sickness happen, and that meeting's going to be to blame you. Now, I wouldn't encourage those who feel as mean and full of malice as that by paying any attention to them. I'd just go about my business and let them talk. If you go down and start a fight with them—"

"Huh! You mean to say Jim Baxter's feeling so holy he's refusing money he doesn't even have to work for?"

"Well, that's what the little girl said. Her name's Mabel, and she's very neat and willing. Not like Susie. I'm sure I'm sorry. Well, you go along now. I've got all the work to do myself this morning and I won't have any time to waste. Tomorrow I'll try to find somebody. Where do you think you'll be in case anybody calls?"

"I'll probably be down at the Evarts place before the morning's over."

"Well, now, someone from Torrington called you up. A Doctor Moses. I told them to ring down there."

"Sure. He's going to be the new doctor around here, I daresay."

"Well, he's a very polite and pleasant man."

"That's right. He'd better be."

*

Eric Cadbury spoke emphatically, with short, undramatic gestures. Informally at ease, he paused sometimes, murmured a question to Matthew Herring—even questioned the answer and got another—while nobody showed impatience.

This audience liked him for not being too glib in a serious matter. What he said seemed all the more reliable when he took the trouble to ask questions, consult papers; without confusion, to stop and correct himself. His short, stocky figure; his clothes, while whole and respectable, not good or new; his expression of absorbed gravity in the task of saying what he meant; kept out any hint of oratory—professional talking for effect to a crowd. Nothing Eric Cadbury said, and no phrase he used to say it, would have sounded absurd if he had been talking only to one man.

Having heard it all before—the investigation of the camp; the latrines; the drainage; Doctor Bull's statements; the laboratory reports—Walter Bates did not really listen to it. That was the way it was. Really, it was kind of a miracle. Of course, it was wonderful that science knew so much, and what it knew certainly ought to be used. Another time, they would know that it wasn't safe to put a camp up there. Yet, in one way, whether they knew it or not hardly mattered now; last summer was the time to know it. Not likely there'd ever again be occasion for such a camp. As Mr. Banning had implied, unless you wanted blood, it seemed sort of futile at this point. Matthew was probably going to have his way, and plenty of people, like Emma, would think that was fine. As far as his wife went, Walter realized that she had her heart in it. Something—but what?—would be better if, squaring matters for Geraldine's being sick, they made life pretty hard for Doc Bull. The Bannings, he saw, hadn't come; and Walter Bates wished that he had been able not to come himself.

Seated in the chair, his elbow on the small table, Walter Bates acted as though he were listening, but he kept his anxious bright eyes busy on individual faces in the two hundred odd visible to him. He had the perceptions of long experience with these same people. Years of presiding meekly over the stubborn deadlocking of the clever and resolute gave him insight and that special knowledge of character gained from disinterestedly watching men quarreling about what they wanted. Most of them had become perfectly transparent to him.

Looking at Charles Ordway, he could see that Charley was being adroit. Fundamentally a simple person, he had learned in Hartford that safety lay in listening. There had been a time when he was argumentative, imagining that politics required talk. Now he shunned like death the loud exchange of gratuitous opinions. Observation or experience had taught him that no positive statement could ever be so innocent that, somewhere, it would not give offense. Only a few people—and those not important—might resent

[282]

and remember; but the multitudinous roots of a political career were planted far and wide in popular good will. One root nipped was nothing; even a hundred hardly mattered; but if he just kept talking, good easy man, Hartford would suddenly see him no more. In this business here, Charles Ordway probably had nothing to lose by being against Doctor Bull; but since it had not been demonstrated that he would gain anything, it was better to sit in amiable grave vacancy until a secret ballot gave him expression. When the majority had been determined, it would be time enough to announce that he was with it. Walter Bates did not condemn him. Considering his own life, he saw in it nothing very brave or noble, either. After all, Charley's motives were not malicious. He didn't want to hurt anybody—not even himself.

There were other faces in this blankness of waiting. Some of them, like Howard Upjohn's, showed a distinctive earnest naïveté. Honestly attending, Howard thought that if he listened, he would learn. He wore his funeral expression, reverent but watchful; yet he was his own man and would vote as it seemed to him that he ought. The truth was that any one could convince him, with a little talk, that anything was right: but the formality would have to be gone through with, and it was a delicate one. The first person to make a point which Howard would not have thought of himself, a point whose logic and aptness came to him with the dazzle of unexpected or disregarded evidence, would also make a convert. Eric Cadbury hadn't managed it; perhaps, because he did not seem to be trying to, and Howard was still waiting, not missing a word, lest it be the one he wanted. It was apparent that Eric Cadbury was not going to try. He said: "I guess I've said my say, Walter. I hope that covers the facts."

He sat down without ceremony and Walter Bates struck lightly with the mallet.

"Mr. Chairman."

"Mr. Herring."

Matthew Herring had the advantage of being six or seven inches taller than Eric Cadbury. Since mounting the platform would be considered a suspicious affectation, height had its value in demanding attention on the floor. Turning from the chair, Matthew Herring's composed, parchment-colored face was visible to every one. He said: "You heard Eric Cadbury's summing up of the facts. The question, as I think you all agree, is whether or not these facts, stated without comment or prejudice, constitute just grounds for requesting the resignation of the Health Officer; and, in event of failing to get that, for demanding that the County Health Officer remove him. I need hardly say that in my opinion, they do."

He paused, deliberately and calmly looking around the hall. "I see that Doctor Bull does not consider this meeting of sufficient importance to warrant attendance. Since he has chosen to absent himself, it is necessary to conclude that there is nothing he cares to say in defense or explanation. Perhaps, however, that is just as well. I cannot conceive of an interpretation of facts like these which would in any way improve his position.

"Now it may be objected that Doctor Bull has not shown any wrong intent, or tried in any way to profit personally or irregularly through his office; and that a difference of opinion may therefore fairly exist on whether or not his negligence is actually criminal. This is a matter for the Grand Jury to determine; and the facts will be brought to their attention.

"What we have to determine is whether or not a man in Doctor Bull's responsible position can possibly be blameless in fact, whatever technicalities protect him in law, when he has admittedly neglected his duties. The disastrous results of this neglect, in illness, distress, and death, make the question not altogether academic. Nor is there anything in Doctor Bull's past behavior to suggest that this was the single oversight in a long career of faithful attention to the public welfare. On the contrary! What zeal he has shown seems usually to have been by way of annoying individuals with whom he was not on good terms. Aside from such episodes, I think the general experience is that he has never been known to trouble to perform any duties which he found even slightly inconvenient. A similar carelessness and neglect has distinguished his work in connection with the School Committee. I think that examples of it are known to you all.

"Putting it as mildly as possible, I do not think that Doctor Bull has shown himself to be a careful and conscientious official. I do not think that his personal attitude has ever been one of devotion to his profession, or to the well-being of the people it commits to his charge. Walter, I think we might open the matter to general discussion. I suggest—I move, in fact—that such discussion be limited to two minutes for each speaker, if there are speakers."

"You've heard Mr. Herring's motion. All in favor— Matthew," Walter Bates interposed, "could I trouble you to lend me your watch? Mine doesn't seem to be going—contrary minded—" He took the watch, laid it before him, and raised the mallet.

"No!" said Robert Newell loudly. "I move we limit all discussions to one minute!" He lowered his voice very little, saying ostensibly to James Clark beside him, "Be here the rest of the morning listening to these damn windbags."

"I think the ayes already have it, Robert," Walter Bates said. "Your motion wasn't in order, so I won't put it to vote. All right. Do I hear—"

"My God!" groaned Robert Newell. "Old man Slade in person!" He took out his own watch.

"Mr. Chairman; People of New Winton—" Old man Slade's voice had a quality harsh and querulous. "You'd think he wasn't real," Robert Newell told Mr. Clark. "He ought to be stuffed and put in the library with that skunk Harry Weems gave them."

Mr. Slade clamped his mouth shut, his short gray beard wagging on his gnarled chin. "As I was saying," he resumed viciously, looking at the back of Robert Newell's head, "I think Mr. Herring left out one thing that has a lot of bearing. This town's always been a decent town and stood for decent living and morals. I think George Bull's been a blot on it long enough. He's an immoral, godless—"

"Hey, two minutes up, Walter!" Robert Newell raised his watch.

"I ain't going to stop until I finish," Mr. Slade said. "I ain't had anything like two minutes. Newell's had 'bout minute and a half."

"Please don't interrupt, Robert. You just make it longer."

"Now, those of us who've got sons and daughters growing up into Christian men and women—" a low, sardonic whistle, which might have been Grant Williams, and could have been read to the effect that Mr. Slade didn't know as much about his own daughter's growing up as he might have, rose and fell away, but Mr. Slade decided to ignore it—"well, what sort of an impression do their growing minds get when they see a man in Doc Bull's position doing the things he's well-known to do? I ain't afraid to name names. Let him and Miss Cardmaker—"

From the back, Harry Weems called: "Ah, leave your names out of it, Slade. Tell us what you know, not what you think."

"I know, young fellow—" Mr. Slade said, turning about.

"If he don't," called Joel Parry, "I do. Ask Doc Bull where his car was last night. Ask him where his car has been plenty of nights before! I see Belle Rogers over there. Ask her what—"

Walter Bates began banging with the mallet. "Order!" he said. "Order! Sit down, Mr. Parry. You can't have the floor until you're properly recognized." He went on banging against the mounting uproar. "I want to say," he shouted as loud as he could, "that as chairman of this meeting, I think Mr. Herring left out what he did for good reasons. We aren't considering any private affairs of Doctor Bull's. I'm going to treat

[287]

any more discussion of them as out of order. Mr. Slade, your time is up. Do I hear any one address the chair?"

"Yes, you hear me, Walter," his wife said, standing up. "I don't believe you have any right to limit discussions just because you don't like them; but never mind that. I've been talking to Mrs. Ordway and Mrs. Vogel, and I think I can say I'm speaking for the mothers of—"

"Oh, God!" Robert Newell groaned.

"Don't you interrupt me, Robert Newell! There's plenty that could be said about you, too. You just keep quiet! Those of us who have children sick at home due to Doctor Bull's ignorant incompetence aren't interested in your scoffing. You ought to be ashamed of yourself! New Winton ought to be just as ashamed of having you for a Selectman as having Doctor Bull for a doctor. We're good and tired of the one; you look out we don't get tired of the other—if we're not already, as I am. Now, I think we ought to take a vote, and never mind about all this speechmaking. There's no reason to mix everybody up." She sat down.

Walter Bates said: "Do I hear any others?"

John Ely, arising, said: "Mr. Chairman, I think there's another thing ought to be gone into—" He had to pause while continued conversation made it impossible to hear him; and he might have sat down, but Mrs. Ely gave him several sharp confirming nods. "Mr. Chairman—"

Walter Bates hammered again. "Mr. Ely has the floor! Please come to order—"

"I just wanted to say," Mr. Ely continued, his startled pale blue eyes turning in his whitish face,

"I think another thing we ought to know about is Mrs. Talbot's being sent away. We all know Mary Talbot; known her since she was that high. When was she ever crazy? How did they get to send her away when her own cousin, Mrs. Darrow, and Clarence Upjohn will bear me out because he and Doctor Bull had a set-to about it, said herself she didn't really think she was anything but kind of upset. Now, it looks funny to some of us. First there's Mamie dying; and I guess everybody knows Doc Bull never came near her the whole day. I guess you might say he just let her die. Not three weeks later, he finds a way to get rid of Mary Talbot. She won't be around reproaching him for killing her daughter. She won't—"

"Ah," said Robert Newell, "be your age, John!"

Mrs. Bates shrilled out. "You stay out of this! Everybody knows you don't care anything about this town's welfare—don't you hit that hammer at me, Walter, when you let him keep making his smart remarks! We have our own opinions about Mamie's death, and what happened to her mother. Any man who can treat a woman the way Robert Newell is well known to treat Alice wouldn't be expected to mind seeing another woman put in the asylum for life—"

The uproar regained its volume instantly. Whether they had come for this or not, it was only human to be gratified by so rich a type of the entertainment any town meeting under Walter Bates was always on the verge of presenting. In this case, while it would be generally felt that Emma Bates over-reached herself and had no right to make Alice Newell's probably hard and unhappy life a matter of what amounted to public record, still it was a show of gumption; you couldn't walk all over Emma Bates and get away with it!

Perfectly recognizing the complications to be expected in heating up some such side issue, Matthew Herring got to his feet, stood looking about the hall patiently.

"Mr. Chairman," he said when he could, "I think Mrs. Bates's first suggestion, that we ought to proceed with a vote, was sensible. I think the details of Doctor Bull's behavior are familiar, and his attitude well enough understood—"

"What do you mean, Matthew?" said Henry Harris. "Do you mean that you believe that Doc Bull put Mrs. Talbot in the asylum to shut her up? If you don't mean that, better say so. People might think you did."

"In answer to Mr. Harris's interruption, I'll say that I don't mean that. That seems to be the opinion of Mr. Ely and some others; but those who hold it ought to know that Doctor Bull did not and could not act alone in such a matter. Sympathy, which I am sure every one feels for Mrs. Talbot's misfortunes, is one thing; the assumption that Doctor Bull would behave so improperly is another, and I think, not justified. I will now ask the chairman to read to the meeting a resolution which will be offered for your adoption. In event of its being satisfactory to you, it will be forwarded to the proper—"

He stopped, for one of the double doors at the back had been thrown open, admitting a long shaft of brilliant cold sunlight. There was a universal quick turning, a prompt amazing dead silence. At the back, the people standing parted; the door went banging shut, and George Bull came down the aisle. He had reached the center of the hall, with no one moving and no one saying anything.

In this hush, Henry Harris's voice arose abruptly, distinct and cheerful. "Well, George," he said, "late again!"

George Bull stood still. "Somebody knows why I'm late," he said. "Who cut the tires on my car last night? He's here, all right. Is he man enough to stand up and say he did it? Well! I'm waiting!"

"Yeah," cried a voice, suddenly revived, "and where was your car when he cut 'em? You've been chasing around here long enough——"

"I'll take care of my business. I'll take care of where I go and what I do. Who doesn't like it?"

There was a stir now of general recovery, and, jumping to answer the challenge, a low growling murmur. "What are you going to do, George? Lick the whole town?" Robert Newell had faced about in his chair, grinning.

"Mr. Chairman," Matthew Herring said, "I think Doctor Bull is out of order."

"Sit down, Herring! First thing you know, you'll be out of order for a month."

"I have the floor at present, Doctor. I suggest that you sit down until you're recognized by the chair——"

"Do you want me to come and sit you down?"

Matthew Herring looked at him, unmoved. "You don't impress me with your threats, Doctor Bull. If you have anything to say, we are ready to listen to it; but I would advise you not to begin by attempting to bully the meeting. We have been patient for a long time; but I think the moment for a reckoning has finally come. You won't help yourself by—"

"So that's how you stand, is it? All right, Walter. Let me have this floor he's so worried about, and I'll tell you how I stand. I don't know who's doing all this grunting and groaning I hear, but let 'em keep still—" The murmur rose louder and he roared out: "I came here to try to make you half-wits see sense. Are you going to let me try or aren't you?"

"Throw him out!"

"Well, well, Joel!" He wheeled about. "I'll be seeing you afterwards. Unless you think you'd better start running now—"

Walter Bates began to hammer again on the table, but the hubbub had risen beyond that. The roar had a sharp edge, angry, chattering, a score of voices shouting their separate answers together. "So you don't want to hear, huh? Well, you'll hear this, you jabbering baboons! I can shout louder than the lot of you!" George Bull's tremendous voice went up in thunder; and he was right, he could. "What I have to say to you is, you and Mat Herring's meeting can go to blazes. I'll see you all in hell before I'll oblige you by resigning! If you can get me out, if you have any case, and the sense to handle it, why, God damn you, do it!"

Turning, he went down the aisle, with people recoiling before him, people, outraged, yelling after him. At the closed door, he put a hand on Grant Williams's shoulder, spun him aside. The sunlight poured dazzling in, his great shadow dropped down the aisle, and he cut it off, closing the door behind him so that all the windows shook.

FOUR

Henry Harris, standing up, said: "A man who
loses his temper in a matter like this never makes
a very favorable impression. Instead of helping,
he hurts himself. When he cusses out his listeners,
they resent it. They get all hot and start shouting
back, and there you are. It's a pity."

He paused, letting his gaze move about. "Putting all that down for the *Times*, Miss Kimball?"
he asked. "I hope you mention my name." He
grinned at her a moment, and raising his voice a
little, clear and sharp, said: "I've heard tell that
they who draw the sword, shall perish by the
sword. That means it's a risky thing to start a
fight, because, once fighting's in the air, you can't
tell where it'll stop. No, sir! Anything might happen. Well, I'll have to say what's on my mind anyway. Suppose Doc Bull's not perfect? Who is?
Well, I don't want to start an argument now,
Matthew, so I'll say I guess you're pretty near
perfect. And Herbert Banning's perfect, of
course. I'm not denying it. But you two aside,
most of us just do the best we can, and usually it's
not so good.

"You saw George Bull go out of here pretty mad. A lot of enthusiasts yelled him down. They don't want him to get a hearing. Those who are setting them on may be scared that, if they could hear George, they might get mixed up and think he wasn't so bad after all—

"You've heard people tell you he ought to have done this. He ought to have done that. Sure, he should. Sure, we all should have done God knows how many things we never did do. I can see now that I ought never to have let that camp site to the Interstate Company without making sure about the drainage first. I didn't bother. All I wanted was the rent money. Now, let me ask you, which one of you knows all about the drainage of any piece of land he might own back in the hills? Which one of you gives a damn? Which one of you wouldn't try to realize some money on it first chance he got without fooling around trying to make all kinds of crazy investigations?"

A voice called out, "We ain't blaming you, Henry. You can sit down now."

"Now, let me say my say, if you will. I'm going to sit down in a minute. Who here thinks when he goes to get a drink whether the water with which he's filling a glass from the faucet is pure water? He ought to know by this time that the only way to be sure is boil it. Does he take that ordinary common-sense precaution? He does not. He thinks it's probably all right the way it is; it always has been all right. Well, what do you suppose Doc Bull thought about the reservoir? He hadn't seen any reason to worry. Who had? Who didn't know that there was this construction camp up there? Who worried about that? Who cared?

"Most every one with any sense realizes that living from day to day is taking a pretty big chance. I was thinking about that this morning. A while ago, I invested a hundred and fifty dollars in a little proposition which looked fool-proof to me. I didn't see how I could lose. Well, I find now that I'm just out that money. I didn't see any reason to worry, but it so happens that my agent in the matter took sick at the critical moment. It's hard luck, but will I get anywhere by raising a howl? I took my chance on that, even if at the time I didn't happen to reflect that I was taking such a chance. I don't know what you think of a person who is willing to take a chance, hoping he'll win or be all right; yet, when he finds he's lost, lies down and yells. I know what I think of him—

"Are things bad enough, or aren't they? Seems to me with the Evarts place full of patients, and Doc Bull working his head off for the sick, we could shut up about who's to blame and help him. If we can't, it must be because somebody won't let us. Who won't let us? Well, I hate to suggest what I haven't documentary proof of— there's been quite a little of that so far this morning and we don't need any more—but this I know. Banning—or Mrs. Banning; she wears that pair of pants—has been working for a long time to get Doc Bull. They don't think he's cultured enough; he can't be, when he don't appreciate that they're worth ten times as much worry and care as plain ordinary people. Maybe the idea of the Bannings not getting enough respect makes you mad, but before you try to fix it for them, you ought to reflect some."

In one sense, Henry Harris had been talking against time, holding the floor to prevent the interruption of a process of reaction begun the minute the door slammed after Doctor Bull. The effect was a good deal like going out with a light gun to hunt a rabbit, and suddenly turning up a bear. The fact that the bear retired couldn't altogether erase the first ringing shock of the face to face encounter. The more you reflected, the nearer supper time it seemed, the less advisable to hunt further here today. A certain withdrawal would go on all around the obstinate and courageous few who meant to have some skin, whether bear or rabbit, on the barn door.

Henry Harris could feel the warm slow spread inside him of the amusement which generally blossomed in his matchless mocking smile. He did not smile now. He went on: "I say to you, for near forty years Doc Bull has had the health of this town, the life and death of the people in it, in his charge. For that matter, I wonder just how many people in this room came out of their mother's wombs with Doc Bull standing by. Winter and summer he's been on the job without a break. He's spent practically his whole life working to relieve the bodily ailments of our people. Some paid him and some didn't, but he never worried over that. Now, what about it?"

He held up a paper. "Those hostile to him have been telling you how everybody knew this, and this was generally understood, and in their opinion, it would certainly seem—I guess you recognize it. It's the way people talk when they don't happen to have the facts, or maybe have them, and find they won't do. Well, here they are. Here are the figures they weren't so anxious to give you. In the vital statistics of this state, over a period of twenty years, the death rate per thousand in New Winton has never in any year ranked poorer than tenth lowest, out of one hundred and sixty-nine Connecticut towns listed. That means that you could name at least one hundred and fifty-nine places in this state every year for the last twenty years where life and health was less secure than here. One year could be an accident, but twenty consecutive years? How'll you square that with Doc Bull being as bad a doctor and as careless of public health as I've heard some tell you he is? This is a letter from the State Health Department, Matthew. Maybe you'd like to make sure it isn't a forgery. Maybe you'd like a copy of it for your newspaper piece, Miss Kimball."

His quick glance showed him at once that he had scored. He could see Howard Upjohn's face, surprised and gratified. Mrs. Vogel and Mrs. Ely exchanged glances; Emma Bates had a blank, jolted expression. He went on: "That's what I thought you ought to know. That's the record behind the present emergency. To my mind, right feeling, human justice, are against kicking a man down through no demonstrable fault of his; and the simple, plain, printed facts nobody can laugh off don't give much of a foothold to those who like logic better than sentiment. In fact about everything seems to be against what you're asked to do.

"I can speak my mind, because I happen to be in the minority party—or what has been the minority; next fall the people of this town may decide different. I don't have to toe any line, or keep in right with any one. So I'll say I think this is nothing but a political plot, engineered to work off a well-known grudge, by certain parties who've always tried to hold control of this town and run it to suit themselves. I'll speak plainer. I see Mr. Banning isn't present. I don't blame him. Why should he come and do his own dirty work when plenty of people just jump at the chance to associate themselves with him by doing it for him—yes, Miss Kimball, I guess you're one of them; but let me finish. Those of you who think that money and influence aren't everything in this world; those of you who believe in fair play and the right of a man to be given the facts, and from them, freely to decide what's right and do it, probably won't feel so anxious to fall in line. Mine's one name will never be on their petition of town officers. I hope no friend of mine has a vote for them. I'm through."

From the anonymous rear a voice or two cried, "That's telling them, Henry!" But in the hesitant silence, Matthew Herring, erecting his tall figure above the seated rows, said: "Mr. Chairman! Now that Mr. Harris seems to have finished his misrepresentations, may I suggest that we proceed with the business of the meeting. I don't think there's any need to waste time pointing out to intelligent people the irrelevance of such points as Mr. Harris could be said to have made. His interpretation of the vital statistics won't stand up a moment when you recall that this has always been a prosperous and isolated agricultural community in one of the healthiest sections of the state. No one here has denied that it is hu-

[298]

man to make mistakes; Mr. Harris appears to feel that it is also divine and ought to be encouraged. His attack on a person not present, and on the motives of those who are, can only be called contemptible and, I am sure, has been recognized as only that. May we get on, Mr. Chairman?"

"Yes, I guess so," Walter Bates said. He hit the table with the mallet. "Please don't make so much noise back there. Now the proposition, I mean, the resolution offered is—I got it written down here somewhere. Just a moment—"

This small inadvertency—Walter Bates's flustered search for his paper—was plainly fatal.

"Ah!" said Robert Newell. There was a hard click of his boot heels striking the floor as he stood up, and he stopped, staring about him, for he could feel the crowded hall in psychological crisis. He had meant only to say that he was going home, but aware now of the delicate balance, his violent, destructive instinct was to bring it down. He shouted again, "Ah, to hell with it! Never mind that paper! We know who wrote it! This meeting's been nothing but a lot of foolishness and a waste of busy men's time. Harris said the things most of us probably believe—"

A quick mounting roar, which might be protest, but which had an indubitable note of cheering made him pause.

"Mr. Chairman!" came Matthew Herring's voice, edged and distinct.

Walter Bates lifted his mallet, but Robert Newell put a foot on the chair seat, stood on it, rising that much higher than Herring. He shouted: "If you ask me, I think Doc Bull's all right, and I know more about it than some. During the average summer, he probably is up to my camp a dozen times. He's never killed anybody yet. I've never seen a guest who wasn't satisfied with the treatment given him. Now, let's adjourn and get out of here. We don't want any resolution; we aren't going to sign anything——"

Mrs. Bates had got up, livid in an inarticulate fury. "Just let every one who feels that way go," she said. "I believe there are enough decent and responsible people here to——"

"Sure," agreed Newell, "let the hens stay and scratch until they're tired! Good place for 'em. Who's chairman here, Walter, you or your wife? How long is this gang of yowling females going to run this town, anyway?"

In the back they were shouting, delighted, "Move we adjourn. Second it! Hell, I third it! You can't do that. Sure I can, I just did——"

Harry Weems cupped his hands and yelled, "Say, how about a vote of confidence in Doc Bull? All in favor——"

Miss Kimball, standing up, cried, "Shame! Shame!——" The stir and confusion of voices drowned them both out; so Harry called, "All right, let's go!" Some one opened the doors, and they began to move.

"Will every one please take his seat?" began Matthew Herring, but it was plain that very few were going to. "Let them go," Miss Kimball said. "They won't think so well of themselves when they see it in print. That much I'm sure of——"

"You don't mean to tell me," said Henry Harris, "that the *Times* would print it all?"

"I certainly do, and——"

Over the disordered front rows, over empty chairs, Matthew Herring said, "Henry, you're quite a speaker! You've beaten me. But I don't think you can beat truth and decency. Not every time, at any rate."

"Why, Matthew," Henry Harris answered, turning his delighted grin from Miss Kimball and her notebook. "I never have any quarrel with intangibles."

Unhurried, he went out, crossed slowly over to the station and stepped into a telephone booth. When his dropped coin got him Doris Clark, he said, "Doris, I want Sansbury one-six-two."

Smiling, leaning against the closed door, he reflected that matters could have been worse. Of course, it was too bad that Lester had to get sick and as he'd said—he grinned again, relishing the circumstances of his saying it—he'd never see his hundred and fifty dollars again; but after all, Matthew Herring couldn't have been any madder, or in any less doubt about who cooked his goose.

"Hello," he said. "Sansbury *Times?* Mr. Marden in? Yes. Oh, Marden. Harris. Listen, will you do me a favor? No, you don't. You don't have to do anything; I'm just asking if you will. I think it would be a good idea to kill the New Winton correspondent's story this week. Well, we've had a kind of hot town meeting, and she hasn't much judgment. No sense in spreading our troubles all over the state. Sure, that's all. No, after that, it'll be all right. She knows her business when she doesn't get excited. Fine. Much obliged. I'll do something for you sometime."

Emerging, he crossed the open space, saluting

with a casual lift of hand various drivers of cars starting and backing. Reaching Gosselin Brothers' store, he went in. "Give me a dozen of those big Florida oranges you have that poetry about pasted on the front window," he said. "It is poetry, isn't it? I tell you what, put them in a bag and send them down to the Evarts place for Mr. Dunn, will you?"

*

Bending down, Mr. Banning brushed the thin crust of mud from the wooden tag, read the words: *Mevrouw Van Gendt*. Remembering at once the long pointed buds, the flowers in salmon shading out of yellow and pink, he applied his pruning shears. That was the last of the four beds, leaving him only the narrow strip of old-fashioned remontants in a curve beyond the sundial—*General McArthur, Jonkheer Mock, Mrs. John Laing.* They were varieties his mother had favored for a rose jar—he could even remember the jar, three quarters full of curled petals in a pungent, arrested decay. It was hard to think of anything more useless.

Straightening up, he pulled off his loose yellow horsehide gloves, laid them with the pruning shears on the sundial while he looked at his watch. It was half-past ten, and, refilling his pipe slowly, he wondered how the town meeting was getting on. He meant, more particularly, how his absence and Lucile's would be interpreted, supposing it was noticed at all in the excitement.

The truth was that he couldn't quite make up his mind, which always proved a great help in taking the easier course. Not regarding the business with any warm approval, he none the less wouldn't object to Matthew's success. The resulting picture of himself didn't please him. It had a complacently passive quality. When other men had got the unpleasantness over, he would be content to join them in what resulting profit there was. The one frank and correct course would probably be for him to oppose the whole scheme; not vaguely and half-heartedly in private, but publicly: *"I do not think any good or just purpose will be served—"*

That was, of course, impossible. Lucile would consider it too outrageous of him. If she thought about them at all, she probably made some distinctively feminine allowance for opinions he might express which were not hers. She didn't mind if it amused him to say what no one expected him to in casual conversation; but when it came to matters she considered serious, she would see it as a wanton betrayal of things which she couldn't help believing they both stood for. Matthew would naturally see it the same way; he would be deeply astonished, unable or perhaps unwilling to explain so irresponsible an attitude.

Sighing unconsciously, he roused himself, struck a match and laid the flame to the packed tobacco. A thick privet hedge sheltered him from the north wind and it was almost warm. He could feel the vehemence of the March sun on the turf, the spaced rose beds, the flagged path; he could even feel it through the suède jacket on his back, and it cheered him with the promise of an eventual peaceful summer, all this business somehow settled and largely forgotten. Taking up the

[303]

shears and his gloves, he uncovered the swash letter script encircling the old dial plate: *It is later than you think.*

He was reminded again of his mother, who had placed the sundial and done, by fits and starts, a little general flower-growing around it. The inscription had, to her, he knew, a religious value. You were to think how little time remained to prepare to face your Maker, not how little time remained in which to be happy. Of course, having thought of it, that was enough. She would not expect that any person in her garden would be in the vulgar need of reforming his life. Gentlefolk meeting had no reason to exchange admonitions: Do not commit adultery. Do not kill. Do not steal. Do not bear false witness. Defraud not. Honor thy father and mother. Propriety would take ample care of the commandments. Manners and morals all fitted together, all made for the placid positiveness with which his mother accepted life.

So sure of it all, she was much less devoted to church work than Lucile. Her religious relationship was to God, not to the Rector. Only a very rude person would suggest it, but the Church, in its sense of the Episcopal parishes, undoubtedly meant more to Lucile than religion did. She thought of the Church with a comfortable sense of its formal beauty and dignity. In this particular fellowship in Christ, all was easy; the people everywhere would be approximately her own kind; their attitudes and interests would be comprehensible to her and in keeping with an ecclesiastical tradition of means, breeding, and education.

That was all very well, Mr. Banning could see, but it was not static any more. It would not be the end. Virginia, in a next generation of Banning women, would undoubtedly have no religion, nor any interest in a surviving tradition. At Virginia's age, he could feel intuitively his parents' sober, perhaps smug, acceptance. What Virginia felt would be his unspoken indifference; and little better, Lucile's preoccupation with the formal aspects. Presumably his parents would have taken disciplinary measures if he had failed in a sober, godly, and righteous attitude. Lucile, by doing nothing, acknowledged her failure. If Virginia went to church, it was distinctly as a favor to her mother and tacitly recognized as that. As far as Virginia was concerned, there was no sense in it. For her to go alone—that was, without any reason—would be unthinkable. Churchgoing was simply a form—fortunately growing milder as she got older—of that adult tyranny to which she submitted because she must. Lucile really would not dare speak to her about God or the teachings of Jesus. It would be safer not to bring up the issue of Virginia's real thoughts and sentiments.

What those were, he couldn't presume to know. Virginia didn't consider him or her mother suitable people to confide in. Probably she expected nothing from them but interference. What, she might reasonably argue, was the point in their declarations of love and interest when most of their time was spent in forbidding her to do what she wanted to do, or finding means to punish her when she did it anyway? Possibly she distrusted her mother more than him—sometimes he could see a skittish, wary approach to frankness or affection; but it never really got there. Prematurely, she would be emboldened to hope, would risk one more of her unpredictable requests; and, necessarily refused, draw back to nurse her new hurts.

There was nothing to be done about it, he knew now. His instincts, from the first to help her, defend her, cherish her—she was not like Guy, who never from the time he could walk and begin to speak was anything but the competent, reasonable, and assured master of his world—got him nowhere. Probably, as in other things, his inability to express himself, except in the most stiff and formal terms, hampered him. Perhaps, in any event, there could have been no explaining to Virginia. She did not care about explanations. If he answered indirectly, she would wait only until she was sure that the answer was going to be no. The light of her unquenched hope, the wild impossible appeal, went out. Wordless, she went away at once; or, if required to stay, stayed not really listening, never agreeing or assenting; as though she could not imagine why he found it necessary to talk so much when he had already said all that mattered.

Sighing again, he pulled his gloves on, for he could see that never would that difficulty resolve. The time was coming, perhaps was almost here, when saying no could not stop her; when, probably angry and bitter, she would do what she wanted without having to ask anybody. Common sense foresaw the disgraces and disasters almost certain to attend her when life, having no words, corrected her viciously with results. He stood still, looking at the sundial, for he had never been able to defend her, or help her, or save her. Perhaps the most he could expect would be the chance to comfort her when she had hurt herself beyond hope. Unhappy, he could see the fine cut script; *It is later than you think.*

*

"Mrs. Cole!"

"Now, my goodness, who's that? Who's there?"

"It's me."

Aunt Myra came out into the kitchen. The back door was open and she could see Mabel Baxter on the verge of entering. "Well," she said, "what time is this for you to come? Now, don't you let it happen again. You come here before school, and I told you you could have your breakfast."

"Well, I was here before. There isn't any school today; it's Saturday, Mrs. Cole."

"Oh, I forgot. Well, there probably will be next week. You march right up afterwards. If I'm not here, the key's always under the mat, so don't make that an excuse. Now, I'm sure I don't know what you can do this morning. I've done everything myself."

"Well, I just wanted to come back and tell you my father said it would be all right."

"I should hope so! I'm paying you as much as I paid Susie, who'd been here three years. You tell him that if he'd work sometimes himself he wouldn't have to worry so much about what his children were paid."

[307]

"Well, it wasn't that—"

"What wasn't what?"

"Oh, well. I mean, all right. Can I do anything now?"

"No, there's no need. I'm going to Sansbury at one o'clock. I won't be back until supper time. You come tomorrow at half-past seven."

2

On Tuesday, March seventeenth, the sun came up a poor yellow in the gray east. Soon it could not be seen at all. A gradual overcasting deepened evenly; the sky was a seamless cold gray; there was no wind.

Henry Harris, going out to sit on the steps with his paper, presently came in, went back to the round stove and settled down there.

"Get some snow this afternoon," he said contentedly to Walter Bates.

Unfolding his paper, propping his feet on the curved fender, he saw Matthew Herring enter, proceed in silence to the post office and start twisting the dial on his lock box. When he had drawn the mail out and clicked the door closed, he came across to the counter and said, "Walter, let me have a tin of cocoa, will you?"

With sober cordiality, Henry Harris said: "Good morning, Matthew. Looks as if we'd have some snow."

Half turning, Matthew Herring answered: "I should think it very likely."

Henry Harris grinned a little more. "Cold," he agreed. "Seems to be getting kind of cold in

[308]

here, too. Well, we can't expect everything, can we? No, sir! We ought to be content with what we have." Rattling the paper, he got his chair to a more comfortable angle and began to read.

*

Numb in a weariness not really of work, but of prolonged strain and nerves exhausted, Miss Stanley, at the window, had her brooding vacant watch disturbed by a gradual change of tone in the afternoon. Starting a little, she gave it her attention, and saw that a hazy thin fall of snow had begun. Stronger, whiter, it was drawing a curtain of fine flakes down the light wind, spinning over the gray hills.

Doctor Verney, by the bed, made a movement, the chair shifting; and at once Miss Stanley was aware, her own heart seemingly louder, that the long interval was stretching too long. Turning sharply, she saw Doctor Verney start too, as though the same lull of weariness had half stupefied him. His hand went out to the table, drew the waiting hypodermic from the fold of sterilized cloth.

Miss Stanley, instantly beside him, clasped one hand tight over the other, and she could feel the color leaving her face, her cheeks stiffening, her eyes fixing in distraction, for it was going to be a near thing. Unprofessionally, she could experience at once a despair and a kind of desperation, oppressed, consumed with a sense of the great unfairness of this whole struggle. The child started with nothing; there was no flesh to sustain her—not an ounce in the narrow buttocks, nothing on the slight molded arms; on her narrow chest those piteous flat breasts. You would think she lived on nothing but the breath painfully passed out through the cracked, parted lips and the small, dull, stained teeth. Her hair was dragged back, tangled, as though the last thing she had known was that it was too hot. Miss Stanley could see the exposed ear, and stunned by the newness of something often seen but never noticed, she was aware for the first time of the remarkable delicacy of its structure, the astonishing frail beauty of its proportions.

While second went to stuporous second, they stood together, their breaths held, their minds pressing on the familiar physiological progression. Now, the hasty diffusion in the veins, the sudden indescribable biochemics of the absorbed adrenalin; now, the lash laid on, the cardiac muscle shocked alive, the arterioles in tumultuous contraction, the almost stilled blood resurging. Now, now, must come, caught back, quick still, rough from the shades, the gasp in of air; life at once extended a little, letting them breathe again too.

Slowly, first he, then she, did breathe. He looked at her, and she, blankly, back at him.

"Well, it's all up," he said. He dropped Virginia's wrist.

Yet they still waited a moment, facing each other in pointless expectation. Doctor Verney said: "Can you reach the stethoscope on the table there, Miss Stanley?"

Pocketing it finally, while Miss Stanley stood watching, he turned and walked to the door. In the hall, he called quietly: "Mr. Banning. May I speak to you a minute?"

Here in the heavy gloom of the stormy afternoon he waited, close to the door he had closed, while Mr. Banning came out of the upstairs sitting room and approached him. Doctor Verney lowered his voice. He said: "You will know best how to handle it with Mrs. Banning. I have to tell you that Virginia has just passed away."

Mr. Banning had, of course, known it already. Probably he had known it since noon, had not been at all deceived. "Yes," he said, "that was to be expected."

Silent a moment, he then added hastily, as though to make up for his strange way of speaking, his voice low, too: "I see, Doctor. Thank you. Lucile is asleep. I don't think I'll wake her."

Now they were both silent, and then both started uncertainly to speak together. Doctor Verney stopped and Mr. Banning went on. "I only want to say that I know that you've done everything humanly possible. I want you to know what a comfort it has been to be able to feel—"

"It came very quietly," Doctor Verney said. "Of course, she never recovered consciousness. There doesn't seem to be any way for me to—"

"Of course not. We mustn't—I mean, that it will be very difficult for Lucile. She seems to be sleeping quite soundly. Last night—you know. I think that it would be best if I saw that Guy was notified."

Turning, he went to the stairs and down them. There was still enough gray light in the library for him to find the telephone, and holding it, he waited, looking out at the whirl of snow, thinking. After a moment, he was distracted by the sight of Mary in a black coat or cloak making her way from the back toward the stables. In each hand she held a pan and now, dim and boisterous, arose the deep barking of the dogs. Galloping through the haze of falling flakes, they came to meet their suppers halfway.

Mr. Banning lifted the receiver and said: "May I have Western Union in Sansbury, please?"

"I'm sorry," May said. "He seems to have left the Evarts place. Just a moment and I'll try him at home."

She plugged in 11, twitched the key, waiting.

After a while she pulled it, let it snap back. "I'm sorry," she said, "Doctor Bull does not answer."

Another lamp lit, and whipping out the new plug, she slipped it in, thumbed over the key and heard Mr. Banning say, "—Western Union in Sansbury, please—"

Her right hand went out; the number six toll line lamp turned golden.

"Western Union, please," she said to the Sansbury operator.

After a moment a clear voice responded: "Western Union."

May said: "Here's your party, Mr. Banning."

She let go the key, sitting in the twilight, gazing out at the snow whirled over the green, blown around the iron soldier on his stone. This was like winter beginning all over again; but she felt strong enough to stand it; for sooner or later it had to be spring; and Joe would be well.

Content, she began to read, holding up the book to the light, filling herself again with the great harmony of lines which, perhaps at first passed over, you lived to see radiant:

His servants he, with new acquist
Of true experience from this great event
With peace and consolation hath dismissed,
And calm of mind . . .

Automatically she thrust out a hand, pushed back the key to see if her line were still busy.

Into her ear jumped the clear voice in Sansbury saying: "I will repeat the paid telegram to Mr. Guy Banning—" May let go, silence cutting in. Suddenly she thought: "But why does he telegraph instead of telephoning?"

She drew the key back—"Yale College, New Haven, Connecticut. Virginia died at half-past five today. Please come at once. Signed, Father. That name is, V as in victor, I as—"

*

From the kitchen Janet Cardmaker heard the blare of flames softly growing in the Franklin stove, the click and slide of the big chunks of cannel coal, now splitting hot.

Beyond the window the recently begun snow was thickening fast, a whirl of weightless, thin flakes in the early twilight. It hurried unseasonable through the lilac buds. It drove blindly down the sloping meadow. She took the whisky bottle by the neck in one hand. Between the fingers of the other she caught up two of her great-great-grandfather's fine crystal wine glasses.

In the kitchen George Bull sat back, quiet as the room. Janet could just see him, sidelong through the pantry door. Firelight shone across the solid slope of his cheek, making a shadow up from the arrogant hedge of eyebrow. He watched the flames with that bold, calm stare-away, his blue eyes steady. Now he moved, rousing himself, stretching his big legs, grunting in the comfortable heat. Casual, but sonorous and effortlessly true, she could hear him humming to himself.

There was an immortality about him, she thought; her regard fixed and critical. Something unkillable. Something here when the first men walked erect; here now. The last man would twitch with it when the earth expired. A good greedy vitality, surely the very vitality of the world and the flesh, it survived all blunders and injuries, all attacks and misfortunes, never quite fed full. She shook her head a little, the smile half derisive in contemptuous affection. Her lips parted enough to say: "The old bastard!"